Not Even Paris

A Jolene Novel
Book One

REBECCA JONES

NOT EVEN PARIS

Copyright © 2025 Rebecca Jones

Published 2025 by Georgia Publishing
https://rebeccajonesbooks.com/georgia-publishing

ISBN: 979-8-9999681-0-4

First Edition, September 2025

Cover design: Georgia Publishing
Cover art copyright © B.S. | Canva

Not Even Paris is a work of fiction. Names, characters, places, and incidents are products of the author's imagination or are used fictitiously.

For Carl.

AUTHOR NOTE

While the author maintains this book is meant for a wide audience, the reader may take note that the following text includes...

- Offhand references to self-harm.

If you come upon an instance you wish we had warned you about, please visit the website on the back cover, and let us know. Thanks.

* * *

The reader may also take note of the character reference page at the back of the book.

CONTENTS

1 THE BOY I'M NOT AT ALL COMPLETELY CRAZY ABOUT

I don't look at him. I don't need to; I know what he looks like. Instead, I focus my eyes on the finished worksheet in front of me and let my other senses wander. He smells like he just had gym, but in a good way, like he just got out of a cold shower—with a pine tree in it, and maybe a river. Something definitely smells like a river—like he wrestled a bear in a forest, built a fire, and went for a swim.

He grunts, and I almost look at him. Out of the corner of my eye, I make out movement. He erases something on his worksheet and readjusts how he's sitting. I still don't look at him. His brown eyes, dark hair, dark skin, square teeth, rocks-for-arms, little bump of a nose—I look at none of it.

Mrs. Diefenbacher doesn't allow us to have our phones out in class, limiting my ability to distract myself from him. I'd pull my book out and read it, but nothing says, "Don't ever, ever, EVER talk to me," like pulling out a book. Unless you actually don't want people to talk to you, then it works in reverse, but I'm

7

running out of things to act interested in. I've spent as much time as possible pretending that my worksheet isn't done. I look around the room, hoping to find something novel, but it's like every other math class: grayish-blue linoleum floor, pro-mathematical-propaganda posters on the walls, and darkly tinted, large windows keep out any threat of natural light. We're even on the low-traffic side of the building, so there isn't much hope for a passerby. I could busy myself, and maybe draw his attention, by taking off my sweatshirt, but it's so cold. It's never warm before noon in Goleta, even in May. Maybe I'll just look at him for a second. No! No—because that one time I did that, and at like, the exact same time he looked up, and it was the most awkward thing ever. I can't let that happen again—not a third time. And it's not like I need to check in on him. I'm sure he's still there in his Lakers jersey and dark-blue jean shorts. I can picture him in my head, something I do a lot when I'm not in math class; I don't need to look at him.

"Jolene?"

I look at him. Even across the table, I have to tilt my head up to meet his eyes.

"Hm?" is my brilliant response.

"Are you finished?"

I glance at my worksheet to check. Yep. Still done. "Nearly."

Mrs. Diefenbacher has divided our class into small round tables. Our tables are our groups. She's big on group work, which in a math setting, or, to be fair, in any school setting, I hate. I hate the dynamics of it all: the power trips, the egos, the tangents, the wondering

8

if this group is going to function or fail, or in either case suck. But Mrs. Diefenbacher, in typical math teacher fashion, seems to take pride in her ability to make us suffer. So, nearly every project is a group project. Every quiz is a group quiz. Every device of teenage torture is a group device of teenage torture.

"Did you get sixteen for number nineteen?" His eyes meet mine.

I adjust my glasses and try to focus on the problem on my paper. How on this green Earth did he get sixteen? But how to break his mistake to him? He's way too hot to tell him he's wrong. I certainly don't want him to think that I think I'm smarter than him, even though—sixteen...

"No," I say. I try to sound like it's not a big deal, like it's maybe even funny. "No, I did not..."

"What did you get?" He scratches his upper lip.

One of our group mates, Danny, who balances his skateboard on his knee, has green hair, and often needs a bit of assistance with assignments, glances at us, abandoning the question he's on, ready to record my answer.

"Ninety," I say, still prepping up the tone at the end, almost like a question, as if I could be wrong.

"Ninety?" He completely says it like a question and erases his "sixteen."

Danny slouches back in his seat, not erasing his answer. Even he got it right.

"It's a vertical angle." I add another layer of softness to my voice. Anyone could make the mistake he did—my tone suggests. "So, it's the same as the other side..."

"I spent five minutes using fancy math, trying to solve this thing, and you solve it by looking at it." Amused astonishment fills Matt's low, deep, dream-fuel voice, the kind of warm voice you could sink into up to your neck.

"You would have gotten it..." I say, as if there's no chance in the world he wasn't seconds away from figuring it out. Even though—I ask you...

He writes in the new answer. "What would I do without you?"

My face grows hotter than the surface of the sun. I worry it shows or that I'm going to ignite and burn down the entire school. Danny would like that if he, you know, didn't die in the process.

Of course, Matt just means what he said in a friendly, math kind of way, but come on. He chose these exact words: "What would I do without you?" He's gotta know the connotations in there and the power they wield—he's a teenager. So, we're left with why. Why did he choose these words? As far as I can tell, there are only two reasons a high school boy would say these eight words in this succession. Either he, one, is leaving me a subtle clue—a peek through the window into the deep chasm of his undying love for me, or two, is an insincere flirt.

There's, of course, the third option, that he just plain and simply sucks at math and would literally fail without me, but I think we can safely disregard that. No one worries about their math fate enough to vocalize it.

After a moment, he looks up from his paper, leans back in his chair and spins his pencil around his fingers. His worksheet's finished. He must have gone back to double-check some of his answers, and good thing, too—honestly...

I feel his eyes on me, so I pretend to go over my work. There's a problem I'm not sure of, but I don't ask anyone. The fourth kid at our table, the smart kid, is notoriously quiet and speaks only in mouse. He wouldn't give me an answer, not in our human tongue. Danny, even if he knew the answer, I couldn't ask him instead of Matt, it would send the wrong signals, but if I ask Matt he might think less of me, and not know, but I can't concentrate on fixing any of my mistakes either—there are only five more minutes left of class, and then he'll be out of my life forever. Well, sort of, and maybe.

Tonight I find out whether I got accepted into L'Institut du Ballet de Paris, one of the top ballet schools in Europe. My grandma, or mamie, is on the board and encouraged me to send in an audition video for their next season. If accepted, I'll spend a year in Paris studying ballet, living with my mamie, shopping with my aunt Eloise, and sailing in Cannes with my uncle Cass. But if Matt doesn't ask me to Prom within these last five minutes of class, and if I'm accepted as a student, and spend the next year in Paris, he'll be graduated by the time I get back. I have to tell him I might be in Paris for a year. He has to dump his girlfriend and ask me to Prom, and we're running out of time.

I mean, why wouldn't he ask me out? I'm not horrendous. Dancing ballet has kept me somewhat fit. Braces throughout junior high fixed the teeth growing

11

out the side of my mouth. My complexion isn't flawless, but whose is? I do have a nose, though. It's not huge, but it's there, where people can see it. But I know he at least somewhat likes me. I'm only in his group, at his table, because he invited me. Not that it's done any good so far—for my dating life or my grade. It's maddening, though. Why ask a girl to join you if you don't plan to ask her out and make her yours for all eternity? This is why guys are confusing.

"What are you doing this weekend?" he asks.

In surprise, I lift my head. But he's talking to Danny. I watch them and bite the inside of my cheek.

"Nothing," Danny says in his scratchy voice. "Not going to Prom." He chuckles slightly.

Matt fixes his eyes on me and smiles. "What about you, Stansen?"

Did he only ask Danny to make asking me seem less of a big deal? Is hoping so pathetic?

I swallow a lump that wasn't there a second ago, shake my head, press my lips together, and shrug. I can act like things are no big deals, too.

His eyebrows narrow, as if my lack of an interesting weekend displeases him.

"You're not going to Prom?" he asks.

I look at him for a split second, provide a blip of a smile, and shrug exactly one shoulder.

He frowns. "You don't know?"

His question makes me feel like a toddler. Of course I should know if I'm going to Prom this weekend. Of course, most people would have a date already. And of course he's already made plans with Caradine. I'm grasping on to air so thin it's anorexic. The only way he'll ask me is if he breaks plans with, and breaks up with, Caradine—Caradine, who is gorgeous, popular, rich, cheerleads, competes in, and wins, beauty pageants, and spends her summers in her native country of Italy. She's almost exactly like the heroine in the novel I'm reading right now, *Back From London*, except, obviously, in the book she goes to London. And her name's Ysenia, not Caradine.

"You going with Caradine?" Danny asks Matt.

Matt yawns a little bit. "Yeah. Her friends are making a big deal about it."

"Thought you broke up," Danny says.

"Nah. It didn't stick."

I hadn't heard they broke up. Please, for the love of grapefruit, Danny, ask him more!

"How long did it last?" Danny asks. Heaven be praised.

"About a weekend. Jason said Margot told him Caradine hoped Anthony would ask her out, but Anthony's my friend. You know? He wouldn't ask out my ex-girlfriend. But we're back together now, so..."

"You took her back after that?" Danny asks.

Matt shrugs, turns to me. "I thought you'd be going."

I'm worried, thrilled, and confused all at the same time. Worried he might have asked me if he didn't think I was going, thrilled he thinks a guy would have asked me, and confused why he would think that.

"You did?" I ask.

"You're a weird girl, Stansen."

What? How does not going to Prom make me weird? Now I'm a little offended. Worried, thrilled, confused and offended—and still hopeful. Maybe now

13

that he knows I'm not going, he'll ask me, and dump Caradine.

If he doesn't, I'm not sure where to go from there. I guess France. Last year, Aunt Eloise and Mamie invited my sister Mary to join them in France for the summer. When Mary had gone, she was scrawny and weird-looking. When she came back, she was gorgeous. She had just a few months of Aunt Eloise's restyling, and it changed her entire look. People underestimate the power of a good haircut. That— plus puberty and growing two bra sizes—goes a long way. She came back and went from kind of popular to JV cheer co-captain and sophomore class treasurer.

But he's not saying anything. He now knows I don't have a date, and he's still not asking me. Maybe I should tell him he might not get another chance. I might not be here next year. If he ever wants to go to prom with me, this could be it.

"I actually find out this weekend whether or not I'm going to study a year abroad in Paris. I'm one of the finalists for this ballet school, and if I get in, then I might stay there for at least a year, maybe longer..."

I feel my chest tighten. This is it. His response is everything.

He falls to the ground and clings to my leg.

"No!" he screams and wails. "You can't go! I'll never see you again!" We grow old and die on the same day in each other's arms. The End. Story over. Why are you still reading? Fine, but that's how it would go if my life was the ending of the last book I finished, *Timeless Love*, where Charlotte and Nicolas were with other people, but secretly liked each other their entire lives, only to find out in their thirties that they were meant for each other—after their spouses died of the plague.

That's not what happens. What he really does is, he gets quiet, looks at the table, sniffs, and congratulates me.

"You must be a really good dancer," he has the nerve to say.

He rubs his neck and picks up the pencil he had stopped spinning. He looks like he's about to say something else when the fourth kid in our group—Tim, the smart kid, at least I think that's his name, pushes his worksheet toward us and ruins it.

Matt and I look at each other, confused—oh! He must have finished checking and rechecking his work. Matt takes the paper and places it between us while Danny leans over for access.

"So, you're not going to Prom, but you might go to France?" Matt erases an answer and fills in Tim's right one.

"Well, if I go, I'll be invited." I instantly regret saying it. He might misunderstand and think I'm talking about Prom when I'm talking about France. I don't want him to think I'm fishing for an invite. "To France, I mean." But that's not wholly true, because whether or not I go to the prom depends also on if a junior or senior—i.e.: him—invites me. So, I try to clear that up without putting bait on a line. "Or Prom, but I've kind of accepted"—don't admit defeat, you idiot—"it'd be a little late. Not that I wouldn't..." Someone stop me. Hit me with a bat or something, anything to make me shut up.

"What about the rest of your weekend? No plans?" He looks up at the last part, then back at Tim's paper. Why is he so curious about my weekend? Is he hoping I ask him about the rest of his? I don't want to hear about his after prom plans. Oh, heck no. But am I obligated to ask now? Ugh.

"Ballet, church." I brace myself. "You?" I ask dutifully, achieving sainthood in doing so—if there's any justice in the world.

"Turn in your worksheets," Mrs. Diefenbacher says, interrupting us. I take back my sainthood—Mrs. Diefenbacher should have it.

Without asking, Matt takes all of ours and places them on Saint Diefenbacher's desk, as our table-mates grab their backpacks and wait by the door. I wait for Matt. He returns and lifts his backpack onto his shoulders with a look I can't place.

"So, we might not be in the same math class next year?" he asks.

"I mean, not unless you take math through a study-abroad online program..." I'm not sure how I'll keep up with my schoolwork while in France, but I'm sure it'll be something like that.

"I don't like it," he says as I throw my backpack on.

"I probably won't get in," I say.

"Yes, you will." He says it as though he's the expert on how well I dance even though I'm pretty sure he's never seen a ballet in his life, let alone one of mine. "How am I supposed to survive math without you?"

"You'll still have Danny and... Tim?" His name's either Tim or it rhymes with Tim. There's a chance

I'm thinking of a time when someone called him, "him..."

"Yes." Matt places a hand over his chest and gazes at the ceiling sentimentally. "I'll always have them."

I can't decide whether I should join him and flick a fake tear out of my eye, and risk looking more dorky than I already do, or laugh and risk being an audience-only contributor. Which one is something a fun girl would do, a girl you'd like to be your girlfriend? The time has passed, and if I did either, it would be awkward, so I do nothing as we make our way toward the door where the rest of the class has gathered.

"I mean, even if I get in, there's a chance I might not take it," I say to the ground.

He stops walking and turns the full force of his unlawfully handsome face to me.

I'm paralyzed. This is it. Make or break. Do or die. He has seconds to confess his love to me and ask me to Prom. Tell me you love me, Matt. Say it. Say it!

"Why wouldn't you take it?" he asks. His eyes are big and soft, genuine and curious.

I suffer from internal sighing. It's not fair that I have to be the one to say I like him first. He's putting it all on me when I'm supposed to be putting it all on him. It's asking too much. It's asking me to have courage I don't have. I don't even know what to do. Do I admit everything and say, "Honestly, Matt, it's 100 percent dependent on you. I know that's pathetic because you're dating someone else, but I literally will not leave this country if you want me to stay"? Is that even true? Can I hint at it and see where it goes? See if he picks up on it—I give a little—he gives a little until we both solidly understand each other and can stop playing these stupid games?

"Well, it's a lot of time away from..." I trail off, leaving him to fill in the blanks for once.

"Yeah," he says. "But you'd be crazy to pass that up. I don't think I would for anything."

I feel like there's nothing inside of me. All my guts, bones, and organs have been scooped out, like a Jack-o'-lantern. Essentially, he wouldn't give up a year in Paris for me, and wouldn't expect me to either. It's my answer. It's what I expected, deep down, but realizing your life isn't the ending of a young adult romance novel still hurts. A blow is a blow. My mouth gapes, and I can't stop blinking. I reel it in and speak to his chest instead of his face. Or I almost speak. Nothing comes out. I shrug, take off my glasses in case we have an "Oh! She's cute without her glasses" moment, and try speaking again.

"Maybe I'm just scared."

I glance up into his eyes. There's warmth and a soft smile.

"Of what? France should be scared of you." He scrunches up his features. "I mean that in a nice way. They don't know what they've got coming."

The sides of my lips slightly rise. At least it's a complimentary decimation of my entire being.

2 THE AFTERMATH AFTER MATH

I put my glasses back on as we trickle out the doorway. Once we enter the outside hall, the cool air sinks into my bones, but in a few seconds we step out from under the shade of the awnings into the walkway through the grass. The sun hits us, and it's actually a little warm.

I wish I had removed my hoodie. I'd take it off now, but I don't want him to leave if I stop walking. This is usually where he leaves me, if we even get this far.

"You have to admit to missing something about Winchester Canyon High School," he says, possibly hinting that he wants me to miss him. Yet again, if he has something to reveal, he's trying to get me to go first. Unfair. I'm the underclassman. He should go first—set an example. But he's probably got nothing to reveal. All the more reason I shouldn't reveal anything either.

"I'll miss Mrs. Diefenbacher yelling at Danny in German," I say.

He laughs. "She should start the day yelling at all of us in German, wake us up a little."

19

"I don't know," I say, joining his laughter. "I feel like, if I'm going to yell at Danny, I'd want him to understand it. But I think Danny takes German, so maybe we're good there."

"That's giving Danny a lot of credit," he says.

We laugh together.

"Aww," I say. "I like Danny."

"Danny?" He almost shouts and looks down at me.

"Not like that."

"I was gonna say, aim higher, Jolene." He snickers, and I die. "Nothing against him, but..."

It's weird talking to the guy you like about liking guys. It shouldn't be allowed to happen. It's too full of awkwardness.

"Remember when—" I say, right as he says, "If you're not—"

We both smile like we're in physical pain. He shifts his stance and gives a kind of sigh, letting me know, in his way that I've studied and gotten familiar with over the past year, he's giving me the floor.

"I was just going to bring up the time Danny fell asleep, and Mrs. Diefenbacher threw a book at him." I laugh at the memory of Danny falling off his chair, Mrs. Diefenbacher realizing she had really hurt him, and how hard the class laughed as she asked the teacher next door to watch us while she took Danny to the health office.

Matt smiles, maybe remembering, too.

"What were you going to say?" I ask.

"If you're not..." He looks serious. He makes eye contact with the pavement below our feet as if he's about to confess something to me.

20

The moment lasts on and on and for forever, but somehow not long enough, and suddenly it's passed, and she's with us—or she's with him, and I'm with myself because nobody's talking to me anymore.

"What's your locker combination?" Caradine asks Matt in the world's most affected and whiny voice, the type of voice that if you heard it in a short-form video online, you'd swipe it away immediately, no matter how glowy her ochre skin is, or how stupid and stunning it looks with her brown and golden eyes and dark-russet hair.

They say girls have low self-esteem because we compare ourselves to photo-enhanced models in magazines and fashion dolls, but it's not true at all; we have low self-esteem because we compare ourselves to girls like her. She's not airbrushed, she didn't have plastic surgery—probably. She's 100 percent real and glorious.

In some ways, the fact Matt dates her makes me think less of him, even though, I mean, I get it. But it's such a shallow thing to do. She's so mean. She's one of those girls who'll put you down, knowing it'll make you desperate for her approval. It's effective, too— she's got one hopeless girl hanging off her arm right now. Caradine's free hand tugs at Matt's jersey.

"You have your own locker," he says.

He doesn't even glance back at me as he walks away with her and her auxiliary.

My reflection catches me in the tinted windows of the math building. No wonder he didn't dump her and ask me out. Compared to her, I'm hideous. My hair color is boring brown, and it's lifeless. I tried to

21

straighten it this morning, but humidity hates me. My shirt, sure, it's kind of cute, the cutest one I have. But who cares when her shirt is form-fitting and exposes a lot more skin? I dress like someone's kid sister. She dresses like someone's girlfriend, someone's girlfriend who makes all the other guys take him aside and ask him what it's like to go out with her.

I pout through the stupid courtyard and turn to walk into my stupid locker hall. A large boy I've only ever seen blocking my locker stands there, doing what he does best. Sometimes he has some friends with him, like now. So I pull off my stupid backpack, unzip the stupid zipper, shove in my stupid sweatshirt, and yank the zipper back up, throwing the backpack back around me, and wait for the large boy and his stupid friends to leave my locker in peace.

I lean against a pillar supporting the awning in the middle of the hallway. My foot slips on some loose gravel. A chunk has come out of the ground. I kick it and lean back up against the pillar.

"That'll show it," a voice says.

My best, well, my only friend, joins me. He smiles his kind, face-value smile. His blond hair—so blond it's almost-red—still a little sweaty from P.E. I only notice because it's closer to my line-of-sight than it was yesterday. At the start of our freshman year, I was significantly taller than him, and he had a little pudgy belly. But now he's a beanpole and still shooting up. He might even be taller than me.

"Ground's always giving me the side-eye," he says.

I give him a participation chuckle. I'm not in the mood for weird jokes. Unfortunately, that's all Logan's

22

got. He hasn't caught on that most people in high school are trying to blend in and appear normal. Logan's never been much for caring about what other people think. I keep expecting him to realize there's a hierarchy, and he'd do better if he played the game. At the same time, I'd be devastated if he changed. He's easy as he is, easy to be around. I don't have to worry about whether he'll think I'm a geek since he is twelve times the geek I am, and proud of it. If they gave out medals at comic conventions for Supreme Geek, Logan—well, he might not place, but he'd score better than I would.

And before you get any ideas, like—"Gee, Jolene, Matt doesn't seem to care about you, but there's a fine young man right here who'd make a lovely boyfriend"—no. Logan's like a brother to me, and I—I don't know, I don't feel that way about him. He doesn't excite me when he bumps my arm. You know what I mean? There's no spark there, and I'm sure he feels the same way about me, or he wouldn't bump my arm so much.

LOGAN

Jolene almost laughs at my side-eye joke. An effort was made anyway. It's okay. She was kicking the ground for a reason; can't expect her to snap out of whatever funk she's in just because of me. If I could lift Jolene out of a bad mood just by walking up to her—you know, it's really not worth even thinking about at this point. She's just a friend, and a good one, and I don't want that to change.

She's not one of those friends who'll eat lunch with you one day but not another, or who'll be weird if you're still gaming at her house when she gets back from ballet rehearsal. She lets me talk for hours if something's stuck in my head, and she'll even have a thoughtful comment afterward, proving that not only did she listen—she thought about it.

The smelly log that sits next to me in Algebra keeps telling me I should ask her out and that he would if he were me. But I know something he doesn't know, she's completely obsessed with Matt Craddick. If a guy could steal her attention away from him, it would be a guy she'd love forever. And yes, alright? He'd be lucky. She's funny, witty, and cute. She has full pink lips and dark-hazel eyes. When she blushes, her entire face turns pink because her skin's almost translucent.

I'm lucky just to be her friend. I get to be the guy she's comfortable around, the guy she confides in, jokes with, teases, the guy who notices when she breaks from her usual jeans, and band t-shirt routine to jean shorts, and a cute baseball-style shirt, her long dark-brown hair, usually up in a ponytail, down, and straightened.

"You look nice. Is there an occasion?" I ask her teasingly, a note of mock accusation in my tone.

"No." She sighs. "Not really."

Every word she says is a lie. I try to read the truth out of her face, but she just looks put out, with a frown and lacking her usual energy. How this skinny, pale thing has any energy, I leave to you.

Matt and Caradine come around a corner, holding hands. Jolene snarls and turns around a pillar, facing away from them, toward me. There it is.

"Oh, a Matt occasion," I say. The awed expression on her face confirming it. "A 'Maccasion'."

She lets out a sigh so big, if it was a fart, half the school would be gagging.

"This was my last chance for him to ask me to Prom."

Jolene's plan ever since she fell for Matt around the first week of school has been for him to ask her out. So far, no luck. Honestly, though, I think she's right. He probably likes her a lot, but I don't think he'll dump Caradine, who's popular, hot, and loaded. He should, but high school is less about how we feel and more about risk assessment. Social hierarchy is everything. Sometimes, I wonder if Jolene doesn't get that at all.

"Guess I'll just—go to France." She huffs out her nose.

"Were you planning on not going to France?" I ask her.

"Well," she takes a moment as if deciding how to phrase it. "I find out tonight if I'm accepted."

"Right."

"Right." The word gets trapped a few times on its way out. "And I thought telling him I might go away for a year would make him ask me to Prom, but it didn't, and it won't."

"Oh," I say. "So, you were going to tell him you might go to France for a year, and he was going to dump the girl he's been dating since before you met him, and then just deal with having a girlfriend in Paris for his senior year, going stag to all the dances—"

25

"Love would tear him apart until I got home..." She's clearly off in this fairy world.

"Not super realistic, though," I say. "He doesn't want a girlfriend half a world away, even if he was madly in love with you."

"Shut up with your logic," she says, looking dejected. "We'll have none of it here." She laughs a little and I smile, glad she's brightening up. But then she frowns again. "But he could have asked me not to go."

"People don't really go from friends to 'Don't go to Paris,' in the course of fifty minutes." That definitely hasn't softened her mood, so I add, "I mean, they go from friends to 'Don't go to Rome,' all the time, probably, but not Paris." That gets a smile. "Were we going to your locker?"

"Can't. It's blocked." She squints her eyes together, looks toward her locker, and I see what she means: A big, beefy dude and several swooners stand guard, preventing her access.

"Could ask them to move."

"I have before. They never do."

"Hey!" Matt's voice sounds out of nowhere. Jolene jumps next to me, so I guess she didn't realize how close he was either. "You're blocking Jolene's locker."

The loiterers look in the direction Matt's pointing—at us. Has he been listening to us, or does he just know it's her locker and that she needs to get to it?

"Oh, sorry," the beef says. He and his groupies clear away.

Jolene gives a kind of lopsided smirk in Matt's direction. It's almost painful to witness, and not only for me. If Caradine's scowl could produce the physical

26

amount of venom it figuratively possesses, an adult human male in good health would be dead in under two seconds. Little Jolene wouldn't stand a chance.

Caradine turns her attention to her boyfriend, grabs Matt around the neck, and pulls his face down toward hers in a big, hard, random kiss. I hear the teeth in Jolene's skull grind down about an inch.

She manhandles a few books from backpack to locker, gives up, slams the door, turns, and leans against the row of metal locks and hinges.

"I don't know what I was thinking," she says so low I'm almost not sure she's talking to me. "Of course he didn't ask me out. The only way to get what you want in high school is to be pretty and popular, and I'm neither."

"Who said that?" I ask.

"No one needed to. I know I'm not pretty. If I were, I'd have a boyfriend—"

"No, I mean, who said you have to be pretty and popular?"

"Life? You just do." She takes a novel out of her backpack and puts it in her locker.

"I'm not either of those things, and I'm happy."

She doesn't seem to hear me. She just takes the novel back out of her locker, returning it to her backpack.

"How many of those do you read a day?" I ask.

"It's not a theory I got from a book," she says, reading my mind.

I give her a look that says I'm not falling for her lies.

"And if it is, it doesn't matter. It's true, and you know it. Hi Mary."

27

Jolene's older sister and one of her many friends, Piper—as luck has it, struts our way. Well, not our way. They're not coming to us as much as they're coming near us.

I choke on my saliva and cough.

Mary gives Jolene only enough attention to deliver a scoff.

I don't understand why they don't get along. Mary looks a lot like Jolene in the sense that they're both about 5'7", have long brown hair, and are absurdly pretty, but Mary wears more and darker makeup, has a pointier chin, and testier eyes.

"Does she always dress like that?" Piper asks while adding to Mary's daily scoff-at-Jolene quota.

They walk on, laughing. Piper flips her hair out of her face and over her tan, bare shoulder. She wears a mustard sleeveless turtleneck. She wears a lot of yellow for someone so mean. You saw how she didn't even bother sending one of those scoffs to me. It makes me feel like some alien force has snapped me into dust. I hate Piper Thompson, and of course, by that, I mean I'm absolutely in love with her. For two strange weeks in junior high, she agreed to go out with me, which, in junior high, meant she'd hold my hand during lunch, and sometimes we'd kiss. They were the two most incredible weeks of my life. We sat near each other in band because we both played the clarinet. Something she didn't continue into high school. I stopped as well. It wasn't as fun without her. Now I play the trumpet.

I don't know if it's normal, but I haven't kissed a girl since. She's kissed boys—a lot, and by "a lot," I mean "a lot." She's had many boyfriends, some also only lasting two weeks, but I haven't dated at all, not even band girls. Maybe not finding love anywhere else is why I cling to the idea that we'll be together again someday, or maybe it's because she has beautiful strawberry blond hair that was shoulder-length last Christmas when she weaved red tinsel in it but is down to her mid-back now. Or maybe it's because she has a beautiful olive complexion. I don't know how some people never get zits because I always have zits, but she never has zits. They're probably too scared of her.

Normally, Jolene would just shrug off Mary's constantly annoyed attitude, but today, she doesn't. She bites the corner of her mouth and stares at a trash can.

"She mad at you?" I add a lot of the teenage angst my mom says I have into my question, sounding properly annoyed. I should probably throw in an eye roll. Hopefully, she takes my finding Mary obnoxious as a sign she shouldn't take her seriously, either. But she sighs again. She's an excellent sigher.

"Nah," she says. "She never says hi to me at school. Oh! Yeah. She is mad. She's jealous because I might go to France for an entire year, and she only went for a summer."

"Why would she go to France for a year?" I ask. "She doesn't even dance."

"Just to go!" Jolene laughs. I'm happy to see I've managed to somewhat lift those spirits of hers. Hopefully, this time it lasts longer than three seconds. "Not everyone who goes to France got into a prestigious ballet program."

"Don't be mad, but your grandma works at the school, right?" I ask. "Are you a finalist because she pulled some strings?"

She scoffs. "I'm really good!"

"No, I know!" I backtrack.

"But yeah, she pulled strings."

3 DOGBERRY, HORATIO, AND THE OBVIOUS CONCLUSION

JOLENE

After school, I lug myself up the hill to the student parking lot. My older sister is a sophomore, so neither of us drives. Sometimes she'll get a ride with her friends, but when she doesn't, she, like I, takes the bus.

I climb inside and there she is. We look a lot alike, except she's beautiful and has an actual form, while I'm more of a skeletal waif, not unlike the ones Logan and I battle on our laptops.

She has long, bouncy brown hair and brown eyes. She's tan and wears her black and purple cheer uniform, sitting with a fellow cheerleader next to her, two behind her, and two other students I don't know but can tell are popular in front of her. Dutifully, I try not to make eye contact and find a seat closer to the front.

I don't know how the popular kids always get seats in the back. They never seem to be in a hurry to be anywhere, but they're always on the bus early enough to get the back seats. Do they not go to class and go straight to the bus, or is it that the other kids know our lives will be rough if we dare sit back there? If I got on the bus first, I wouldn't sit back there.

The bus gets to our stop last because our house isn't on a street with other houses; it's off by itself through a path in the woods, about a fourth of a mile past the farthest-out bus stop.

Mary, as usual, walks ten feet ahead of me the whole way home.

Our house stands at the end of a winding dirt path through the eucalyptus. Mary and I both prefer to take this path rather than walk along the road parallel. The road's not well used, and if at one time it was anything but gravel, you wouldn't know it, but the dirt path through the trees is faster, slightly more secluded, and more beautiful.

It gets quieter the closer we get to the house. When we're not having a drought, sometimes the creek bed gathers a little bit of water, slightly resembling a stream. One summer, when I was a kid, Mary and I found tadpoles. We caught a few and took them home. Mary said she would take care of them. They were all dead within two weeks. Since then, I haven't searched for any. They could have come back. I wouldn't know.

I walk out from behind a tree and there's our large, light-pink house. Vines with pink blossoms spread up its front. Long white windows beckon the sunlight, and a dark-blue, almost black door stands locked in front of me. Mary, as always, locked it after going inside.

I don't know why I even tried the handle.

I huff out my nose, swing my book-filled backpack around to my front, balance it on a bush, take the keys from the small pocket, and unlock the door.

Mary had taken pains to shut the foyer's doors, too. We never shut these. I open the white doors separating our foyer from the rest of the house and step into the hallway.

Dogberry, my Border Collie, charges me so fast he almost knocks me over. I give him a rubdown.

"Did you miss me?"

He tells me he did by licking my face.

We head up to the third-floor attic, walk past the landing/storage area, my bathroom, and come to a bright-pink door with a large, wooden "J" on the front—my room.

I flip a switch and turn on my pink, glittering chandelier overhead, then toss my backpack on my soft-pink queen bed, careful not to hit my sleeping white cat, Horatio. The bed's against my slanted, distressed, and peeling light-blue wall.

When I push my bookcase, it rotates, granting me access to my closet behind it; an almost empty room, depressingly underutilized—a place where clothes go to lie on the floor.

I kick off my shoes, take my bra off without taking off my shirt, and peel away my jeans. I leave them where they fall and go back out my bookcase door.

I don't have ballet for a few hours, so I pull out my book, cross to my sliding glass door, lilt the balcony curtains apart, and pull the door open.

The breath of the beach past the trees wafts over me. Dogberry hops up, and we settle onto my couch made of wood pallets and cushions. I lay my pink knit blanket over us and flip through the book. *Back From London* is a young adult novel about a girl who goes to high school but has to be careful because ever since she got back from her summer abroad, dinosaurs keep randomly attacking. I'm not that far into it. So far she's just been dumped by the love of her life, and now has to travel through the land of the dinosaurs to—wait. I sit up straight, making Dogberry jump. How did I miss it? I've been thinking this was the end of my story, but what if it's the beginning? That would explain why everything sucks right now. Nothing goes the way you want it to before you go to Paris! You go to Paris, you glow up like your sister did, you become a ballet rockstar, you come back, everyone loves you and the guy of your dreams dumps his vapid girlfriend, asks you to the school dance, and your life is perfect. It's so obviously what is going to happen. I was ridiculous for not figuring it out sooner.

4 PULLED STRINGS

JOLENE

We're not rehearsing for a performance right now, so ballet comprises technique training. It's a bit boring compared to learning new choreography, but I always enjoy it when we get to the *grand jetés* across the floor. Those are always fun.

When class is over, I pack up my stuff. I'm still wrapping the ribbons around my pointe shoes when the next class starts coming in, the third to highest class in the school—Lindsey Calisher, to be exact. This year she danced roles usually reserved for girls in the second-highest or highest classes.

She puts her bag down on the back cabinets, removes her street clothes, tugs on her ballet slippers to warm up, and effortlessly slides into the splits, her toes so pointed they touch the floor, and stretches her arms to her feet, leaning her entire torso against her leg. She's only stretching, but her movements are swanlike and so graceful it makes me want to jump out

35

the window. And she's blond and pretty—I bet she has no problem getting a guy to notice her.

I heave my dance bag over my shoulder, knowing all too well that even if I get into the French ballet school, I'll never be able to dance like her.

"Guess what?" my mom asks as I slide into her Lexus after class.

My mom's the type of woman who always has perfectly manicured hands, coiffed blond hair, and pairs her impeccably-white whites with pristine-white whites.

You hear people complain about turning into their moms. Maybe I'd be more like her if she were around more often, but she works in Hollywood as a costumer for a major studio, and we hardly ever see her. It's funny; she's the one who hates Los Angeles, and didn't want to build a home there, but she's the one who lives there.

She doesn't wait for my guess. "You got in!"

I scream and hug her.

She tells me how proud she is and starts making plans while pulling away from the dance school, but I don't pick up much: my mind is spinning.

I honestly didn't think I'd get in. I shouldn't have. Mamie must have donated money or pulled more strings. It's too much. I can't ever repay her, and I can't not go. It'd be so ungrateful—and I want to go! Of course I want to, but all I can think of is that if I go, I'll never see Matt again. Oh, come on! Would I seriously not go to Paris because a guy might ask me out if I stay?! There's a chance we wouldn't even be in the same math class next year anyway, and then I'd never see him again even if I stayed. Staying would be rude and pathetic. Ah, but going—going to Paris for a year, dancing with the rain outside the open window overlooking the Eiffel Tower, eating a chocolate croissant under the awning of a corner café, shopping, taking style tips from my fashion mogul mamie and Aunt Eloise—it could change my life.

5 WHY DID I EVEN BUY A YEARBOOK?

JOLENE

Do me a favor and act a little surprised when I tell you, the rest of the school year passes without Matt asking me out.

After graduation and the seniors are set free of WCHS, Logan comes to my house. We grab some snacks and hike past the second story up to my attic.

I wasn't always supposed to have an attic. My dad built our house for a family of three. All was well and good until, surprise—I came along. They crammed me in with Mary for a while until our constant fighting drove them insane. Rather than give up his office, my dad had a sizeable chunk of the attic made up for me. Mary rubbed it in my face that I had to be the one to move to the attic, but when it was finished, and she laid eyes on it, she pouted, went to her much smaller room, slammed the door, and has been slamming it ever since.

Logan takes his seat at my desk and starts setting up his gaming laptop. When my dad was replacing my last laptop, which decided it was time to die last spring, Logan told me to ask for a gaming laptop, which I did. When it arrived, my dad and Logan spent the evening loading all sorts of things they thought were necessary onto it. I mean, it can do a lot, but I don't know what that lot is—I only use it for schoolwork and to game with Logan. It's on my bed, ready to play, but I'm not. I sit at my vanity, inspecting my face.

"My sister, Jess, got a computer for her birthday," Logan says as if I don't know who Jess is. "I tried to get her to let me set it up, but she insisted on doing it herself."

"Uh-huh."

There's a tiny hair that wants to stand out and upstage the rest of my eyebrows. Where are my tweezers? I search my vanity, find them, and pluck.

"Are you ready?" he asks me.

"Oh, yeah." I move to my bed and reach for my laptop, but it's got my yearbook on it. I toss the book toward Logan. "You haven't signed it yet." and open my laptop and load the game as he flicks through my yearbook, seeing who else has written in it and what they've said. It makes me a little embarrassed, but it's just Logan, so I let him.

"Alice Sistine signed your yearbook?"

"She's nice," I say.

He shrugs. He's not the first to raise his eyebrows because someone like Alice Sistine deigned to sign my book as if cheerleaders couldn't act outside their programming.

"You get Matt's signature?" he asks.

"No. It was against Asimov's Three Laws of Popularity."

I open the front-facing camera on my phone and check if my pores look smaller on camera than they do in the mirror.

"I didn't get the chance," I say. "He's junior class treasurer—"

"I know," Logan says, eyes rolling.

"So he had to help with Senior Week."

Why someone so bad at math would want to be treasurer, I don't understand. I do, however, get why people voted for him.

"I've hardly seen him—"

"Aww," he says, his eyes twinkling.

"What?"

He shows me what.

"You've drawn a little heart around Matt's picture."

I snatch the yearbook away.

"I didn't sign it yet!" he protests.

"Then stop looking through it and sign it." I shove it back at him.

He opens it again.

"Do you think it'd be pathetic if I asked one of his friends where he lived, tracked him down, and asked him to sign it?" I ask on my way back to my vanity. My phone is useless.

"No," he says. "That sounds like something an almost too normal of a person would do, especially if you showed him this cute little heart."

"Guys like girls who dance, right? Is it just cheerleading, or is it like ballet, too?"

"I'm sure it's both." He glares at me for some reason.

40

"What?"

"Are you kidding me?!"

"What?!"

"I'm sure Matt's not going out with Caradine because she's a cheerleader." He maneuvers in game.

"You don't know."

He snorts as a response.

"How was graduation?" I ask.

Maybe I should start wearing my hair in loose curls like Caradine does. I take my hair out of my ponytail.

"I'm quitting band," he says. "I am never playing 'Pomp and Circumstance' for forty minutes ever again. Ever."

"Aww," I say. "But then, who will play the trumpet loudly and off-key?"

He scowls at me in the mirror.

"Oh," he says, a smile creeping into place despite my teasing. "There are others. They're quieter now, but once the loudest among them is gone, they'll rise up. They always rise up."

I laugh and let Logan have some quiet so he can write the world's best cliché in my yearbook. But later, when I read it—it's actually very sweet:

Jolene, I'll miss you while you're gone, but I'll remember you every time I flip past a ballet video you'd want me to stop on, see Matt in the hallway, eat a tangerine, or walk by that puddle that soaked your socks last time it rained.

Your Best and Most Amazing Friend,

Logan Monnel

41

He sets it aside and turns back to his laptop.

"Are we still fighting the bog?" he asks.

"It won't lift!" I say while adding more mascara to my lashes.

"It might help if you played."

"It might not," I admit.

Ugh, I don't want to play. I want to sit in front of my mirror and obsess over why he didn't choose me over Caradine. But of course, he didn't! She has curvy legs; mine look like a cartoon fox is trying to pass for a stork in an archery contest. They certainly wouldn't inspire Matt to dress up like a bird in order to win a kiss from me. Just saying. And my butt? I don't have a butt. I have the butt of a starving child from a third-world country. And my eyebrows? Ugh!

Of course, I don't say any of this. Instead, I look at all these problem areas, also known as my entire body, in my mirror while Logan tries to game but occasionally shoots a concerned glance my way.

"What are you doing?" he asks.

"Nothing," I say, switching between pulling my shirt tighter over my waist and letting it billow out.

Someone knocks. I look at Logan, who looks back at me with a curious expression. Who on earth is knocking? Hopefully, it's not Mary and one of her evil friends—but those don't knock.

"Come in?" I ask.

It's just my mom. She comes into my room wearing jeans and a light-pink button-up blouse. If it were me, and I were in my late thirties on my day off, I'd be

42

wearing pajama shorts and a camisole. Oh, look, that's what I'm wearing.

"You didn't show me your yearbook," she says, eyeing the one Logan tossed back on my bed. "When I was in high school, I'd go through the entire thing and bookmark which pages I was on—"

"I'm on one," I say.

"Well, you're not on any teams," she says. "I was a class officer and a cheerleader, and on yearbook, and the president of the fashion club—"

"I'm on two pages," Logan says.

My mom gives him a smile as a little present. "Because you're on band?"

"Uh-huh," he says, oblivious to her condescending tone.

"Did you get all the signatures you wanted?" she asks me.

"A lot of the junior class officers weren't around when the yearbooks came out," I say. "I mean, I'm sure they got theirs, but I haven't seen them since..."

My mom sees right through me.

"Any junior class officer in particular?" she asks.

Logan and I answer simultaneously: him in the affirmative, me in the negative.

I exhale and roll my eyes at him. Traitor.

"Just this guy in my math class," I say. "We were kind of friends."

"A junior in a freshman math class?"

I don't like the note of shame in her voice.

"What?" I ask. "He was cool."

What a failure my mom would see me as if she knew how hard I tried to get him to like me, and sucked at it.

"The best time to buy airline tickets is tonight if you want to get there in time to have a few days before class starts," she says. "So I need a definitive answer by eight."

Logan looks at me confused. "I thought you were going."

"I haven't completely decided," I say as my mom leaves.

"What's there to think about?" His question jars things into perspective. It would sound so stupid to say out loud all the things I've been thinking: who would watch my cat? Stupid. What if Matt wants to marry me? Stupid.

After Logan leaves, I flip through my yearbook, reading what people have written today. Everything except Logan's is bland and impersonal. "Have a nice summer" written over and over again. Several people didn't even get that far—they wrote their names and left it at that. I'm a nobody. Invisible.

I trade my yearbook for the novel I finished back in May, *Back From London*. Much like Mary's summer in France, Yesenia's trip to England transformed her. She returned to her hometown a goddess. If I stay in Goleta, nothing will change. I'll be the same forever. But if I go to Paris—if I let Paris change me—there's a chance I could return and finally get what I want. Maybe I'll never see Matt again, but who knows, maybe I will, or maybe I'll meet another guy, and this time I'll be the kind of girl he asks to the school dance and brags about dating to his friends.

I go down to the second story and find my mom in her room on her laptop. She looks up at me as I enter and sit on the edge of her bed.

I open my mouth, then shut it, then open it again. "I want to go to Paris."

The rest of my time in California I spend hanging out with Logan and being ignored by Mary. You'd think your sister—who knows full well she won't see you for an entire year—would say more than three words to you in the weeks before you left, but no. She's off here and there with her cheerleading friends. I only see her during meals or when we bump into each other on the stairs, during which times our conversation consists of grunts and "move."

6 MARY

MARY

You'd think in the days before she left for a year, my sister would do more than be in the way and annoy me. It's as if she's trying to get in enough obnoxiousness to last the whole year she'll be gone.

I wish I remembered the days before Jolene was born or even conceived. But it was only a few months after I came screaming into the world that Mom got pregnant by Jolene's dad, and they had her. I only got to enjoy being an only child for a split second—and don't think that being the oldest child gives me any privileges. That may be true in other families. They all get more photos taken of them as babies, get better clothes, and get more attention. I don't relate to any of it. But I don't have youngest-child syndrome either. I don't know what I have—neglected child syndrome?

Dad has never restrained from letting anyone and everyone know which of his daughters he prefers, and of course, it's his own. I can't even fault him for that, but it would be nice if he loved me at all or even liked me.

And it's not like I haven't tried to get him to like me, I have! I study hard—I'm quiet. He always tells us about his glory days playing high school football, so I tried out for cheer as a freshman and moved up the ranks. I thought he'd be excited when I made varsity, but I made the mistake of telling him the same day Jolene got an A on a math final. I aced all my finals, but she got one A, and it was like Christmas.

But it's okay. I only have to deal with Dad's favoritism when I'm around him, which, now that I'm busier, is less and less and about to be even lesser for an entire year now that Jolene's leaving.

Days before her departure, she bumps into me on the stairs. I punch her arm in greeting.

"Will you take care of Horatio for me?" She has the nerve to ask.

"Cat? Yes. Dog? No." I go to pass her—but she turns when I do and keeps blabbering.

"I'm taking Dogberry."

"Good."

"Horatio gets night terrors if he sleeps alone," she says.

"I said I'd watch him."

"But you didn't say if you'd let him sleep in your bed—"

"I'm not going to give you a written report of everything I'm going to do for your dumb cat."

Of course, I'm going to let Horatio sleep in my bed. I don't know why she's even asking. I walk away, though. Let her worry.

7 FIRST CLASS TO PARIS

JOLENE

I stand barefoot on a grassy cliff, staring over a beach at dusk, the salty air whips my hair and my white, gossamer, flowy dress. Music dances on the air; it swells and crescendos like a score from an old cinematic drama about a love triangle so complicated and painful that not even the Civil War could tear it apart.

He comes to me wearing a billowing white shirt—of course, it's unbuttoned, and black, thigh-high pirate boots with a rapier at his waist. He wraps one arm around me and pulls me close to him roughly, jostling my sleeve off my shoulder.

"Matt," I say. "It's almost sunset. They'll take me away when it rises again."

"Let them try."

He leans down to kiss me, and my dog licks my face.

"Okay. I'm up," I tell Dogberry, who dances around the room anxiously, the way he does every morning.

I rub the sleep crust out of the corner of my eyes, throw back the covers, snatch up my glasses, and pick up my novel that had been on my blankets when I threw them back, toss it on my bed, slide on my flip-flops, grab my nearest sweater, and walk downstairs. I let Dogberry out the back door—a few minutes of me freezing my butt off pass, and Dogberry returns. We run back up the stairs. He curls onto my rug, leaning against my bed, as I pull the still-warm covers back over me.

I try to fall back asleep and return to the dream, but I can't. Like most of my dreams lately, this one seemed to stem from falling asleep in the middle of a chapter; it's almost exactly like my book. I flip it to the page I fell asleep reading. Our heroine stands on a cliff facing the ocean with the man of her dreams. Why does this seriously never happen in real life?

I put the book aside again as Dogberry's traveling crate in the corner of my room draws my attention and pokes my traveling anxiety. I don't know how I'm going to convince him that being inside of it for half a day will be worth it. My mom got some pills to help him sleep during the flight, but I can't help worrying as Horatio crawls onto my face, plops down, and resumes his tiny cat snores. I push him off. Despite often falling asleep on my face, I'll probably miss him more than my sister.

My mom drives Dogberry and me to the little Santa Barbara airport early in the morning. I said goodbye to Mary and my dad at the house, so we'd have room for Dogberry in my mom's car. Mary was moody, and my dad teared up.

My mom parks and helps me grab my luggage, I take Dogberry by the leash, and we enter the airport. My mom flies a lot, so she knows where she's going and we—faster than I expected—reach the check-in counter. We check in my luggage and Dogberry, and an airport employee introduces himself as my guide, puts a lanyard around my neck that says MINOR in fat red letters, and joins us as we head to security. Once there, he takes my carry-on and lays it on the conveyor belt, and my mom gives me a hug.

"Goodbye, honey." She wraps me in a hug. "Look after yourself? Paris isn't a super safe place."

"I will," I assure her.

"Don't talk to strangers, no matter how cute they are."

"I won't," I say. "I saw that movie, too."

"Stay inside if there are any protests."

"I will, Mom."

"Come here." She hugs me tightly again and kisses my cheek. I return it all.

My guide leads me through the airport and to my gate. I get early boarding because of my minor status, so it isn't long before I'm summoned, and my guide tells me what to look for when I land.

I take a deep breath, and look out the airport windows at the hills I won't see for a year. I say goodbye to Santa Barbara, goodbye to Matt, goodbye to my past self, and step on the boarding bridge.

My seat is an aisle seat. I might have been able to get a window, but I took so long to decide to come or not, that there were none left. I have to get up to let the window seat ticket holder in, then again to let in the one with the middle seat. Any second we'll take off— or so I keep thinking. But then something strange happens. Two flight attendants at the front of our section seem confused, and I can't help but feel it has to do with me. Finally, one comes over.

"Jolene Stansen?" she asks.

"Yeah," I say.

"It looks like you've been bumped up to first class."

"Me?"

"That's right. If you'll follow me."

I dance ballet. I know better than to disobey a woman with a bun that tight.

I stand up and reach for my carry-on in the overhead, but a male flight attendant beats me to it.

"I've got it," he says.

I don't mean to, but I make a bewildered face, follow the bun woman to the front of the plane, and up a flight of stairs. Down an aisle of compartments we go until we reach what must be mine.

"Here we are," she says, standing aside so I can enter the enclosed room. "We'll take off in seven minutes. The phone calls me directly, so if you need anything, my name's Joyce. May I get you anything now?"

I take it all in. Everything is either white leather or mahogany. Three small windows let the sun in, and the room smells amazing. It's probably the lilies in the vase on the desk. I inspect them—oh, she asked me a question. What could I possibly want?

"I think I'm good," I tell her. "Thank you."

"Then enjoy your flight."

I buckle myself into the white leather seat and pull out my fantasy-romance about a girl marooned on a magical island. I read all about how she falls in love with a mystical young king while our flight takes us up through the US and into Canada. Some bottomless caviar and a quarrel between our lovers take us over the southernmost tip of Greenland. We fly over the rest of the Atlantic, and one more diet soda, one more kiss between a young woman and king before their relationship is tragically torn to shreds see us safely to Paris.

Joyce knocks and opens my cabin door.

"Did you enjoy your flight?"

I smile and nod. All words would understate. But something's been bugging me, and I figure I might as well ask.

"Do you know why I got bumped to first class?"

"I thought you knew." Joyce smiles and tilts her head. "It was courtesy of the House of Duchene."

8 THE HOUSE OF DUCHENE

JOLENE

I don't think many people at my school have heard of The House of Duchene; the brand's not all that famous, especially in the States, so I seldom talk about it. I mean, I don't want to come across as bragging. I learned way later than I should have that it makes people hate you. In junior high, I used to eat lunch with a group of girls, even though I only knew one of them, Lindsey Calisher. I told you about her—she's a year ahead of me in school and ballet. Anyway, one of her friends asked me where I got my shoes. Usually, I didn't talk much, and they didn't really talk to me. I didn't super fit in with the group and just sat with them because I had no one else to sit with, and they let me. But when I told this girl, "They were a birthday present from my aunt in Paris," she sneered, lifted her nose, and made a face at the girl on her other side. I couldn't understand it for the longest time. You got laughed at if you shopped at places too cheap, but if you had something expensive, that wasn't okay either.

Luckily, it wasn't long after that I started hanging out with Logan. One year, he sat next to me in history. We never spoke to each other until he randomly asked me if I had read the assignment. A few days later he suggested I join a horror book club that met during lunch, and one lunch period the club disbanded so we ate together anyway, and have been eating together ever since.

He's so easy to be around that sometimes I forget he's there. He'll just be places without me even remembering I invited him, which is fine. Like, he was at our Thanksgiving last year. I don't know what his mom and little sister did, but he spent the entire day with us.

One time he randomly rode his bike over and when he got to my house, we were leaving for church, so he just joined us, stayed until I told him I needed to get ready for bed, and then rode all the way home in the dark with my dad following him in his car, so Logan could see. It was crazy. Logan lives all the way across town, so far from me he almost went to Turnpike High. Meanwhile, I live about as far west as you can before the beach curves and you end up in the ocean.

The house my father built literally overlooks the Pacific. There's a wall around our backyard and a gate that leads right to the sand. We're also about a hundred yards from the closest building, so we don't have a lot of neighborhood issues, but we also don't get our pizza within twenty minutes, our mail is often who-knows-where, and the wildlife isn't afraid of us. One summer, a mountain lion stalked us, and we couldn't leave the house until animal control hauled it away. Even then, it was three days before I'd go out the front door. We also get surfers crossing through our property, but apart from the litter, they don't bother us. I definitely don't mind them.

Last summer, after my dad made me pick up after the surfers and Logan helped me, we got some boards and tried to learn how to surf. After a day of failing to stand up, we quit. Logan never tried again, but after relentless attempts I finally got it, but it was long after Logan had gone inside.

My parents always told us to never swim in the ocean alone. But the older and more rebellious we got, the more slacked-in-their-rules they got. We could finally pacify them by wearing smartwatches and wetsuits. The water was so cold we wanted them anyway.

I didn't even bring a wetsuit to France. I wonder what the beaches will be like, and how often I'll be able to go to them. Uncle Caspian spends a great deal of time at the beaches in the South, but that doesn't mean I'll be able to. I have so much on my list of things to do, but I'm sure a year, even a busy year, will ensure my entire list is all checked off.

Although, stepping out of the car that was sent for me and being greeted by Marnie's Rococo home, I wonder if I couldn't be perfectly happy staying indoors all year. Her mansion is ancient, but of course remodeled. It looks like a museum, has six stories, a million windows, and is in the Seventh Arrondissement by the Eiffel Tower, Seine, and the Champ de Mars.

I've been here before—once when I was small, like five or something, and then my dad made it a point to take his daughters to France when we turned twelve—something he didn't decide to do until after Mary turned thirteen.

A man in a tux opens one of the front doors, and Dogberry and I step inside. The entryway is all white marble, which makes a satisfying clack when my aunt Eloise runs up to me.

"Jolene!" She wraps her tiny arms around me tightly, and I get a whiff of something that smells like cucumber and elegance.

She pulls away, holding my shoulders in her small hands and surveying me with a huge grin, as I do the same to her. She's a bit taller than I am, but that might be the heels. She's thin and perfectly manicured with her shock-white hair—chicly contrasted by her deep olive skin—pulled up into a neat pony. A pair of large round glasses sits above her smile. There's a subtle perfection in her look, simple, understated, and classic. No wonder she's taken over Mamie's fashion empire. She could style a goat and send it down a runway to applause.

"Everyone is waiting for you." She takes my hand and leads me through the lobby and halls, all with marble floors covered in expensive and ancient-looking carpets I cringe to step on. But Dogberry and Eloise traipse right across them, so I try to ignore my gut feeling to take off my shoes.

We enter a large room, with tall windows and an unlit fireplace boasting a huge mantel with a giant picture of my mamie when she was younger.

Mamie, my grandmother, rises from her couch where she's been sitting with my uncle Caspian, Eloise's husband.

"There's *ma chérie*, Jolie!" Mamie stretches out her arms, and I run to them.

Like Eloise, she smells amazing and cool, has shock-white hair, but worn short and straight, and wears oversized round glasses. She's a little stiff in matching capris and jacket in a deep-blue couch fabric with embroidered flowers and birds. Her neck, wrists and fingers display an abundance of accessories, but to hear her take on it, everyone else under-accessorizes.

"Who is this?" asks Caspian as he waits to hug me. "This can't be little Jo-Jo! You're too tall! Call the airport. We've got the wrong girl."

He gives me a tight hug, lifting me off the ground.

"Did you mean to get an orphan boy instead?" I ask.

He looks at me quizzically, then pets Dogberry. Good job, Jolene. I haven't seen Uncle Cass in years, and I make it awkward. Maybe I should have guessed he didn't grow up reading *Anne of Green Gables*. Maybe I'll stick to referencing things like *Moby Dick* or maybe some book about nautical knots. I honestly know little about Cass apart from his love of sailing. Even right now, he looks like he could be on a boat. He's got five o'clock shadow because, well, you wouldn't want the other pirates making fun of your baby face, wears khaki capris, loafers, and a rope sweater that smells like salt water.

"I'm going to show Jolene where she'll be staying," Eloise says.

"I'll catch up with you in a bit," Mamie tells me, hugging me again.

Eloise leads Dogberry and me out and up the stairs, through doors upon doors of rooms and halls until she gets to a door I don't remember seeing before.

She throws it open and reveals the Eiffel Tower, not in a painting, but huge and right outside my balcony. By the way, I have a balcony. I don't even notice the rest of the room for a whole three minutes. I remain absolutely transfixed by the view until a man in a tux enters and places a charcuterie board, pastries, and lemonade on a round glass and gold table in the entryway. My room has an entryway, by the way. I smile at the inclusion of a few dog biscuits and water in a dog bowl.

Eloise pays this man no mind. "Over here is your ensuite, your closet, your shoe closet, your winter closet—did you bring winter clothes?"

"I don't have winter clothes." It's not entirely true. I have a ski ensemble, but I didn't bring it. Other than that, though, my warmest jacket is a black quilted puff jacket—that I also didn't bring because I packed when it was hot out, and it didn't occur to me that a year in France would include all four seasons.

"Another excuse to shop," Eloise says. "The phone on your end table calls Pierre, the butler, if you need anything, day or night. If he doesn't answer, it'll be one of the others on call. Marietta picks up laundry every morning. Breakfast is at seven o'clock, but they'll bring you a tray if you miss it. Mamie has quite a few little pups, so the staff is well-trained for dogs, and Dogberry will have company. The masseuse comes at four o'clock on Thursdays. Mamie's arranged for the hairdresser to visit us this Friday, but Caspian is bugging me to let him steal you to Cannes for the weekend to sail. I told him those trips end up being seven-day weekends, and there'll be plenty of time later, but it's up to you. Let's see, what else? Mamie usually meets me for lunch—if it aligns with your schedule, you're, of course, always welcome to join us—oh!" She crosses to the table with the snacks and picks up a small notecard with numbers on it. "This is the Wi-Fi. I know you have your phone, but did you bring your laptop?"

I nod without using words—arriving in Paris has left me speechless. Mamie, Caspian, and Eloise are all so glamorous that I feel grungy and less-than, like I just crawled out of the ocean. I mean, Eloise has been nothing but warm and accommodating; it's just—I worry I'm not worth the effort.

"Let us know if you'd rather we got you a desktop to do your studies," she says. "I know from experience typing on a laptop all day can get odious. I wrote my second book on a laptop in bed. It should have been comfortable, but it was far from it. That was when we were redoing my office, so it was that or at work. What else? I don't know. I'm sure I'll think of it—oh! Dinner tonight, and then my friend Iphigeneia's party. It's her cat Chocolate's birthday, so she's rented La Ménagerie Rouge. The theme is 'Golden.' Did you bring anything gold?"

It's almost too much to process. She said something about a friend, a chocolate cat, and were we going to see a show? Eventually, enough fragments of thoughts materialize and my mind wraps around her question.

"No," I say.

"Good. Another excuse to shop. I'm sorry, you must be tired. Do you want to rest or shop?"

It takes me another moment to process what she's asking. No one's ever put a question like that to me before. Essentially, my aunt's asking me if I want to go with her to buy a golden dress to wear to a private party at La Ménagerie Rouge, or if I want to go to sleep.

"I'm not tired."

9 CHOCOLATE'S BIRTHDAY PARTY

JOLENE

Mamie's butler, Pierre, calls ahead and gets us reservations to peruse a few stores. Mamie buys me new luggage, saying I need to hurl mine into the Seine—new shoes, new underwear, several new outfits, some dresses, and we even squeeze in a hair and makeup appointment—canceling the hairdresser she had scheduled for Friday. We also visit Eloise's friend's boutique, a little pink and black shop with a French name I can't pronounce written in black letters above the door.

I slip inside one of the two dressing rooms and pull the black velvet curtain shut. I hate when they use curtains instead of doors. It makes me feel like anyone can burst in, but Mamie and Eloise stand just outside, and don't seem the bursting type.

I try on a golden sequin top that surprisingly flatters my pale skin and pair it with a slate-blue, ruffled skirt that has guitars and music notes on it. The print makes the ensemble less high-class, perhaps, but playful, which suits me fine.

I look in the mirror. Suddenly, everything I used to think about fashion shifts. Maybe there weren't awkward body types. Maybe there was only fashion. Dressed right, you could probably make any body look chic. My legs, which I thought were too skinny, in this skirt and paired with these shoes, look long and elegant. My chest, which hasn't quite grown in—at least I hope this isn't my final form—looks perfect in this shirt. I would be overflowing if I had any more to flow. I look—I don't know, is it okay if I say "good"?

I get rave reviews on exiting the dressing room, especially from the shop owner, who, to be fair, acquired it.

Mamie makes the purchases, we dine out, drop Mamie off at home, and head off to Eloise's friend Iphigeneia's cat's birthday party.

The thing about La Ménagerie Rouge is that when they say "Rouge," they mean "Rouge." Everything is red—everything. There's a giant red water wheel that mimics the larger one outside, a red stage, the dance floor in front of the mountain of red seats is red; the tables on the mezzanine are red; you step inside, and you, in fact, become red. I've never been redder than I am at this moment.

Several feet from us, a red Iphigeneia Mischka welcomes her guests—or her cat's guests. But where Chocolate is is anyone's guess. Iphigeneia certainly isn't holding him or her. Is Chocolate a boy cat name or a girl cat name? Either way, I'm bummed it isn't here. I had plans to spend my night petting it and ignoring humans. Although that would have been hard—the humans are everywhere and showing more skin than I've ever shown in my entire life. Even when I have a leotard on, I don't show this much leg. I've never felt self-conscious because I had a lot of clothes on before, but everyone is slender and fit and in a hurry to show it off. They're not dressed like Eloise. I kind of thought they would be. But she wears black pants and a sequin top. The guys, however, dress much like Caspian, who's donned a black, ribbed tee with four buttons down the top front of his chest.

Eloise takes my elbow. It's loud, so she has to lean in close to my ear to speak.

"There are a few things I would warn you about concerning Iphigeneia." Eloise presses her lips together and a crease forms between her eyebrows as though needing a moment to figure out how to tell me bad news.

"Too late," Caspian says. "She's coming."

Iphigeneia Mischka, breathtakingly beautiful, with porcelain skin and a round, timeless face, makes her way toward us wearing a short, sleeveless, golden dress with a gathered ruffle on one side. Sequins, crystals, and golden beads gleam in the red lights, and despite already being obviously intoxicated, she doesn't trip when she topples around on her golden stilettos, which are, perhaps, literally gold.

Her eyes drift in my direction but don't quite reach me before whipping back to Eloise and Caspian.

She reminds me of Matt's girlfriend, Caradine, who could never bring herself to actually look at me.

I bet Caradine is horrible to him, and he's miserable whenever he's around her. He never smiled when she was with him. I wonder where he is right now. I think it's noon in California. He's probably having lunch. Do you think what he used to eat at school is the same as what he eats at home? Whenever I saw him sitting with Caradine and her friends, he was always eating a sandwich, an apple, and a soda.

"It's not too much, is it?" Iphigeneia flips one of her blond locks back to join its friends. "If one more columnist calls my parties too extravagant, I'm going to scream!"

Uncle Caspian smirks, raises his eyebrows, grins at me, then turns to Iphigeneia. "If you don't rent out La Ménagerie Rouge for your cat's birthday, do you even care?"

I stifle a laugh but can't beat back my smile, so I turn my face away and take in the room, now that I'm properly in it.

The party is too much, but wonderfully so, like eating all your candy on Halloween, or staying up all night at a slumber party, or having two Thanksgivings in one day because both grandparents are in town and don't get along with each other.

"I think the party's great," I say.

But complimenting this person is a mistake. In two steps, she is on top of me, patting my hair, wrapping her arms around me, and leaning on my neck.

"You know," she swirls my hair in her fingers, "when I met you a second ago, I did not like you. But now you're my favorite person at the party!"

64

I widen my eyes and aim them at Eloise. She receives my distress call but remains inactive—stunned.

A man brushes past me—his broad, bronze-skinned arm grazing my shoulder. I recognize him from various period-drama movie posters and the cover art on *The Count of Monte Cristo West End* cast recording album. There's a possibility I may have sung along with him, pretending to be his love interest, Eugénie, so often that I permanently hurt my voice going for the high notes.

He's slightly older now than when he played Albert, maybe late teens or early twenties, older enough to be properly broad-shouldered and large-forearmed. He keeps his dark hair long, probably to cut back on wig fittings, has a cleft chin like only men in novels and cartoon chauvinists have, and I know it's so cliché to say he has a crooked smile, but so help me he has a crooked smile, and I don't mean his teeth are crooked—his teeth are abnormally straight and blindingly white, but when he smiles, half his mouth rises and the other half resists—probably conscientiously objecting to such frivolity as smiling when there are more serious matters to attend to, like wrestling bears or rescuing damsels.

I try not to stare as he pulls Iphigeneia off of me, interrupting her tracing my cheek with her pinky.

It's crowded, and he's pressed right up against me. Apart from my dad, Logan, and the guys behind me in line at theme parks, I've literally never been this close to a man before. Even then, none of those guys made my chest pound like it wanted to escape the bounds that kept it separated from this specimen of men. It makes me warm, and I'm not sure if the warmth is coming from him, the room, or if my body is about to spontaneously combust.

"Tragic news tonight," the newscaster will say. "La Ménagerie Rouge was set ablaze by a *Carrie*-like incident, when an American teenaged girl ignited, setting the entire place on fire, killing 200 guests, including one boiling hot celebrity with a singing voice so pure, it made choir boys cry, and a cat."

"Come on, Geneia. It's time to say hello to the other guests," Oscar Ivanov tells Iphigeneia.

"But I want to stay with Jojo! She's the only one who gets it!" Iphigeneia protests against his pulling arms by pulling mine.

Without my approval, my eyes bug out of my head—another distress call, this time to Oscar Ivanov, of all people!

"Your other guests want to wish Chocolate a happy birthday," he says.

That does the trick. He pivots her by the shoulders and nudges her toward a neighboring cluster of red cat lovers. After setting my new bestie upon this new group of victims, he returns to Eloise, Caspian, and me.

"You two are on again, I'm assuming," Caspian says.

Oscar rolls his eyes as an answer. Then he looks at me and back at Cass.

"This is my niece," Eloise says. "Jolene, this is Oscar."

"Now it makes sense," he says. "Far too gorgeous to be related to Cass."

Caspian smirks as Oscar smiles his half smile again.

66

Despite knowing he's just flattering me, and Eloise while he's at it—I can't help but blush. Thankfully, under these lights, no one knows it.

The rest of the night is a red blur, until finally—far too late in the early morning—we drive back to Mamie's.

The drive is calm, somber, and beautiful. Away from the red of La Ménagerie Rouge, all the pink lights seem pale. The romance of the city seems melancholy. The old architecture, the trees, and the river run deep with secrets they whisper of gallant men, beautiful women, and stolen kisses on bridges.

Somewhere along the way, I doze off because the next thing I know, the sun is shining through my open window, a tray topped with croissants, cream, milk, fruit, cheese, and eggs lays on top of my bedside table, and I'm wearing the shirt, and skirt I wore the night before—my shoes on the floor.

It can't be earlier than six, but Dogberry hasn't woken me up to go outside yet. Did he die? I reach down and feel his back. He's still breathing. Maybe he's off schedule, or maybe someone came, took him out, and brought him back already.

I sit up and pull a million bobby pins out of my hair. Its shorter length surprises me—oh yeah, I got it cut. I give it a good few rubs and a flip, try a grape, and notice a note slipped in under the cream, reading:

Meet us at eleven o'clock for lunch. Pierre knows where. I suggest acquainting yourself with the pool in the meantime.

— Eloise

The pool is massive, of course, and surrounded by gardens. Flowers for days and hedges stretch so far that I wonder how the city allows them to take up this much space.

It's warm out, and the water feels nice, especially after the sticky heat of the night before.

After a few laps, I head into my bathroom. The walls, floors, and counters are tan marble. Off-white, fluffy rugs cover the floor and feel as though they've never been stepped on.

I turn on the water and let it heat up while rinsing my bikini in the sink. Once I ring it out, I fling it over the shower door as steam starts to rise. Inside, I'm greeted by an array of soaps. My bathroom back home had shampoo, conditioner, and body wash. This shower has shampoo, conditioner, deep conditioner, hair oil, body wash, body moisturizer, shave foam, face soap, face moisturizer, face exfoliant, body exfoliant, hair exfoliant—I don't even know what that is—foot scrub, hand moisturizer, pumice stone, a puff, a razor, all name brand, and all smell like exotic citrus.

I finish, put on a robe I find behind the bathroom door, and turn to the sink and mirror. A whole new assortment of tubs, bottles, hair curlers, straighteners, blow dryers, brushes, sprays, and moisturizers await me.

I try out some creams in my hair, blow dry it, then braid it to the side. I brought my own makeup, but Mamie and Eloise have taken care of that, too, and expertly so. The bottles of foundation perfectly match my skin, better than what I brought, and they apply flawlessly.

I finish my makeup and appreciate that I've never looked better. If Matt could see me now, he'd probably look at me, say something sweet, then take Caradine to Prom all over again. Let's face it.

I meet Mamie and Eloise for lunch at a little patio café near the St. Quentin Market and order a cheeseburger. As the waiter refills my drink, Mamie hands an envelope to me.

"Here," she says as I open it and find a black credit card inside. "It doesn't have a credit limit, but Jolie, I do. No more than twenty thousand a month, please."

My mouth falls open. I don't know the exchange rate, but I know enough to know that's quite a bit.

"Wow. Thank you, Mamie..."

"*Vous êtes les bienvenus, chéri.*[1] Now excuse me a moment."

Mamie walks in the direction of the bathrooms, and Eloise tilts her head toward me.

"If you go over, Maman will one, never know, and two, never care."

But I make a mental note to stick to Mamie's more-than-generous parameters. I'm not even sure I could spend more if I tried. What do rich people find to spend their money on? That question is answered after days of shopping, eating, swimming, parties, premieres, museums, plays, ballets, and operas, and just when I start getting used to the routine, able to

---

[1] You are welcome, darling.

find my way around, and it's looking like life might just be amazing, my ballet classes begin.

10 L'INSTITUT DU BALLET DE PARIS

JOLENE

The ballet school is such that it feeds into a rather impressive company. Many who graduate get offered positions, and those still in the school have the chance to audition for small *corps de ballet* roles. I don't dare wish to graduate into the company, especially not at fifteen or sixteen, but I do hope to get a *corps* position in *The Nutcracker* coming up.

With all my dreams gathered up in the pit of my stomach, I step out of the car and let the chauffeur shut the door behind me. I want to keep my eyes on the floor, too scared of being intimidated by the building before me, but I force myself to look up at its beautiful centuries-old architecture. I feel tiny and insignificant.

The ballet studio occupies the entire building, but my class is on the thirteenth floor—in a foreboding way.

But just when I think everything is class and elegance, I approach the woman at the front counter who wears pineapple earrings and hot-pink lipstick on her teeth.

"Nouvelle?" she asks.

I respond with the little French my mother insisted I learn after assessing the results of the month I spent on a language app.

"Je vous demande pardon. Je ne parle pas français,"[2] I say.

"Are you new?" she asks again, pointedly emphasizing the consonants, as if she missed breakfast, and chewing on her words must tie her over until lunch.

"Oh—yes. *Oui.*"

She smirks, and stretches out her hand toward me, palm up. I glance at it, then at her, not understanding her unspoken French.

"Identifiant, s'il vous plaît."[3] Her spoken French isn't much plainer.

In eloquent response, I balk.

"Identification." But her accented English isn't any more clear than her French. She might as well go back to nonverbal foreign communication.

Then it dawns on me. "Oh!" I pull out my passport and hand it to her.

She rolls her eyes, types, and then hands me a security badge. "This gets you in and out of the building. While you are in the building, perhaps not during classes, you will have this on your person. *Oui?"*

---

[2] I beg your pardon. I don't speak French.
[3] Identify yourself, please.

I can tell she thinks I ought to have responded already, only I just now finished deciphering and decoding what she said. As quickly as I can, I reply, *"Oui!"*

She rolls her eyes for the fiftieth time and waves me off toward the elevator.

I don't look back. I push the thirteen, wait, exit on the wrong floor, get back in, exit on the correct floor, and face a long hallway. They said my class would be in room 671, but none of the doors have numbers. I finally find one with a number 792. I turn around and there's 784. I follow this direction—as the numbers seem to be declining—the odd ones I find.

At last, I come upon the room. Inside, several teenage boys and girls stretch, put on their ballet slippers, and chat in the large mirrored room with barres, Degas paintings, a piano in the corner, and windows overlooking the city. The instructor stands by the door, going over some music. She smiles at me as I enter.

"You must be Jolene Stansen," she says.

"Yes."

"I am Madame Patenaude. How much French do you speak?"

"Hardly any," I say.

"Don't let that slow you down."

"I won't."

"You're the only one who doesn't speak it, and I won't slow down or repeat myself."

I'm about to respond when she plows on ahead—as promised, not slowing down even a little bit. "Take your spot at the barre, *s'il vous plaît.*"

73

Let me fill you in on ballet etiquette. Your spot at the barre is sacred, and once it's yours, it remains yours for the entire season. Anyone who tries to claim your spot—well, I don't know what happens to them because I've never seen it done.

I don't want to be greedy, so I don't rush for the best spot—the one right next to the teacher. Whoever gets this spot always gets extra attention, favoritism, and inevitably more solos.

Everyone settles in and, to my surprise, none of them take the best spot. Maybe things are different here. Or maybe they're scared to be so close to Mme. Patenaude. Should I show her I'm not afraid? Why not?

I walk to the barre, place my hand on it, and feel an icy chill gust over me. The dancers around me stare—unsure? Suspicious? I don't know what they mean by acting so cold until a guy, who looks like he broke out in muscles, enters with horror and disgust on his strikingly gorgeous face.

"Qui est-ce? Qu'est-ce que cela veut dire? Pourquoi cette petite fille est-elle à ma place?"[4] He yells in my direction.

I don't need to speak French to know he's more than a little angry with me. And I can guess why, although I don't think he needs to sneer so much, just between you and me.

"I'm sorry," I say. "I didn't know it was taken."

He's not pacified despite my hasty retreat.

---

[4] Who is this? What does that mean? Why is this little girl in my place?

"Bien sûr c'est pris. C'est le meilleur endroit de la pièce! Stupide idiot."[5] He says some other things I think are swear words while I rush past him.

A few girls laugh as I take a spot as far from him as possible, putting me in the farthest back corner. Right where I don't want to be.

"He always stands there." I trace the voice to a girl on the other side of the barre I've just grabbed. She very nearly smiles.

"I thought it was the first day of class," I say.

Does he reserve the spot even when a new class starts? Even when there are a bunch of new students in the room? I've never seen that before.

"No talking!" Mme. Patenaude yells in English.

She stands in the front corner, where I was, and calls out the barre routine.

My teacher in Goleta would call out the routine and demonstrate it for us while she did it. I never realized before how dependent I was on the visuals for some of these terms. But with a few glances around me, I catch on quickly and manage to keep up. It's just barre work, after all. I've been doing this since I was eight years old. How often Mme. Patenaude rushes over to correct me, however, makes me feel like a beginner, and her insults seep through her French.

"Étendre. Coude vers le haut. Je suis furieuse! C'est une technique de base!"[6]

As the class progresses and we move on to center, I slowly realize Mamie pulling strings to get me into the

---

[5] Of course it's taken. This is the best place in the room, stupid idiot.
[6] Extend. Elbow up. I am furious! It is a basic technique!

program might not have been the best idea. It seems like everyone else has danced with Mme. Patenaude before. They anticipate her, seem at ease, and don't get called out for tiny mistakes that aren't exactly wrong as much as they are stylistically not what Mme. Patenaude prefers. Not only that, but I'm at least a year behind everyone else. They're way more flexible and stronger than I am, can do more rotations, have better balance, better turnout, and *port de tête.*

When class is over, Mme. Patenaude leads us in a bow. We clap—she accepts the praise and quiets us.

"Go have lunch. After, during our *pas de deux* class, I will match you with your partner for the season based on how you performed today."

Oh. All of that is in French. I only understand, "Go have lunch," but I guess at the rest and think I do a pretty decent job of it, as when I return, Mme. Patenaude partners me with none other than Captain Temper, whose actual name is Beau Martin, which I know not because he told me in any friendly type of introduction, but because Mme. Patenaude says so when she pushes me across the room by my shoulders to stand by him.

He doesn't speak to me. He doesn't even acknowledge me, but to be fair, being his partner isn't all bad. For one, it's not exactly a struggle to look at him. He could be confused for a model. In short, he's terrifying. He towers over me too, and I wonder if, when we do lifts, he'll send me flying through the roof. He looks like he'd like to.

After pairing everyone, Mme. Patenaude stands in front of the group, glowering at me.

"Pas de jupes autorisées,"[7] she says, rolling her eyes, an action which she also manages to do in French. I know you're thinking eye-rolling is universal and the same in every language. Well, I've had people roll their eyes at me in English, Spanish, and now French. French is the worst, by a lot.

I look around for help. No one is forthcoming.

Mme. Patenaude lets out a deep sigh, strides over to me, and in one quick gesture rips off my ballet skirt.

"Pas de jupes dans la classe pas de deux!"[8] she yells as she throws my skirt to the side of the room.

My eyes stare, large, shocked, mortified. I stand there, paralyzed, in the center of the room. But she isn't done. She slaps my arm, motioning for me to move to the side.

"Rejoignez votre partenaire et apprenez un peu de français pendant que vous y êtes."[9]

She faces the others and calls forward Beau and, shockingly enough, a girl standing on his other side. Somehow, I missed that I wasn't his only partner. But now that I've done the math, there aren't enough guys in the class for every girl to be paired evenly. Of course, some of us would have to share. "Some of us" means me and whoever this girl is.

And whoever she is, she is a personified ballet goddess. Mme. Patenaude has Beau, and this queen of women demonstrate weight transfers, and when they finish, expertly so, they return to the rest of us so we

---

[7] No skirts allowed.
[8] No skirts in pair dance class!
[9] Join your partner and learn some French while you're at it.

underlings can attempt the majestic duo's moves. The movements themselves are fairly straightforward. I *relevé en pointe* in *sous-sus,* with my left foot in front, and arms in first position. I hold stiff as he is to tilt me side-to-side, then back-to-front. Super simple, or at least, it should be.

He motions for me to stand before him.

"Vous Américain?"[10] he asks.

"Um, yes?" I ask.

"Pas de bavarage!"[11] yells Mme. Patenaude, as though volume might help me decipher her foreign tongue.

"Vous danses comme ça," [12] Beau says. I don't understand any of it.

I stand in front of him. I can't remember standing ever being this terrifying. He puts his large hands around my waist, and I'm hit in the face with nine thousand different self-conscious thoughts. Mostly, I wonder if I should say I've never done partner work before. Does that matter? Would they laugh? Would Beau laugh?

He speaks, and I feel his breath on my neck.

"At your leisure, little Jolie," he says in his intoxicating French accent.

I *relevé en pointe* into *sous-sus* into panic. I definitely should have said something, because I didn't understand any of the tips or pointers she might have given during the incomprehensible demonstration. But it's too late. I'm being tilted. I try to keep still, to trust that he's got me. Is it so hard to believe I can trust

---

[10] You American?
[11] No chatter.
[12] You dance like it.

78

him? It feels like even his hands have gigantic muscles, and even on pointe I only come up to his chin.

I look at us in the mirror. If we were a silhouette, you wouldn't be able to see me at all. His entire frame engulfs me. But something embedded deep in my psyche screams that I am too heavy for partner work. I have to be. I can't possibly be acceptable! And so I am not holding rigidly straight. I bend. I fall off *relevé*.

Beau swears, and his other partner laughs. She comes over. I'm sure she'd flip her red hair over her shoulder if she didn't have it pinned up in a bun, probably piercing the part of her brain that controls smug self-admiration.

"Try again," she says.

I obey and *revelé* again, holding *sous-sus*. "It's not hard. Stay straight. Let him do what he needs to. He does it right. You don't need to fight him."

I try and fail again.

"Je ne sais pas pourquoi je m'embête." [13] She sighs. "Again!"

We try again, this time successfully. But praise, there is none. I guess that's fair.

"Learn some French, understand Mme. Patenaude, and maybe you'll pick it up faster," Beau says.

I don't make it into *The Nutcracker*.

---

[13] I don't know why I bother.

11 THE CHAOS OF SWANS

JOLENE

I'm tossing and turning backstage in a giant theater I've never seen before. People dressed as ballet swans fly frantically around me like a whirlpool, except not in any circular spiral. In fact, there's no rhyme or reason to anything anyone's doing.

I look down at my costume. I can't be Odette, the swan princess! But when I reach up to my head, and feel a tiara—yep. My dream role! But I don't know the choreography. I don't know anything.

Hoping for some answers, I grab a passing swan. "What's going on? I haven't been to any of the rehearsals."

She rolls her eyes and pushes me aside. Again and again I try asking the masses swirling about for help, but they all sigh and shove me away.

"Places!" someone yells, and everyone falls into position.

Am I supposed to be on stage? How come nobody is helping me? Who's in charge of this chaos? This is no way to run a ballet company!

I wake up with a jolt in the back of Mamie's car. I must have dozed off on my way home from rehearsal. A flood of relief fills me as reality sweeps back into my mind. It was just a dream, but the relief is short-lived as I remember I'm just as lost in my actual ballet class as in my dream one. It's been months, and I still feel woefully behind.

I sigh and gaze out the car window. Rain glistens down random pathways.

At home, I'd be rehearsing my no doubt minor role in *The Nutcracker,* shopping for Christmas gifts for my family, searching for seasonal loot in-game with Logan, "suffering" through math with Matt...

Maybe coming here was a mistake. So far, I've got nothing to show for it except a worse sense of self than when I started. Not only am I a loser in California, but I've managed to epically spread my loser-dom abroad.

12 BUTT APPEAL

MARY

So far, I've gotta tell ya, I do not mind Jolene being gone. Life is just—easier. The air itself smells better without her stank wafting down from the attic. I even like school better, knowing I won't run into her. She can't embarrass me anymore with her messy hair and dorky shirts. I hope Aunt Eloise is putting a stop to all that. Mom—I love her, but she did nothing to end Jolene's fashion disasters. It's so irresponsible—especially when my mom literally works in fashion. I mean, some of us have reputations we'd actually like to maintain—friends we'd like to hang on to.

Ever since half-way through freshman year, I've started hanging out with Tay-Tay Breiman. She's like the blond version of me—if I were meaner. I appreciate how she doesn't put up with anyone's crap—it's why we're friends.

Tay-Tay and I take algebra third period. We're the only juniors on varsity cheer—they're particular, and they only take twelve girls.

Tonight's an away game, so we wear our purple uniforms with black trim to school. I prefer our black home-game uniforms with purple trim, but a cheer uniform's a cheer uniform.

It's almost time for class to start when Tay-Tay, remaking her long ponytail, leans over to me.

"Do you like Justin Granite?" It's out of nowhere and carries a strange edge of accusation.

The obvious answer is, of course. Who doesn't like that cocky little Viking?

"Psh." I scoff. "No. Why? Did he say something?"

"Not to me."

I think of eight ways to kill her if she doesn't tell me more—five of them fun.

"What did you hear?" I ask.

She sighs. "I heard Tyson telling Anthony that Justin said your butt's hot."

I put on my best impression of girls who act offended by stuff like this. "Ew."

"I thought you said you liked him."

"I'm not a piece of meat." That's something they say, right? "If he had any courage, he'd tell me himself."

"You want him to tell you he thinks your butt's hot?"

"A real man would."

She snorts and takes her ponytail out again.

Only a few guys in school meet the Acceptable Boyfriend Standard or ABS. Justin meets all my criteria. He's stupid wealthy. His dad owns, like, a major company, and his company owns a youth charity that everyone's enrolled in. He's popular, of course, and he's hot. He's got high, tanned cheekbones, and his arm muscles are so large he could probably tear me in half...

Forty minutes later, the bell rings and I realize I've spent the entire class period thinking about letting him try.

13 JUST LIKE CARADINE'S

JOLENE

Christmas break turns out to be a little lonely in France. I get time off from ballet and school, but Eloise, Mamie, and even Cass keep their tight schedules. I've almost made a friend in ballet, but we haven't gotten to the part where we communicate outside of class. So today I shop alone.

I ask the chauffeur to drive me to a store I went into last week with Eloise. They had some cute clothes, but, as usual, Eloise sent back everything I picked out, and pushed her own choices on me. It was hard to complain when she paid for it all—it didn't even come out of the ridiculously enormous budget Mamie set. But there were pieces I haven't been able to get off my mind.

I act like I'm a normal human, and don't dash for the skirt right when I walk in the store. I meander and make my way toward it. Thankfully, they still have it—and in my size.

The attendant finds me a changing room, and I put it on. I don't know why Eloise didn't like it. It's cute. It's really, really short though. But hear me out. I've never worn a skirt this short before, but no one cared that everyone was almost naked at Iphigeneia's party. It might not be as big of a deal as my entire being keeps telling me it is. And I'm wearing it to ballet— over tights.

Okay, yes. Caradine had a skirt just like it, and I want Beau to see me in it. I don't know why! I'm trying not to dig too deep into it. But I know he hates me, and he's cute, and I want him to stop thinking about how bad I am at ballet, and start thinking, "She's bad at ballet, but hot." Okay?! Is that so wrong!?

The morning after break, I dress for class and pull my new skirt on over my leotard and tights, strap on my boots, zip up my jacket, and throw on a hat and scarf. I go downstairs, eat breakfast, and right as I'm about to go out the door, Eloise calls from behind me.

"Jolene?" She bites her bottom lip as I turn to her. "What are you wearing?"

"I went shopping."

"You forgot to buy something." She steps closer to me, inspecting me. "You don't need to dress like this."

"My leotard is shorter."

"You're not walking down the street in your leotard. Here's what I wish someone had told me when I wore my first miniskirt: you'll attract guys, all of them, even the nice guys, but they won't approach you. The ones who'll approach you will be the ones you don't want to approach you."

86

I nod. I can't think of anything else to do. Ashamed and feeling naive, I change into jeans and head to ballet.

14 DESPICABILITY

JOLENE

As months go on, I slowly pick up some French. For example, *"Espèce de stupide petit Américain,"* means, "You stupid little American." *"Je ne peux pas croire que quelqu'un puisse être aussi dépourvu de talent,"* means, "I can't believe anyone could be so untalented," and *"Comment n'oublies-tu pas comment respirer, espèce d'excuse stupide, sans talent, insignifiante pour une petite fille,"* means, "How do you not forget how to breathe, you stupid, talentless, insignificant excuse for a little girl?"

Mme. Patenaude bumped up Beau's other partner—who was in *The Nutcracker*—to the higher class, leaving him all to myself, which I have mixed feelings about. On the one hand, he's gorgeous and talented, but on the other, I sometimes wonder if I would be doing better if I had a partner I was more comfortable around. Although who that would be I couldn't tell you. Show me a man I'm comfortable around besides Logan, my dad, my grandpa, and Uncle Cass, and I'll show you a man that doesn't exist.

But France isn't all bad. There are plenty of times when I'm not in ballet, and those times are incredible. Even school's enjoyable. I take all my classes online through a program my mom set up. A lot of teenage actors use it on location. It's pretty painless. Learning math online, in many ways, is simpler than in a classroom. Online, I'm not too terrified to message my teacher stupid questions. History is a lot of reading and watching short films, then answering short essay questions and multiple choice. For English, I read books, join the class chat about what we've read, write essays, and repeat. The program offers more science classes than the general type at WCHS. I'm taking astronomy, and again it's just a bunch of videos and multiple-choice quizzes. I'm supposed to submit my own video of a science project in a few weeks. I'm still trying to work out what that's gonna be. Maybe it'll be something about the effect *pas de deux* class has on capillaries in my face, but that might be better suited for a biology class. My online French class might be my favorite of the ones I've listed so far, just because it's the most essential to my survival at the moment. Physical education is ballet, as always, and because I'm abroad, my extracurricular coursework is literally sightseeing. I'm taking a photography and French architecture course, so I take photos, write reports about museums and palaces, and I'm not gonna lie, it's pretty posh.

I often accompany Eloise to the office and do schoolwork with her there. Sometimes, she'll ask my opinion about various garments, and she's even allowed me backstage at a few of her runways. I'm low-key hoping a model sprains her ankle or gains too much weight, and I have to step in for her on the catwalk, but so far, that hasn't happened. Plus, I'm pretty sure if any of them gained weight, I'd still be heavier. And most of them are much taller than me.

We've taken a few trips south to sail with Caspian and his sailing friends. When we're on a ship, I always think he'll bark orders at me, the way my dad does when I help him check the fire alarm batteries. But he doesn't. He yells, for sure, but only because he has to be heard over the wind and chaotic chatter of his shipmates.

Sometimes, among Cass's friends is Oscar, the movie star from the cat party. He's only just turned nineteen, and I'm almost sixteen, so I let myself dream I stand a chance, as absurd as it is.

Imagine if he liked me, though. I know—shut up. But sometimes celebrities date normal people, and he's close friends with my aunt and uncle, and I've got novelty on my side. That's a thing, right? Please don't say it's just a book thing. You know how, like in some novels, she moves to a new town, and suddenly, lots of guys are interested in her, whereas before, she was pretty much ignored? There's gotta be some truth to it, or it wouldn't be a trope. In the books, everyone talks about the new girl and assumes things. If it were real, you'd have to hit the ground running to keep up the momentum, or it might slip and you'd be right back where you started. It would be the most powerful thing on Earth if it could get someone like Oscar

Ivanov to like me. Applied correctly, with such power, you could rule the world.

Maybe coming home after being gone for a year will have the same effect as being completely new. But honestly, with my luck, I'll probably slide right back into the slot I left vacant when I went away. Although I've gotten prettier. I'm not gorgeous by any means, but a girl changes a lot between fourteen and almost sixteen—and it's more than just a haircut and better makeup. It's more than just clothing, although how I dress now is worlds different from how I used to— even without the miniskirt. In part, the change is because of Mamie and Eloise refusing to let me shop in stores that sell off-brand baggy jeans and pop culture t-shirts. But they've also drilled into me an appreciation of finer fabrics, staple pieces, clothes that actually fit and flatter me. I've even started gravitating toward shoes that are more than just functional. I can dance for hours on pointe, but I can't walk around the Champs-Élysées in heels? Come on.

But any change I've undergone has only had a negative effect on Beau. He's gone from flat-out rude to flat-out obnoxious. He's evolved from talking to me like a child to talking to me like a princess—and not in a "Duchess of Wales" way, but in a "Don't break a nail, little helpless baby" way—which is stupid, because breaking a nail hurts worse than anything.

He stands a few people behind me as I situate myself to do the combination across the floor: *piqué tour, piqué tour, sauté, chassé, glissade, grand jeté.*

It isn't *pas de deux* class, so I don't have to dance with him, and so I don't. Instead, I get ready to dance across the floor with Helene in front of me.

She's short, has brown hair, and looks like a Bulldog was granted human existence. I don't mean that in a rude way; she isn't ugly. It's just that all her features are right in the middle of her face, and her hair pulled back into a bun isn't drawing attention from her long, angular chin. But she is cute and charming. She talks too much, though, so the other girls won't dance near her, worried they'll be collateral damage when Mme. Patenaude inevitably yells at her.

I suppose you could say we're friends—if a friend is someone who helps you stretch your point, then laughs and tells the other dancers how much better hers is—not even bothering to use French or waiting for you to be out of earshot. But she's more of a friend than any of the other girls have offered to be, so I get ready to dance behind her when I notice Beau is, in fact, next to me, waiting for his and his partner's turn.

"You do your stretches, little Jolie?" he asks in French, probably assuming I still can't understand him, which is fair. Much of what he says goes over my head, but not this.

"You do yours?" I ask, also in French, sure I am all things witty and brilliant, giving myself slight pleasure that I may have caught him off guard.

Helene and I dance and end up across the room from everyone who hasn't gone yet.

We wait for them where we've ended, so we can dance back the same moves—leading with our left foot instead of our right, so we work our good sides and our bad sides. We're meant to organize ourselves back into our same lines, but it's easy enough to remember our order without literally standing in it, so I linger a moment to adjust a bobby pin that's come loose.

After Beau and his partner finish, he regretfully stands by me.

"Your leaps are getting flatter," he says, this time in English. I move to the back of the line, but he keeps up. "While you yourself have gotten less so." I glare at him. "Don't look so outraged. Girls want to be shapely. No? Maybe not ballerina girls, but you maybe can't help it. But maybe it'd be better to drop out now. Why waste all the effort when you can only topple over?"

I turn away from him. But there's a mirror in front of me. There are mirrors everywhere. At any angle, he's able to see every angle of me. There's nowhere to hide. I cross my arms over my chest and shift so I'm standing with Helene between myself and my front reflection.

I'd try to excuse his inexcusable behavior by suggesting his English perhaps isn't so good or that in France, it's not impolite to tell fifteen-year-old girls that their chests are too big for ballet, but I choose not to give him any benefit of any doubt. And this is the guy I have to dance with! Why Mme. Patenaude never gets after him for talking is beyond me. I wish she would. I wish she would throw him out the window.

In *pas de deux* class, we moved on from tilting a while ago and are now working on *pirouettes*. Mme.

Patenaude has a different couple show how it's done, and then, girding my loins, I stand in front of Beau.

"When you're ready, little Jolie," he says. "Or maybe I can no longer call you 'little'."

Having already prepped my *pirouette* and being completely thrown off by his despicability, I forget to bring in my arms when I spin. Not only do I hit him, I send him to the floor in a big crash everybody notices. Ballerinas everywhere stop dancing and stare, gasp, laugh, and roll their eyes.

I hate that I'm mortified, that I care at all about this guy—this slime bucket, who treats me worse than my older sister treats the other poor souls auditioning for cheer. But I stammer out, "I'm so sorry!"

He glares at me.

Maybe I don't care that I've hurt him because a part of me is glad I did. Maybe I'm only mortified because I know this will lessen his opinion of me, as if it could get any lower than it is. I hate that I care. I hate that I hate myself for caring more than I hate him.

"Beginning ballet students are down the hall, Jolene," Mme. Patenaude says in French. She extends an arm to Beau and continues her rage against me, no doubt to a sympathetic ear.

After we bow, thank Mme. Patenaude, and end class, she—looking somber and scary—pulls me to the side.

"If you can't keep up, you're going to find yourself on the first flight home, understood?"

I want to defend myself. I want to tell her Beau's throwing me off, talking too much, and pervy. But what I actually do is sheepishly nod.

She turns away from me with an almost apologetic sigh. Almost.

"Get out of my sight," she says in French.

I've never left a room faster.

15 LES MISÉRABLES

JOLENE

When I get back to my room, it's late. I unravel my toe shoes so they can breathe overnight, then toss my ballet bag into its corner, undress, shower, and curl up in short pajamas and a camisole. The driver, Marc, per my request, stopped at a café on the way home, as I was starving, and knew the others had probably already eaten. I get all set up to read my new favorite book, but the thought of being sent home won't stop haunting me.

Maybe I should call my mom and let her know I might come back early. Maybe I should just leave. We tried it, and it didn't work. I'm no better at ballet, and any glow-up I've undergone has only drawn a target on my chest.

That's the other thing; if I go home, I'll never have to see Beau again. Why does he seek me out? Why do I let him get to me so much? Why do his eyes follow me around during the entirety of every class when he

96

obviously hates me so much? Why do I care what he thinks?

As fun as it would be to let him consume me the entire weekend, I'm sick of thinking about him. Time for a distraction. Time for a new new favorite book.

I walk into Mamie's library. I've actually come to know it as Eloise's library, as she's the one who curates and tends to it. It's extensive, but mostly the books are in French. They fill up every cranny, but the room itself is small.

I go to my section, or the section in English that's off in a corner by a large window. Waiting for me, just where I've left it and often returned to consider it, is an unabridged copy of *Les Misérables*. It's a long book, but I still have months and months left to read it before I have to go.

Eloise enters and crosses to me.

"I thought I'd find you in here." She sees what I'm holding. "That's one of my favorites."

"I've wanted to read it since we saw the musical in Solvang."

"Take it home if you don't finish." She puts her hands a foot apart and mouths the words, "It's big."

"Puis-je vraiment?"[14] I ask her if she really means it. I've been encouraging myself to try out my French around her—too scared to do so in front of Mamie or Caspian, worried they may think I'm silly, but Eloise is more forgiving.

---

[14] Can I really?

"I rarely read classic French literature in English," Eloise says, then laughs. "That came out rather snobbish."

"What's a little snobbery among family?" I ask.

She looks at me almost sadly. "You're not like Mary at all. She tilts her head as if trying to make out similar features between us.

"Well, you know. She's..." but I struggle for words. She's what? She's pretty? She's talented? She's funny? She's only related to me through our mom?

Maybe Eloise is right. Maybe I'm hardly like Mary at all. Maybe Mary's known this all along, and that's why she keeps her distance, and for the obvious reason that I embarrass her.

"When she spent last summer with us, she hardly spoke," Eloise says. "She didn't express interest or excitement about anything. We asked her what she wanted to do, and nothing..."

"Maybe she doesn't feel like you guys are her family."

"But we've known her, her whole life." Eloise adjusts her glasses. "We haven't treated her differently—"

"You haven't, but I think it bothers her that I get to come to Paris for a year and she only went for a summer."

"But she doesn't take ballet—"

"That's what Logan said!" I laugh at the memory of my friend in the locker hall.

"Logan is your friend," Eloise smirks. "Or boyfriend?"

"He's just a friend."

She smiles an obnoxious, knowing smile that's wrong on all accounts.

"All friends are 'just friends' until they're suddenly more than friends," she says. "I refuse to believe that one of you—at least one—doesn't like the other."

I roll my eyes at her. Why is this always the consensus? I'm determined to change the masses' minds. If it's one at a time, so be it. So, I focus on her and say, "You can have platonic relationships. Look at Harry and Hermione."

"They're fiction," Eloise says. "Once again, I'll have to ask you to use an example outside the Wizarding World of Harry Potter."

Oops. I didn't realize I had a habit of doing that.

"Logan likes his junior high ex-girlfriend, and I like..." Shoot. It's out there now. I like someone, and she won't rest until she knows everything.

I wasn't going to talk about him—I was going to leave him in California and forget about him.

Screw it. It's not like I haven't been thinking about him—even if I haven't spoken his name. Every time I get a second, I spend it in my mind with him, like I'm freaking Eponine spending her nights walking around Paris with an imaginary Marius. I wonder if that's in the book I'm holding, or just the musical version.

"Who?" Eloise asks after I don't finish my sentence.

"Someone else," I say, prolonging the inevitable.

"Out with it." Her tone scolds me like a child hiding a stolen macaron from the butler's pantry.

"There was this guy in my math class last year," I say. "But he had a girlfriend. I thought he may have liked me more, but, I mean, he didn't dump her for me, so..."

"Did you tell him you liked him?" Eloise asks.

"No!" I shock myself with how loud it comes out. "No," I add quietly, resignedly.

"Why? If you're never going to see him again anyway...?"

"Because I don't want to be humiliated!" I say while laughing. "And chances are, it wouldn't have changed anything—his girlfriend's way hotter than me, and popular. He might have liked being around me more, but I'm sure he liked being seen with her. Telling him would have just been a waste of words, and if I ever ran into him again, at a grocery store or something, I'd have to, like, duck behind the apples instead of being like, 'Hey Matt! It's been a long time,' and he'd be like, 'Yeah. Caradine died. We should catch up sometime'. And by that time, I'd be all like super cute, and it would work out between us, and all because I didn't completely embarrass myself as a freshman by confessing to him that I liked him."

"You've given this some thought," she says—an understatement. It's all I ever think about.

She leaves me to my thoughts, so I plop down on a cushy window seat and let them engulf me. Maybe the difference between Caradine and someone like me is courage. Eloise is right; I didn't tell Matt I liked him because I'm a coward. I even chickened out of wearing that miniskirt after Eloise made me feel foolish. It's almost like I'm scared to be successful, not surprising, it's not like I've ever had success. It can only be expected that I'd fear it—it comes with responsibility.

You're expected to keep it up. You're looked up to. Your life changes. What would it have meant if Matt had dumped Caradine and asked me to Prom? It would have altered everything—even more so than coming to France! Caradine would have an actual reason for hating me, for one. She'd make sure half the student body followed suit. And going to dance with Matt, being alone with him, dancing with him— nobody has the guts to face that. It's terrifying! What if I said something stupid, or smiled weird in the dance photos? What if his friends started expecting me to behave a certain way, and come out to parties, and be who they think I should be?

I look out the window at the pool. The first time I swam in it, I was surprised at how shallow it was. I scraped the top of my foot searching for the deep end. I never did find one.

The clouds shift, and I make out my reflection.

Is that really all that separates me from girls like Caradine—that she's willing to take risks and put herself out there? She's willing to be beautiful? She's willing to be popular? Instead of hoping for these things, she goes and gets them?

Well, that's just stupid. It's at least stupid not to try, right—see if I like it? I can always back out, transfer schools, or curl up and die.

Once I get back to the States, I'll only have two years of high school left. If I try and fall flat on my face, I only have to live with the shame for a short time. And if I don't go for it now, when? I came to France to let it change me, but so far I've taken a back seat, hoping I'd take it in through osmosis. I can't just wait for it to make me the girl I want to be—I need to demand it.

I take *Les Misérables* back to my room, toss it on my bed—clunk—and do the stretches Mme. Patenaude always tells us we should do at home. Then I tie on my toe shoes and go over my *pirouettes*—imagining I'm dancing with Beau and don't want to smack him in the face again. It's hard to pretend, but I force myself to do it over and over again, past the moment I've got the move right, all the way until it would be difficult to get it wrong. I'll need to break in a new pair of pointe shoes tomorrow, but it was worth it. I won't be nervous the next time I walk into that studio.

16 THE RECITAL

JOLENE

Now that I've been spending over half my free time stretching and practicing, Beau's rude comments have diminished, and while Mme. Patenaude isn't heaping on the praise, she's also not screaming at me, so that's a plus. She also hasn't ordered my dismissal from the country, another plus.

Then one day in the middle of March, I walk into ballet and fewer people are there. Among the missing is Beau. I'm about to ask what happened when Mme. Patenaude approaches me with a young man I've never spoken to but know his name's Jean.

"Your partners have been let go. Failure to keep up." She says all this in French, of course. "You're partners now."

Mme. Patenaude leaves us for her music, and Jean turns to me.

Jean is not as obviously attractive as Beau, but that's probably a good thing. Dancing with a boy makes me nervous enough—do we have to add hotness to it?

"How are you enjoying our school?" he asks in English as I hang up my dance bag.

Jean has curly orange hair that he keeps having to brush out of his kind, green eyes. They're the sort of eyes that laugh even when he doesn't—but not in the mocking way Beau's did—in a friendly, genuine way.

"It's great," I say, not knowing what's coming out of my mouth. "I'm sorry—I'm completely thrown. I thought Beau was keeping up..."

"You didn't notice how he blamed all his mistakes on you?"

"I thought he was right," I say.

Relief doesn't flood over me, it tsunamis over me. Am I actually done with Beau? It can't be true. Despite my improvements, I held the belief that Beau would always be the superior dancer, but now I'm not sure why I thought that. Was it because he acted like it? Was that really all it took for me to accept I was deficient?

"Mme. Patenaude always yells at me," I say.

"She yells at him more. Or at least she did..."

He might actually just be right about that. I've gotten more fluent in the language, but when someone's not speaking directly to me, it's easy to miss what's said.

And certain moves I thought were difficult are relatively easy with Jean as my partner. It seems like Mme. Patenaude noticed what I didn't—Beau was holding me back.

After the next several months of learning lifts, jumps, and killing those *pirouettes*, I finally feel worthy of being at this ballet school.

104

In June, we present to friends and family our final recital, in which each pair is to perform a *pas de deux* from a ballet. We're doing it inside our classroom, with chairs set up on the edges for our invited guests.

Mamie, Eloise and Caspian sit right in the middle. I'm grateful for their support, but their presence slightly adds to my terror of performing in front of the class and Mme. Patenaude. It'd almost be easier if the room were full of strangers, though I'm not sure why.

Jean and I take our places for our combination. The music starts—Odette and Siegfried's *pas de deux* from *Swan Lake*. He stands behind me and takes my hands as I *bourrée en pointe*, my *port de bras* as swanlike as I can make it.

I *piqué* into *passé*—my arms in fourth. The music is longing, romantic, and melancholic. I *développé*, extending my leg into an *attitude*, as he guides me into a *soutenu* turn—clenching my teeth as I dip down to swipe the floor with my hand.

I start to fall, but Jean's on top of it. He strengthens his grip around my waist—not so rough that it hurts or, worse, distracts me, but enough to stabilize and remind me I can depend on him.

We continue with our *promenade penché*—or what I like to call our upside-down spin, where he walks around me—holding me while I'm tilted over, nearly touching the ground. I'm a little off balance, but he straightens me out after we make our rotation.

Then he steadies my hand as I *fouetté* into *arabesque*, and fall into the death drop—as I call it—and it occurs to me Mme. Patenaude gave us this dance as our final,

105

not earlier, because she wants to kill me, but wanted to wait for the end of the season.

Jean holds my right hand as, *en pointe*, I extend my leg up past our shoulders. We face each other, holding our positions for a moment—then I fall backward, stiff as a board, praying he makes it behind me before my head collides with the pinewood floor.

Despite being bent back over his arm, I manage to get a sigh out. It's looking like I might not die today at all.

We do the "death drop" again, the upside-down spin, followed by a few *jetés*, some *pirouettes*, tiny jumps, and huge lifts where he raises me high over his head, which scares me less and is easier than the "death drop."

We go into our ending with the "death turn," where he spins me around, and if he lets go, I'll smash the floor with my face, but that's the worst of it. The rest is just "ballet hugging," *arabesques, pirouettes,* and one final "death lean" to the side, and we're done.

"Bien joué,"[15] Jean says in between large breaths before standing me back upright.

To my surprise, the entire audience, including our classmates, applaud with no sign of stopping. So much so that Jean takes my hand and situates himself as if about to bow. I follow his lead and bow, after which he follows, in ballet fashion.

Our classmates smile and smirk until Mme. Patenaude motions for everyone to be quiet, and for the next couple to begin.

---

[15] Well done.

After it's over and everyone's performed, she approaches Jean and me as we get our ballet bags.

"*Bien joué,* Jean." She turns to me. "You've improved significantly, Jolene." I don't suppress my smile. "But you'll never make it in a large, professional company. Not without," she sighs, "a significant amount of effort, significant."

My heart drops. I know she wants me to understand this above everything she has said all year because she says it in English.

But all the way home, Eloise, Caspian, and Mamie vehemently oppose Mme. Patenaude, congratulate me on my performance, and downplay my more talented classmates.

While I'm not sure I buy their sincerity, it's enough to raise my spirits. But what I keep replaying in my mind is the reception from my fellow dancers, all those I've been intimidated by all year—who've never seemed to pay me any positive attention. Their faces and applause have left me feeling like maybe my year abroad hasn't been a waste. No matter what I face at home, I am different, improved from who I was when I left.

17 THE ELEVEN

JOLENE

I spend my last day in France at work with Eloise. Her office is chic, with windows everywhere and soft, plush, white carpet. She lets me sit at her desk as she's up and about dealing with a photo shoot. It's a little chaotic, so I try to stay out of her way and flip through a portfolio of her modeling career.

"*Non c'est bon. Tout le monde en prend dix.*"[16] She walks to me, takes a sip of her water, and leans against the desk.

"You look so beautiful in these photos," I say. "I wish I was as beautiful as you."

"Psh. *Je suis au bout de ma vie,*"[17] she says, a common term I hear at ballet, meaning the sayer is so frustrated they're about to die. "Who told you you weren't as beautiful as me?"

"Nobody," I say.

---

[16] No. It's fine. Everyone take ten.
[17] I'm at the end of my life.

She raises a hand as if to say, There you have it. But there is far from had.

"If I was," I say, "then guys would ask me out..."

She snorts. "Less attractive people than you get asked out all the time. I shouldn't tell you this; it might support your unfounded theory, but Cass has had to rein in some of his friends."

"What do you mean?" I ask, realizing what she means the second I start talking. "Which ones?"

My mind's audacious enough to let Oscar come across it—that actor I almost died over at Iphigeneia's cat's party.

"Oh, I'm never going to tell you," she says firmly.

A few times since arriving in Paris, I've accompanied Caspian on his sailing adventures in the South of France. These trips usually included a few of his friends, and every so often one of those friends was Oscar Ivanov.

We didn't speak much, as talking is hard to do when you're shy and terrified. But if you ever run into him and ask if he knows who I was, he'll say yes. Probably.

"I'll only say they're near your age," Eloise adds. "So we didn't have any of them thrown over the side of *The Eleven*."

The Eleven is Caspian's latest ship—he sank the previous one. After having the pleasure of going down with it, he awarded me the honor of naming his new boat.

Most people think *The Eleven* has something to do with a TV series, but in truth, it was Matt's high school basketball jersey number.

Pathetic. I know. But what do you want from me?

"I bet Cass wouldn't have had to do any reining a year ago." I admit, thinking of that sad girl in math class—flat-haired, uninspired dancer who was so fearful, she almost missed a year abroad in Paris.

"When you still had training wheels on your bike and couldn't watch PG-13 movies?" Eloise glares at me. "It's amazing how guys don't want to date children."

"A year ago, I had just turned fifteen," I say.

"And you weren't ugly," Eloise insists. "You were young—you're still young."

As I try to pick apart how I feel about what she's said—and if there's any truth in it whatsoever—Mamie enters, flustered.

"We're going to lunch, darlings," she says, and what I read as stress might actually be grief. "Jolene, I've just gotten off the phone with your mother. We'd like to extend an invitation to you to come to Paris for at least a few weeks every summer."

"I'd love to!" I hug her tiny form tightly.

"Oh! I'm going to miss having you around." She pulls back, still keeping her hands on my shoulders, and kisses my cheek. "That's settled then. We'll keep the room for you. But remember, Jolie, you're welcome always, not just in the summer. As far as I'm concerned, that's your room, and my home is your home." She wipes a tear from her cheek. "There. Are your things packed? Are you ready to go home?"

"It'll be weird being back," I tell them.

Mamie nods and leads the way out the door while Eloise takes her handbag from her desk.

"Did we distract you, then?" she asks.

"From what?"

110

"From that boy!" She laughs, hopeful.

"Oh, *j'aimerais que ce soit aussi simple,*"[18] I say. "But it was certainly nice."

"You're worth more than any boy at that school. And if he can't see it, he's stupid. And if you can't see it, then trust that I'm brilliant and always right until you can."

Adults are like pep-talk machines. They all produce the same morale-boosting clichés. Of course, they think the kids in their lives are all fantastic, but if everyone's worth more than everyone else, then everyone's worth less than everyone else. Which of these parents or aunts is right? It's all stupid and nonsense.

We go to lunch at our favorite café. I order a croissant. Eloise and Mamie have salads and skip the pastry.

"Just leave the credit card on your table, and—oh, I have half a mind to just let you keep it." Mamie says.

"Maman," Eloise says in a scolding tone, choking on her lettuce.

"You saw what she came in," Mamie continues. "They're not looking out for her..."

"They're doing fine. I'm sure." Eloise glares and shakes her head with a small smile. "You can't give Jolene a line of credit unless you're prepared to do the same for all your grandchildren."

"I only have Jolene."

---

[18] I wish it were that simple.

For a moment, I'm sure Mamie is going to remember my sister. But a moment passes, and Eloise's distracted by her phone, so I speak up.

"Mary—"

"I meant..." Mamie meant blood grandchildren.

A wind sweeps by, making my legs shiver.

I know they love Mary, but a tiny pit forms in my stomach—not big, but dense.

Mamie chews for a moment before finishing her thought. "Well, I have half a mind to give Mary one, too."

Eloise sets down her phone.

"Maman, we talked about this. For heaven's sake," Eloise says. "Let's not talk anymore about money. It's our last lunch."

After that, I go back to my room and pick up my things. I dig Dogberry's traveling crate out of storage, and Marc, the chauffeur, drops us off at the airport.

With Dogberry asleep among the other traveling pets, I fly first class back home.

18 BACK FROM PARIS

JOLENE

The pictures online have not prepared me for the bright shade of violent fuchsia my sister has dyed her hair. I'm also unprepared for the amount of black she's added to her wardrobe and makeup, and the number of piercings seemingly everywhere. She's almost so unrecognizable that it's hard to believe she's still the same person at all. But when the plane lands and I walk out of the exit, this demon pixie, along with my parents, is waiting for me.

I hug my mom first: "Oh, my girl! How was your flight, sweetheart?" Then Dad: "You've gotten taller! Lori, hasn't she gotten taller? I think she's taller than Mary now." Then, a reluctant Mary, who grumbles a "hello" before my dad takes my carry-on.

We find Dogberry, who's awake and anxious to be free. I let him out, clasp on his leash, and we make our way to luggage claim.

"These are nice," my mom says as she, my dad, and I grab my suitcases off the conveyor belt. "Did Mamie buy these for you?"

"Yeah," I say.

Mary rolls her eyes and lets my fourth piece of luggage circle the belt.

As we drive home, I feel uneasy as everything is the same, but different. Some shops and restaurants on Hollister have changed, or painted the exterior of their buildings, but I can't quite put my finger on what the changes are. The vegetation has also changed. It's home, but not home, familiar but almost like I've only read about the place in a book.

Home is strange, too. My room is exactly how I left it. I don't think anyone's even been in it for a year, except I suspect my mom's recently dusted because my eyes itch almost immediately upon entering.

Dogberry dances around, excited to be home, and licks Horatio, my white cat, who still does nothing but sleep even when enthusiastically licked on the face by a Border Collie.

I'm not sure where he slept during the last year, but the morning after I get home, all his things—his laser, his food tray, and his toys—are haphazardly piled at the foot of the stairs leading up to my attic.

I saved unpacking for the day after getting home, since Mamie and Eloise took me shopping a few days ago, and the idea of unpacking all of it is daunting.

I lug my suitcases through my pivoting bookcase door, and when I'm done hanging everything up, my closet's actually filled. I won't even have to go back-to-school shopping this year, not that I'll let that stop me.

As for ballet, getting back into the routine is like suddenly being thrown into an alternate dimension—again, similar but eerily different. Odd, younger-me insecurities rise in my gut like an old habit. Although I have no reason to be nervous or doubt myself. After the first class, in fact, my teacher bumps me up to the highest class of pre-professional, which—just between you and me—is a little bit behind where I left off in Paris.

I'm not missed by anyone in my old class, since I never became super close with any of them, but if I had hopes of making new friends in this class, those shatter almost instantly.

On the first day, our instructor, Mrs. Reed, has us practice *pirouettes* during partner work. I notice a few of the other girls glare at me as I adjust my partner's hand placement. Then I get even more glares after Mrs. Reed has everyone take turns doing the *pirouettes*, and I do more than everyone else and am the only one Mrs. Reed doesn't correct.

But at least in this class, there's one girl who goes to my school—the same one I ate with in seventh grade for a brief period, Lindsey Calisher. She's had a large role in the ballets for years and was in the junior high choir with me. She's a year ahead of me in school, so we've never become real friends. But maybe now that we're at the same ballet level...

Class ends, and Mrs. Reed asks me to come over.

"Jolene, your year in France has paid off."

115

I'm more than relieved—according to Mme. Patenaude, my dancing was *affreux*,[19] but her school was so much harder, and her standards so much higher. And my classmates seemed to disagree with her assessment of me.

It occurs to me she may have been showing me "tough love" and withholding praise so that I wouldn't stop trying. It wouldn't have been the first time she had done it—she rarely praised anybody. Once I saw her make even the best dancer at the school cry.

"Thank you," I say.

"I hope you're planning on auditioning for the Sugar Plum Fairy."

"Oh..." I steal a quick glance toward Lindsey.

She seems to undo her laces extra slowly as if listening to Mrs. Reed and not paying her shoes any real attention.

"Yeah," I say. "Absolutely."

"Good. Auditions are the third."

Lindsey glares at me as she takes off her toe shoes. There's a chance I won't be making friends with her.

---

[19] Awful

19 BEGINNING AGAIN

JOLENE

She stands at my open door, not knocking.

"Let me borrow your eyeliner." It's not a question.

"What happened to yours?" I ask.

"I lent it to Veronika," she says as if I should know who that is. "I know Mamie bought you a bunch of fancy makeup in France. How many eyeliners do you need?"

"On my vanity."

But she's already crossing to it. She picks up a few lip glosses that are not easily confused with eyeliner by anyone and examines their colors. She places them back where they don't go, and it takes everything inside of me not to get up and start grabbing it all out of her hands. Instead, I grind my teeth and resign myself to fixing it after she leaves.

I've been home for a few weeks, and the first time she's set foot in my room or said more than three words to me is to upend my vanity.

It's not that I blame her for not spending more time with me, not really. We're both busy. Usually, she's out of the house by the time I get out of bed, which isn't exactly late in the day. She's driving now, and Grandpa Stansen sent her a check for a car when she passed her driving test, which, for some reason, she spent on a used black truck that couldn't have cost the entire check. I suspect she pocketed the other fifteen thousand, although what she spent it on, I couldn't tell you—unless pink hair dye is crazy expensive. She doesn't have a job, so it's not like she goes to work. She does have a few friends, but I doubt they're up when the sun's still out. I've seen them a few times when they've come over after dark. They're all ghostly pale, thin, and scurvy, with hair of various shades and cuts and the same accessories as my sister: safety pins needlessly sprinkled around, piercings in surprising places. Mary's never introduced them, but I've started naming them myself. The girl with long black hair, who looks like the ghost from *The Ring*, I call her Samara, obviously. The boy with red hair I call Kvothe. He was with Mary at the school when we went around, teacher to teacher, and registered for classes. They're the two regulars, so they're the only ones I bothered to name. The others come and go, and—wait—I think all the girls I've seen are just Samara with different—oh, my gosh—she's just been changing her hair with wigs; that's the only thing that explains why sometimes she has long black hair, and sometimes it's a short neon blue!

Point is, I thought when I got back from France, Mary would be excited to see me, and anxious to talk to me, and ask how my trip was. But that's not the case. She grunts whenever I say "hello," and when she's home, she's in her room blasting murder-music.

But now she's not only here but asking for a favor. How do I not give her a hard time?

"How was France, Jolene? Oh. It was amazing, Mary. Thanks for asking. What did you do apart from ballet class? I hung out with Eloise, Caspian, and a few of their friends a lot. Did you go to Versailles? Why, yes, we did, in fact."

Mary burps. "Why are you reading a schoolbook? School starts tomorrow."

"It's not a schoolbook. I'm reading it for fun."

She scoffs and wipes something that came out of her mouth off my eyeshadow palette. "No one reads French novels for fun."

"It's translated into English—well, most of it is. The proper nouns are obviously still in French..."

She glares at me.

"I'm sorry," I say. "I mean, the names of stuff."

"I know what proper nouns are."

She tosses down my nail polish a little too roughly, giving me a mini coronary, and turns over and over a tube of eyelash-curling mascara.

"Eloise gave it to me," I say, still discussing the book.

"Spoiler alert: everyone dies."

"That's why reading French novels is fun," I reply.

She sniffs at that and inspects my black eyeliner. I thought she would go for one of my two-dollar pencil liners, not the expensive one in her hands. But I don't really use the black one, so no big deal, although...

119

"Black is too dark for your skin tone," I tell her.

"That's not a thing." She sorts through my face moisturizer, my hand moisturizer, my primer, and my foundation. She picks up my favorite pair of diamond studs Mamie gave me for my birthday and then puts them back down. "I'm going to bed—got a zero period in the morning."

I hold up quote fingers and say, "'Going to bed.'"

"What's that supposed to mean?"

"You're just gonna go read vampire fanfic all night," I say. I've overheard her talking to Samara about it—a lot.

She rolls her eyes as she crosses my room toward my door. "You think you know me so well."

"I know you well enough to know you took my red lipstick."

She turns to me then hurls my lipstick at my face—smacking me on the forehead.

"Ow!" I shout like she's a creature with the capacity to feel sympathy.

"Bet you didn't know I was gonna do that." She smirks and walks out, leaving the door I had shut open.

It's the first day of school. The typical morning mist hasn't drifted off yet, and I regret wearing shorts.

I walk into my first class, expecting a few familiar faces, if not friendly. But there's no one I recognize. I don't even recognize the teacher, but I must have registered for his class, unless this isn't the right class—come to think of it—I'm not sure this is even the right school; it doesn't look anything like the one I used to go to...

120

I get up to leave and bump into some students trying to get to their desks.

"Hey," a student, a boy, says. "I know you! You've been gone."

"Yeah," I say. Maybe it is the right school after all.

"I liked you better that way."

All the students laugh. I glance at the teacher, who's also openly laughing.

Oh, let this please be a dream. Please.

I look down to check if I'm naked. I'm not naked, but I'm wearing a ball gown, and everyone's still pointing and laughing, but now with more force.

Mary comes into the classroom and joins in the laughter.

"Little princess thinks she's better than everyone!" she shouts, and everyone keeps laughing.

I run out of the classroom, smack into Matt. He's exactly like I remember him.

He takes me by the shoulders and looks into my eyes. "You look stupider."

I cry and wake up to Dogberry licking my face— never happier for a dream to be cut short.

20 EVIL LOOPS

MARY

The alarm on my phone goes off at the ridiculous hour of six am, filling the house with the guttural growls of my murder music—the way every home should be—but I can still hear Jolene's footsteps thunder across my ceiling and her window slam shut. Little princess. I bet too many birds were flying in trying to find space on her already bird-laden fingers.

I shower, dry off, use Jolene's black eyeliner on my eyes and lips, spike my short pink hair, pull on my black leather, spikes, chains, rings, grab my backpack, and head down to breakfast.

Mom's there, standing over a frying pan of eggs, reading something on her cell phone.

"You're not supposed to work too hard." I dump my backpack on a chair.

"I'm just taking care of one quick thing," she says— her standard answer—eyes never leaving her phone.

"Do we have Evil Loops?" I ask.

122

Still staring at her screen, my mom's expression turns quizzical, as if her phone asked the question. "Medieval Loops?"

"No." I pull the box of Medieval Loops out of the cupboard. "Evil Loops. See? I crossed out 'Medi' and turned the 'A' into an 'I'." I show her how I improved the box and how in place of a cartoon character on the front, there's now a demon cartoon character.

She smiles but doesn't look at it. "Ah, he's cute."

"Cute?!" I turn the box to face me. "He's ferocious. You're making him look bad in front of the other cereal boxes."

But it's impossible to tell if she even hears me. So I give up, grab a bowl, spoon, milk, and sit at the table. I eat my entire bowl of cereal before my mom looks up even once.

I grab a red marker from the junk drawer and add more piercings and tattoos to the little guy.

Wait—did Jolene describe our mom? Whatever. Even if she did, she probably didn't do it right— probably added a bunch of extra fluff about how she smells like Chanel and smiles like sunshine, or some crap. But what you need to know is, Mom is great. She's beautiful, blond, tall, thin, and impeccably dressed—usually in white suits—all elegant and stuff. What sucks is she works in LA, so she's gone a lot, but it's also kinda cool because she makes enough to sustain my expensive lifestyle—and my expensive driving habits.

She refuses to let me or Jolene audition for anything she costumes, which suits me fine. I'd rather do almost anything than act, but ever since Jolene was a kid, she's been begging for it.

Speaking of begging for it, Dad, clean-shaven, hair combed, bespectacled, wearing a gray suit and forest green tie, joins us.

"Mornin'." He drops bread into the toaster.

"Hey honey," Mom says, still apparently trying to memorize whatever's on her screen.

"You get the butter out?" he asks.

Mom shoots him a glare and points shortly at the counter, then presses her fingertips to her forehead. "Sorry. I'm just trying to read this real quick."

He puts his laptop bag on a chair opposite me and examines my cereal box masterpiece. I should open a gallery.

"You're up early," is his greeting.

"I have a zero period. Failed Spanish last year, so I get to cram it in this year."

He doesn't even bother to lecture me about how I should study harder, get good grades, get into a good college, stop wasting my art skills transforming breakfast leprechauns into evil cereal demons—none of that. He just crosses to the fridge and searches for the milk that's already on the table.

"How is Jolene getting to school?" he asks me, as if I have any idea, or desire for said knowledge.

I shrug and grunt.

"I'll just take her."

"You'll be late," I say. "Who will architect the buildings?"

Leave it to Dad to over-worry. Once he took an entire day off because Jolene sprained her ankle at ballet the evening before. I think he felt guilty that when the ballet called for someone to come get her, he wasn't home from work yet and none of us could get a hold of him. But still.

"Okay, drama queen." He finds the milk where I said it was and sits next to me—my cue to get up and get my lunch.

"I better run," I say.

"Bye, honey!" Mom says, still locked in a staring war with her phone.

"We gave you that truck so you could help us drive you and your sister around," Dad says. I've heard this sentence every day this summer. A year without a sister went by too fast.

"Grandpa gave me the truck, Dad," I say, as I say every day.

And he replies with, "Well, we let him." It's as if he's reading from a script.

"You know, Mamie probably could have gotten me into a fancy French art school if she wanted. I know she's on the ballet board but come on. I'm sure she has a lot of ties in the art community, too."

"Honey, did you get your lunch?" Mom asks.

Of course, I got my lunch. I'm not three. So, I ignore her and keep arguing with Dad.

"Oh wait," I say. "I forgot. They don't have art in Paris."

"Enjoy your first day," Mom says, completely unaffected by my sarcasm.

"You said you didn't like Paris," Dad says.

"Yeah, but the opportunity would have been nice!"

"How should I have known you wanted an opportunity to spend a year in a city you said you didn't like?!" His voice rises in decibel and pitch.

"I don't want it!" I yell.

"Then what are we talking about?!"

"Art school!"

"It's going to be hot today, so don't wear your jacket all day, even if it's what all the cool goths are doing," Mom says.

"Mom, that's not—"

"Bye honey," she says.

I leave the room, then pop my head back in.

"If Jolene wants to travel through time and get ready earlier so she's ready to leave right now, then she's welcome to join me!" I slam the door.

Somehow, I feel less than victorious as I walk to my truck.

It's early and chilly, and the smell of the tarry beach finds its way through the trees to our front yard.

I hear Jolene's window open, and she hurls something into the side yard. It's probably a dead body. My dad probably wouldn't even care if it were.

I shrug, get into my black Tacoma, and drive off toward school, not knowing which of my least favorite locations—home or school—I prefer less.

21 OPERATION MINISKIRT

JOLENE

There are a few things I will not do now that I'm back from Paris. One, I'm not going to pine over a boy all year only to not have him dump his stupid girlfriend and ask me to Prom. It's not going to happen.

Okay, that's the only thing I'm not going to do—no more being slighted for me, no sir. I have a plan: Operation Miniskirt.

Eloise accosted me for trying to wear it to ballet—said I'd attract everyone but only get approached by the guys I don't want to approach me. But the more I think about it, the more I'm unconvinced. Better to attract and then figure it out from there.

I mean, Caradine often wore short skirts to school, and it seemed to work out for her. And unless they've changed the dress code, I don't see why I shouldn't wear one, too. This is what girls who have boyfriends wear, and if it gets back to Matt that I'm hot and all the guys want me now, then fine. Great. See if I care.

127

But wearing a miniskirt isn't for the weak. One has to be sneaky. Step One: Bypass parents.

I brush my teeth, do my makeup, and throw my miniskirt out my window and into the side yard. Then, I pull on a pair of jeans, my cute pink top, and hide the fact it's strapless with my light-blue hoodie.

After hoisting my backpack onto my shoulders—the new, expensive backpack Mamie bought me that's milk-chocolate-brown with light-pink monograms and details—I go downstairs for breakfast.

Our kitchen is white with blue accents and a dark wooden floor. A white table and chairs sit near the side, where a white wall full of family photos and several school photos of myself and Mary hang. You can literally track Mary's dramatic change on this wall: normal, normal, popular cheerleader, insane.

I enter, and my mom, standing at the stove with her cell in her hands, turns to me.

"Hi honey." She smiles. "Do you want some eggs?"

"No, thanks." I open the fridge. "Do we have any croissants?" I can't find the butter, then spot it on the counter next to my mom. "In France, we had pastry and cheese at every meal."

"In America, we shut the refrigerator door, *chérie*," my mom says.

I apologize with a grimace and shut it. "I'll just have a banana."

My dad hands me a banana from the fruit basket on the table. I take it and peel as I lean against the now-closed fridge.

"Eat up. I'll drive you to school," he says.

128

"Um, that's okay," I tell my dad, trying not to hurt his feelings. He looks so eager. "Logan's giving me a ride. He's been in the Grand Canyon since I got back and wants to show me his new car."

"He got a new car at the Grand Canyon?" my mom asks.

"No."

Why do parents take joy in misunderstanding you? It's like the happiest you'll see them all day.

"I'm glad to give you a ride, honey," my dad says.

Ugh. I'm gonna have to spell it out for him, hoping maybe, MAYBE, he'll remember being sixteen and take pity.

"I'm a junior. I can't be seen getting dropped off by my dad in front of all my friends."

"What friends? Logan?"

"I have other friends besides Logan."

Except I really don't. I know people I'm friendly enough with online, but they aren't people I'd call up to do anything with. I had a best friend in fifth grade, but she moved before sixth grade ended. And the people in my ballet school all go to different schools, or are in different grades, so we know each other, and we're nice enough, but never "friends." Like, Lindsey goes to my school, but she's a senior, and she still—as far as I can tell—would prefer if I had died in Paris.

Hold up—is Logan my only friend? For reals? In France, I had Helene. One time, we bumped into each other shopping, and she acted glad to see me, so that was something.

"How about I drop you off around the corner?" I can tell my dad is joking because his eyes dance with excitement at his humor's biannual appearance. But why he thinks I'd be amused at my expense is beyond me. So I glare at him.

"I don't need a ride, Dad." I grab my lunch out of the fridge and leave.

I open the side gate and latch it behind me. My miniskirt waits for me on top of a bush. I shake off the caterpillar on it, slip off my shoes, slide off my jeans, and change into the skirt. I roll up my pants and shove them into my backpack, realizing I could have rolled up my mini and put it in my backpack instead of hurling it out my window like a barbarian—but what are you gonna do? Mental note for next time.

I unhook the gate, shut it behind me, question why we haven't put a lock on it, and wait for Logan.

I hear him coming before he arrives. I thought he was going to show me his car. This is no "car"—this is a beast, a big, blue behemoth, an ancient Volkswagen microbus, complete with peeling paneling.

I consider letting my dad drive me to school after all—in his Lexus. Minus two points on the social scale for being dropped off by my dad, but come on—is it cooler to show up with a friend in this? This is a step backward in my plan to get a guy to dump his mean girlfriend for me—or just ask me out, not having a prior girlfriend, which would also be acceptable.

But he's got the world's biggest grin on his sweet face. I've never seen his brown eyes so big with delirium—they almost reach his blond hair, which is impressive because he wears it pretty short.

I get in the colossal vehicle and find we're not alone. It's not just me, Logan, and the tank. A little red-headed figure with a black beanie says hi in the second row of seats.

"Jess!" I shout. "I forgot you're a freshman this year!"

"Awesome," she says, sounding like it's anything but.

I turn toward Logan, who's still beaming with pride. I guess anyone who's vanquished such a monster deserves to gloat about it.

"So...?" he asks.

"Did you at least win the demolition derby?" I gently tease.

"And what do you drive?" he asks.

"Alright. Shut up."

He takes a moment to maneuver the stick shift, but eventually he grinds it into first, and we lurch down my street.

"What's the deal? Why are you wearing a belt as a skirt? Is that a French thing?" he asks.

I almost choke. I don't think he's ever noticed I'm a girl before.

"In Paris, it's actually a hat," I say.

"Really?"

"No," I say, and to push off my embarrassment, firmly transferring it to him, I add, "Oh, my gosh. It's made you so awkward."

"No, no." He scoffs, tilting his head back. "All my friends wear skirts that short."

I laugh. He hasn't changed. A sense of relief warms me. Even though we've kept in contact online, I was a little worried he'd be different.

131

"You don't have any other friends." Jess rubs her nose while staring out the window.

"I have friends on band—"

"You quit band," she says.

"What?" I ask, afraid he has changed after all. "You quit band?"

A memory unlocks of him sitting at my desk, laughing and vowing never to play "Pomp and Circumstance" again.

"I swim now. Okay?" he asks.

How did I miss something as big as him making the swim team?!

"I swim, and you wear your dolls' clothes."

Before I left, I could tell Logan anything. We've known each other since junior high. Eloise said there's no such thing as a purely platonic relationship between the sexes and that either Logan, myself, or both must like the other romantically. But I don't feel that way toward him, and I've never seen anything to suggest he doesn't feel the same way. It's just that being around him is as easy as singing in the shower and as fun as jumping in a puddle when you're four.

"I just don't want to spend another year liking a guy who doesn't like me back."

"Matt liked you," he says with authority, as if he could know.

"Not enough," I say. "Not enough to dump his girlfriend."

"And that skirt is the answer?"

"One thing I learned in Paris, skirts are always the answer."

It's not true at all. Skirts actually caused me a lot of problems in France, with Mme. Patenaude ripping off my dance skirt and throwing it to the side of the room while screaming at me, but it sounds good, so I leave it.

He glares at my knees and grinds the gears. A little bit of unease wafts over me, and not just from the fumes coming out of the van. I've been worrying about his being different—I didn't concern myself with how changed I'd seem to him.

22 MYTH

JOLENE

The walk from the car, through the school to our first period is turning out to be the longest walk I have ever taken, obviously not in distance—but in observance of it. I had no idea a little miniskirt would turn absolutely everyone's heads. I don't look back at them—I pointedly don't—but I feel their eyes on me so intensely it almost hurts. I wasn't expecting this.

We finally get to the H block, and duck inside the classroom.

Freshmen and sophomores take Frosh English and Soph English. Now that we're juniors, we join the seniors and can choose from more interesting classes that fulfill the English requirements. Logan and I picked mythology with everyone's favorite teacher— well, everyone who doesn't care which college they get into—Mr. Laramie.

Mr. Laramie decorates his classroom from skylight to floor with artwork—not good artwork, student artwork, and not something they made for art class. I don't know how it started, but art kids bring in the random stuff they work on, and Laramie puts it up on his walls. Some of it is pretty interesting: someone's pet snake shopping downtown, freaking everyone out; a charcoal drawing of someone who looks too much like one of the biology teachers sawing off a student's leg. But there's also the random terrible self-portrait, or well-done but unimaginative watercolor of their cat. But I kind of love that he never turns anyone's art away. He ran out of room on the walls and started decorating the ceiling. Then the sculptures came. It was just one on his desk of a dragon someone had made. Now he has shelves of them. And I don't know if he did it, or if a student brought in a couch, but there's now a three-seat sofa that smells like stale feet under the windows, a faux plant with leaves of four, and a mini fridge. It's like a weird museum but also how I picture a college dorm—smell included.

Mr. Laramie sits at his desk, leaning in his chair against the front wall. He's probably in his fifties, has some gray hair, mostly in his unkempt beard. He never doesn't wear Hawaiian shirts and shorts, with sandals. It can rain, and he'll change nothing, but maybe add a frayed navy-blue unzipped zip-up hoodie.

Logan and I squeeze in among the other students, somewhat in the middle of the class, he behind me.

They all stare at my legs. I ignore them and look at the clock behind Laramie's desk—8:05.

My mistake dawns on me—why did I wear this skirt if I'll be in my seat when most of the class comes in? I should have dawdled, waited for the class to fill up. I scan the room to inventory who's seen me. To my horror—and, by her expression, hers too—Mary glares at me from the far wall.

I wave. She rolls her eyes and turns away.

She's sitting by two girls I recognize—Quinn Wayne and Courtney Usher. If you get them confused, it's probably okay. I used to, too, back when we went to the same grade school and they called me "Joke-lene."

They each wear black and purple cheer uniforms with matching jackets; they must be on varsity cheer, which for a junior is rare—or was a year ago. They're each cute but not overly gorgeous. Quinn is dark-skinned and wears her brown hair long and straight. Her features are sharp and angular.

She holds her phone up and away, taking a selfie with her best friend Courtney, who's darker, softer, with rounder features and shorter, curlier hair.

"Did she text you last night?" Quinn asks Courtney, who scoffs.

"Yes. I told her it's not our fault she didn't make cheer."

As I put my backpack on my desk, I remember something that had escaped my mind during Operation Bypass Parents.

"Oh! I got you a gift." I turn to him carefully. Already, this skirt is a hassle.

His eyes light up. "French gifts?" he asks, a goofy expression on his face.

"*Oui,*" I say, matching his excitement. "Did you get me any grand gifts from the Grand Canyon?"

"Grandest darn gifts you ever saw." His wide grin makes me laugh.

"Did you hike down?" I ask.

"No. We took those little helicopter things like in *Superman III.*"

"Really?"

He laughs, assumedly at my gullibility. "No. We—"

But I don't get to hear what he actually did because a few things happen all at once—Quinn says, "Oh! Shh! Here she comes"—and in walks Piper Thompson.

Logan and I both sigh, but for different reasons. I, because this girl has been tormenting my poor friend since she broke his heart in eighth grade, and he sighs because—well, I guess our reasons aren't that different.

Piper is tan after a long summer and wears dark jeans, no-lace tennis shoes, and a yellow T-shirt, jacketless even though it's freezing and not even nine yet. She has long, strawberry-blond hair with long bangs—I don't get why she still hasn't grown them out. She can't possibly like them this length. It's maddening. There's still something about her that reminds me of a horse—I think it's her long face and broad chin. How this girl has any power over my good friend Logan, I will never understand. Maybe it's her eyes—she has perfectly pretty green eyes.

They started dating after he asked her to go to the movies. Two weeks later, he was standing on her porch, heartbroken. Since then, she keeps up a steady pace of leading him on and rejecting him, and he keeps getting over her and falling back under. You can tell which way the tide ebbs easily enough. Like right now, she sees him, flips her hair over her shoulder,

137

and finds a seat near the far wall with Quinn and Courtney.

Since they're juniors on varsity cheer, I imagine it says something that Piper's friends with them. They're kind of a clique.

I only pay attention to where she sits because I'm watching Logan do the same with his jaw on the floor. I don't get it. A smarter young boy would drool over Quinn or Courtney instead. I mean, they're just as mean, but a lot cuter. I don't get it.

"You guys, I have to tell you," Piper says to the group surrounding her, comprising more than just Quinn and Courtney, but also Quinn's boyfriend, his friend, some other football players, and some other girls. "So, I'm in Spanish zero period, and—"

"Wait—" Kaila Jones, having gone unnoticed when she entered the class in her own cheer uniform, stands at the entrance of Piper's row with long, gorgeous red hair flowing, and long, gorgeous thin legs glowing, and gawks at Piper. "Where am I supposed to sit?"

Is that a glare at Mary?

"Just sit back there," Courtney points for Kaila to sit a few seats behind her in an empty seat back by Tyrus Kreuger, a super hot football player—but we don't have time to get into that.

"Or"—Kaila says with a sneer and a glare that's definitely for Mary—"scary Mary could crawl back under whatever rock she slithered out of this morning."

Mary stares straight ahead of her—so different from the confident snob she once was.

I know what she must be feeling inside. It can't be much different than how I do. My throat is dry, and I haven't been breathing.

I should say something.

When Kaila gets no response from Mary, she huffs out her nose and struts down Mary's aisle toward the seat Courtney suggested.

If I weren't already watching, I'd have missed it. Mary shifts in her seat, and Kaila crashes onto the floor. Everyone who saw it laughs, except me. I don't know if Logan saw it, but he doesn't laugh either.

Kaila stands and snarls at Mary.

"I wish I'd got that on video," Quinn says. "Can you do it again?"

That makes Courtney laugh harder.

The whole thing doesn't escape Mr. Laramie's notice, who still sits at the front of the class, talking to some students at his desk.

"You fall, Jones?" he asks Kaila.

"I'm fine," she says.

"Use your walking skills next time."

"Will do," she says, trying to blow it off, but wincing as she places her backpack next to her seat and turns her knees under her desk.

I assume it's over. But I'm not that lucky.

"Mr. Laramie, she didn't fall." It's Mary. "Piper tripped her."

Piper scoffs as Mary grins maliciously, like her artwork on the cereal box.

"You tripped her, Thompson?" he asks.

"No," Piper says, pointedly. "Mary did."

"This true, Mary?"

"It's not my fault her feet are so big," Mary says casually, examining one of her chrome, balled bracelets. She looks up to add, "and smelly. I was doing the class a favor. Hopefully, she'd break her leg, and we wouldn't have to smell her. You're welcome!"

A few kids laugh, including Logan—although you'd only know it if you were sitting right in front of him.

Mr. Laramie points his thumb toward the door.

"Office." He says it more as an obvious consequence. He doesn't seem to want to discipline.

Mary gathers her clay-motion skeleton backpack and, chin lifted, walks toward the door. Kaila—cheerleader that she is—claps.

Mary turns and growls at her. "Clap again and I'll trip you down the Greek!"

"Go shave your head!" Kaila shouts.

"I'll shave yours!" Mary yells.

Mr. Laramie stands and starts physically ushering my sister outside.

She keeps yelling. "BUT I DON'T HAVE A RAZOR SHARP ENOUGH TO CUT THROUGH THAT RAT'S NEST!"

"No one believes that!" Kaila shouts back.

Mary stops screaming once Mr. Laramie gets her outside, and in a moment he returns, Maryless, goes back to his desk, and writes up what I assume is a referral.

I should have said something.

Throughout the rest of class, all I can think about is Mary tripping Kaila and blaming it on Piper. These are girls I'm trying to impress! I always imagined Mary would help me rise through the social hierarchy, not be my barrier to it.

This is a setback, but it's not the end of Operation Miniskirt. If I learned anything from Caradine, it's that when the guys like you, the girls will be your friends, even if they secretly hate you. Fine. Let them hate me—just let them let me into their group!

When class is almost over and students line up at the door, I try to get to Piper to explain and apologize for Mary. But the bell rings, and she leaves before I can. I'd find Kaila and try to explain to her, but she left class slightly after Mary—bleeding.

Logan and I step out into the hall, and I scoop my hair out from behind my backpack.

I'll have to try again later, maybe tomorrow. But it'll be so awkward waiting any longer. I'll have to be all like, "Hey, Piper, remember yesterday when my sister tripped Kaila and blamed you?" It's bad enough I'll have to do that with Kaila. Hopefully, I can catch her before the end of the day. It'll be so much better to catch them as soon as possible.

But she's too far ahead of me, and I can't call out to her. She's only ever been mean to me—the very few times we've interacted. We're not friends. We'll never be friends—shut up! This is freshman me talk, back when I was intimidated by people, and terrified.

I take a breath and grab on to my backpack straps at the shoulders. "Hang on a minute," I tell Logan, then call out: "Piper!"

Quinn, Courtney, and Piper all turn to glare at me. The two cheerleaders stand on either side of her, like terrifying popular guards.

141

Piper waits for me to catch up. I leave Logan, trusting he'll wait for me.

"Hey." I should have planned what I was going to say. It already sounds stupid. "Um..." Also stupid. I take a breath to get my head right, but there's no righting this. "I'm sorry about Mary."

The face Piper gives me is that of a feral dog deciding to bite or not. Her jaw is tense, but her teeth don't quite meet, and her mouth pulls back, judging.

Thinking if I go on I'll make things better, I continue. "I was so horrified she tripped Kaila and blamed it on you..."

But her eternal glaring does not fade.

Maybe she doesn't remember that Mary and I are related.

"She's my sister," I say. "HALF! Half-sister."

"Oh!" Piper's eyes lighten. "I almost didn't remember you."

It kinda sounds like she didn't recognize me—which I would almost like to hear, in a way—but it's not, and I'm not sure if she means it that way, or the way she said it. Like you probably are after reading that, I'm very confused.

I stand there, trying to figure it out, when Courtney calls her away, and they leave. I'm halfway through replaying the interaction when Logan's standing beside me.

"Ack, you should warn me when you're going to do something like that," he says. "I was so unprepared for that much secondhand embarrassment."

"Sorry." I watch Piper and her friends turn the corner around the building. I can't get over how different everything is.

"What happened to Mary?" I ask.

"I don't know. She just one day ditched all her friends, quit cheer, started wearing a lot of black, dyed her hair bright pink, and made friends with the more goth-inspired art kids—all, like, overnight."

I knew a lot of that already. "I had no idea." What I didn't know was the abruptness.

I try to make sense of it all on our way to science.

23 THE CUTEST BOY I'VE EVER SEEN IN A SCIENCE CLASS

JOLENE

"Welcome to chemistry. Welcome, welcome. Take your seats, people. Choose wisely; once it's on the roster, it's yours for the year."

Ms. Magpali is adorable and tiny, with the world's cutest haircut. It's straight, black, buzzed around the sides but long on top, and she combs it to one side. Trust me, it works for her. It's a little bit of an edgy look for a teacher, but she has to do something to offset how cute and tiny she is. She's loud too, which makes no sense physically.

The four rows of desks at the front of the classroom fill up first. I sit as fast as I can, now hoping that nobody sees me in this skirt. The entire walk over here from myth people stared, called me slut, or loudly suggested to their friends: "Somebody needs attention."

Anyway, I take my seat in front of Logan again, and when the late-comers arrive, they take stools at the lab

144

tables in the back. To my surprise, some of these tardy students include Piper, Courtney, Quinn, Quinn's boyfriend, his friend, and Tyrus, the cute football player Kaila sat by—after she tripped and smacked into the linoleum floor.

I take off my light-blue hoodie. It has nothing to do with how attractive Tyrus is, or that he's sitting only a few feet behind me with nothing between us but air— well, and Logan. It's just getting warmer now that the morning ocean fog is dissipating. And Ms. Magpali, no doubt because she is so tiny and must be freezing every second of her life, probably yanks up the heater the second she gets to class in the morning.

The thing is, my hoodie was covering my bare shoulders, and without it, I'm not only in the world's tiniest skirt, but I'm also in a ridiculous, sleeveless top. Ridiculous but cute.

An exasperated noise comes from behind me. "You've got to be kidding me."

I turn to Logan, not quite indignant but somewhat embarrassed. "Pull it together. It's warm in here."

His smirk says he's just messing with me, so I send a friendly glare at him in return.

During this, Danny Vegas, who used to sit at my math table with Matt, Tim and me, takes the seat by my side.

I know Danny, but we're not on, like, greeting terms, so I take notice, but keep chatting with Logan until Ms. Magpali asks for assistance. "Can someone tall help me pull the chart down?"

I thought Tyrus was going to be the hottest guy in chemistry this year, or perhaps in the entire school, but in walks one of the most incredibly attractive guys I have ever seen: short blond hair, blue eyes, and a bone structure so sharp he could use his jaw as a can opener. He also mercifully has expensive fashion taste, the kind you wish all boys had, and wears a maroon tee, designer jeans, and stylish brown shoes.

Having been blessed with height, and after entering our once dismal cave and now glorious realm, he deigns to pull down Ms. Magpali's chart. As he does, he glances over his shoulder—why? I can't tell, but his eyes find me, and he smiles.

Panic fills my chest up to my nasal passages, and I feel sick, mortified at being caught staring at him.

I look down at my desk and busy myself searching for my pencil.

The last thing I need is for him to tell his friends I was looking at him. It'd be even worse if Piper and the cheerleaders at the back of the class noticed. They'd spread it around the entire school how sad and weird Mary's little sister was staring at a guy so obviously out of her league.

PIPER

Ms. Magpali cinches her brows together, frowning. "Oh, actually, that's the map. We want the Periodic Table..."

But Justin doesn't hear her. He keeps his eyes fixed on Mary's half-sister, who's, frankly, dressed like a prostitute. Like, he openly and visibly stares at her with a cocky grin as he walks to our lab table and slides into the seat across from me.

146

I wait for him to snap out of it, but the longer I wait, the more ridiculous he gets, so I offer him an out.

"What's going on this weekend?" I wait for an answer. It doesn't come, so I clear my throat, which seems to do the trick.

"Anthony's game," Justin says, as if I, of all people, would forget the first football game of the year and, coincidentally, Anthony's first as quarterback. "Throwing a victory party afterward."

I take a long breath through my nose and out again to sound annoyed and make him think I might not come. "Isn't that a little premature?" I ask, not really asking.

He scoffs, as if I'm not the most popular junior, whom he should, if he had any decency, at least act like I'm the least bit intimidating.

"Have you seen Anthony play?" he dares ask.

I don't care how tall he is, how cute his fluffy hair is, or how big his freaking blue eyes are—he does not get to insult me like that. Have I seen Anthony play? I'm his claim holder, and if I ever give him up, Courtney's next. But as such, I have certain made-up responsibilities, like going to his games.

See, with a guy like Anthony, you have to stake your claim early—let everyone know you saw him first, and that if anyone tries anything, flirting, or asking him out, or accepting an invitation from him—they'll have to answer to you. So far, I'm successful. He's not dating anyone anyway. Honestly, though, like, that might not be my doing. He's the quarterback this year, but he's also kind of a loner. I think that's what I like about him, though. He's hot, but he doesn't know it.

147

He should be popular, but all he does at parties is stand against the wall—out of the way, and out of the fun.

"Of course I've seen him play!" I cast as much shame as I can into my voice.

He's unfazed. "If we don't win, we'll just call it a party." He leans back and has to catch himself, maybe forgetting he's on a bench, not a chair.

Why do all boys do this? Like they can't get enough of an adrenaline rush from sitting in a chair normally, they have to risk tipping over. His almost fall reminds me of something—

"Oh!" I say, parting my long bangs that keep slipping down to the side. "I have to tell you what happened first."

"You tripped Kaila," he says.

"No!" I yell. "Who said I tripped her?"

"Tay-Tay. She wants me to punch you in the face."

Crap. No—it's not that I'm scared of Justin punching me, it's just that Tay-Tay's a senior, like Justin and Anthony, and Tay-Tay's cheer captain. I spent the whole of last year kissing up to her, and she still didn't pick me for the team. She'll have some sway for next year's team, so I still have to make nice, and if she needs to kick someone off the team and fill the spot—it's happened before—maybe she'll pick me. I am her boyfriend Justin's close friend. Which is why you'd think she would have picked me for the team. I'm just as good as Courtney and Quinn, if not better. Courtney's kind of chunky, to be honest, and Quinn doesn't have a lot of rhythm. They were on JV cheer last year, but still. I bet their parents, like, bought the team all new uniforms, or something, and that's why Tay let them in, cause I'm not a bad dancer. Like, I can't do the splits, or anything, or a cartwheel, or that almost-flip-thing, but I'm not bad, and this year I thought I was definitely going to make cheer because who I thought was my friend—Tay-Tay—was the captain and in charge of try-outs! But here we are—not on cheer.

It's whatever. Sometimes they have auditions at the semester break. Maybe I can talk my parents into making a large donation. Unlikely. I barely got them to buy me a car.

Anyway, I need Tay to like me irregardless. It's not just that she's in charge of whether or not I make cheer. She's also dating Justin. So, she's a few pegs above me on the social ladder. I'm junior class secretary and the ASB president's friend. She's cheer captain and the ASB president's girlfriend. I might as well play softball or something; that's how invisible I am in comparison.

"Tell her I didn't do it. Mary did," I tell him.

His face freezes. His eyes dart to the side. "Stansen?" he asks quietly.

I give him a face that says, "Obviously!" and add, "Will you tell her, please?" I say the "please" less like "please" and more like, "do it!"

"Okay." He sounds annoyed, scratches his ear, and looks away.

"Are you going to!?"

He turns back to me. "Yes!"

"Okay," I say as he turns away again. "Thank you."

149

I bring my arms back, stick out my chest, and crack my back, then watch Justin as he watches Mary's little sister.

"Why did Mary do it?" he asks.

"Hm?" I'm not really taking in his question until after I "hm." "Oh, I don't know. Kaila was being Kaila."

I thought I knew Justin. But he smirks and laughs, as if finding something about the story charming—not the reaction I expected at all.

"So, she tripped her?"

"Yeah," I say. "Kaila was just gonna shake it off, but then Mary told Mr. Laramie I tripped her."

I raise an arm in a shrug, and to show off my gorgeous red nails. I just got them done yesterday at a new place downtown. The place smelled like chemicals, and they didn't have massage chairs, but they did a decent job.

"Why?" he asks again. I roll my eyes and continue.

"She and Kaila ended up screaming at each other as Mr. Laramie dragged Mary out."

He gapes at me for a solid minute, then comes alive again. "That is not at all what Tay told me."

"She got it secondhand from a super embarrassed Kaila," I say.

"But she didn't even mention Mary—"

I don't know why he's so obsessed with Mary, but I don't have to deal with it anymore because all the sudden Jesse Morrison, ASB vice president—kinda cute but not Anthony—leans over me to talk to Justin.

"You see that girl?" he asks.

I tilt my head to see who he's looking at and roll my eyes.

150

"She keeps looking at me," he says, getting the attention of all the surrounding guys.

I can feel their eyes combing over her body. The only thing worse than guys doing it to you is guys doing it to someone else around you.

"Who is she?" Jesse asks.

Ugh. "She" is Mary's half-sister, of course, the slut who's been pilfering Justin's attention on-and-off since the start of class. The girl who weirdly tried to apologize for her sister earlier. The girl who I liked better when she was across the Pacific.

She turns around, glancing at Justin, then looks at the rest of us watching her. She flushes bright-red— adding an obnoxious glow to her abnormally dewy skin—and snaps her head back to her chemistry book.

I scoff. This girl. Who does she think she is— waltzing in here, back from France, with her long brown hair in a romantically messy side-braid, perfectly-peach shoulders, and long legs? If I were naked, I wouldn't be showing that much skin. I hate her—all mysterious. If she had stayed in town, like any normal teenage girl—I mean, we all go through puberty. It's not like she's the only one—she would have slowly gotten pretty right in front of everyone's faces, and the slow burn would have gone unnoticed, and in everyone's minds she'd still be the frumpy little fourteen-year-old we knew before. But no, she had to go off and transition in solitude like an overly dramatic, self-important caterpillar.

She's so obvious when she turns again toward us, attempting to be subtle, acting like she's looking at the clock.

151

I stare her down, hoping my expression lets her know we're not all obsessing over her. She faces the front again and flips through her science book for the eightieth time.

Justin smirks out of the corner of my eye, a smirk that seems to know what I know: she wasn't looking at Jesse.

24 THE ASB PRESIDENT

JOLENE

I'm getting like really sick of the skirt. I can't walk to my locker without guys staring at me, and not in a dignified way. And the girls all glare at me, loudly whispering insults.

I could probably change into my jeans, but I don't want to be called out on that: "She changed her clothes; she probably got tired of everyone calling her a slut." I mean, obviously! And what's worse, admitting you don't like being called a slut, or being called a slut? I can't bring myself to be okay with either, so I do nothing.

When I reach my locker, Logan's already there, sitting on the ground by his, transferring books to and from his backpack, then zipping it up. As he does it, the specimen from our chem class turns down the locker hall with Piper and a few football players he was sitting with.

He walks by—still looking at me like I'm a piece of hard candy. It both electrifies me and sets me on edge.

153

It reminds me of the way Beau would look at me in the mirror. I draw my arms around my waist.

"Who is that?" I ask.

Logan turns his head, still on the floor. I wish he'd stand up, crouch, or kneel, like any dignified high schooler would.

"Justin Granite?" he asks. "ASB president? You don't know him?"

"I was gone."

Logan scoffs. "So? The whole town knows him. He's a Granite. His dad owns Granite Forge."

"That Granite?!"

"Yeah."

Wow, Granite Forge employs half the county. Even Logan's mom works for them.

I adjust my glasses as Justin and his group stop across the hall at one of their lockers. He's so pretty. He almost looks like a decent person when he's not ogling me. But once at his locker, he turns and moves his eyes over me again—my cue to turn away.

"He keeps giving me this look..."

A part of me wonders if he'd be looking so much if it weren't for Operation Miniskirt. This is both what I wanted this morning when I put the skirt on, and what Eloise warned me about, all tied up in a neat little package with a bow. Now if only I could shove it back in the mailbox—return to sender!

"He has a girlfriend," Logan says.

"No, I'm not interested." A fact I didn't totally realize until I say it. It's a relief—I can stop this wishy-washy back-and-forth that's been going on in my head—no, not my head. I very much doubt my head's involved in this. I've just never had a guy this attractive look at me this way before—or in any way. Okay, besides Beau, and Matt obviously looked at me. He had to; I was his trusty math partner. But it was so different, it almost didn't count. Like if your brother looked at you, you wouldn't say he was looking at you. Ugh, I need to never again liken Matt to a brother. I need my mind to go somewhere else.

I look down the hall. It leads out to the grassy courtyard in front of the "temporary" classrooms. A bird picks at someone's discarded bag of chips on a bench.

"I bet he's at Yale or something..." I say, not really aware I'm talking. "He was really smart."

"Who?"

"Oh, Matt."

Logan grunts. "He was a junior in your freshman math class..."

Oh yeah, and I often had to help him.

"So, maybe not Yale?" I ask.

"He didn't tell you where he applied?"

"He was a junior." I shrug.

25 ALWAYS A SUPERINTENDENT, NEVER A CUSTODIAN

MATT

There's no way my grandpa knows how awesome his apartment building is. He's gotta be completely unaware leading Jason and me into one of the unit's large living spaces, and I mean large. The room's the size of a basketball court. The ceilings go up forever, and a huge window smacks you in the face with sunlight right when you walk in. Most of the walls expose red brick. It looks industrial with a twisted iron staircase leading up to what I guess is a loft bedroom or something overlooking the rest of the apartment. It can't be any bigger than the kitchen, but I like the idea of being up there, looking down.

It's not what I pictured two weeks ago when he offered me an apartment and a job as superintendent of the complex. But I also didn't expect to get into UC Santa Barbara, which I only did after my grandpa made a few calls. My grades were not good. I almost didn't even take the SATs, but Grandpa said he knew a few people and told me I ought to give it a try.

"Could use a bigger living space," Jason says. I know he's joking because I know Jason, and anyone with any sense would pick up on his obvious sarcastic humor, unless they were my Grandpa Craddick.

Jason would be in high school right now if he hadn't dropped out, and at work right now if he hadn't overslept one too many times and gotten fired from bagging groceries. He's half-Vietnamese and keeps his hair in an outdated cut that he's had since we were kids. I'd make fun of him for it, but he's too easygoing to make fun of. It doesn't work. You've gotta send that energy to Justin or somebody. It rolls right off of Jason.

Most people like him because he's so chill; it's like hanging out with a turtle or something. Seriously, nothing gets to him. But my grandpa's not having it.

He turns to me, his lip curling. "This one moving in with you?"

"No." I scratch the back of my head—only partly lying. Jason's crashing with me indefinitely, but his name won't be on the lease. "He's just a friend. I found a roommate online."

My grandpa's letting me stay as part of my salary, but I'm not going to miss an opportunity to make a few extra bucks. That's why I put out an ad for a roommate. I am my entrepreneurial, ambitious grandpa's grandson.

"I'm gonna head out." He hands me the keys. "There's storage in the basement if you need more space."

"Grandpa, it's fine. Jase was making a joke. There's plenty of space."

"Start work Monday?" It's less of a question than it is a confirmation.

"I can start earlier than that." It comes out maybe a little too eagerly.

My grandpa served his country, was awarded the Purple Heart, and donated a building for a new public library and a wing at the local hospital. If he can do all that, I can start work before the weekend.

"Just don't work too hard." He pats my shoulder before he leaves.

I look at the keys in my hand—two sets: one key ring with all the keys to the building, and one key ring with just two keys: for the top and bottom lock of my very own apartment—with Jason and a roommate.

"Where do you sleep, though?" Jason asks. I shouldn't be surprised that's where his mind is. I woke him up to come see the apartment with me. There's a good chance he would have slept another five hours.

"In the loft, I guess. It's crammed, but how much room do you need to sleep, right?"

"If you take the loft, where is your roommate sleeping? Or me?"

"What was I supposed to say? He's giving me this apartment rent-free, and a job I'm way underqualified for."

"Custodian?"

"Superintendent."

"What happened to custodian?"

"It was always superintendent."

"Hello?" A female voice calls from the door my grandpa must have left ajar, probably assuming we were right behind him.

"Come in," I say.

JASON

The apartment door opens wider and two girls, one with long, straight, blond hair, and the other with red hair that's only slightly shorter, enter. They both wear tiny shorts, flip-flops, and tank tops. They're tan and smell like coconuts and like they just jumped off their surfboards half a minute ago—which they could have, cause the beach is literally ten feet out the backdoor of Matt's apartment.

When they see me—well, I actually can't confirm they do see me. When they see Matt, their expressions shift from casual to surprised to downright giddy. Frankly, it's a little embarrassing. They should be embarrassed.

"Sorry," the blonde says, literally batting her eyes. I didn't know girls actually did that. "But do you guys have a screwdriver? We're building our furniture."

"I don't have one on me," Matt tells her. "But I can get one from the supply closet. I'm the new superintendent."

I almost laugh out loud. Of course he has to slide that in, and it works, not that it needed to. The girls were already one foot down the aisle.

"Awesome. Thanks," the blonde says. "I'm Charlene, by the way. This is Dillon."

"We're in number eleven," Dillon says.

"I'll be there in a minute," Matt tells them instead of introducing me the way the blonde made sure to introduce her friend.

The girls leave. I turn to Matt.

"So...?" I wait for an answer. Something must explain why he is the way he is.

"What?" Matt plays dumb, as usual.

"She was giving you the face," I tell him.

"What face?"

"The face, face! You should ask her out."

He looks at me all wide-eyed. This guy, I tell ya. Halfway through last year, we were sitting in the Greek theater at school eating lunch, and he showed me a picture on his phone of a girl in a white bikini on a sailboat and said, "I had math class with this girl last year." And he's gotten stupider and weirder ever since.

He broke up with his girlfriend, saying she was manipulative and controlling, which hadn't bothered him until then, and he didn't ask out her friend, who was also crazy hot and made it very clear she was into him. He ignored girls so much that none of them asked him to the girl-ask-boy dance, Sadie Hawkins, and for Prom, he asked a friend of Justin's date and ignored her the whole time. I know all this can't be because he's gotten it into his head that he's in love with this boat chick, but I honestly can't help thinking that's exactly what it is.

"Yeah, but," he says, about to confirm my suspicions—just watch. "I might run into Jolene..."

Yup.

26 THE GREEK

JOLENE

"Who did you eat lunch with while I was gone?" I bite my apple, swallow, and turn to Logan.

At lunch, most students sit in the Greek theater to eat. Some eat in the overlooking cafeteria, and some outliers eat under trees or on benches scattered around campus, but most people are in the Greek. The Associated Student Body presidency plays music over loudspeakers they set up on the stage. Once a week, they host class competitions down there. But we don't have to worry about that today, since it's not Friday.

I'm actually not sure they still do class comps, but I suspect they do. It's weird being back. At times, I feel like I haven't missed a beat, and at others, it's like I've never been here in my life.

"I joined a lot of clubs," he says before sipping his juice. He drinks from a juice box like a little kid. He's probably the only one in the Greek not drinking a bottle or can of something. "Gamer Group met on

161

Mondays, Jazz Band on Tuesdays and Thursdays, Star Warriors every other Wednesday—"

"So, you're still doing band?!"

"Well," he takes another sip. "Jazz Band doesn't play at graduation, but you still get to compete and go to Mystic Mountain at the end of the year."

"What's with the skirt?" Mary plops herself down on the step above the one Logan and I sit on.

"It's just a skirt," I say.

"I can't believe Dad let you out of the house like that." It's rich coming from the girl with an exposed belly button ring, and whose fishnet tights are the only things preventing the entire world from seeing her butt sticking out below her skirt.

"Your skirt is shorter than mine."

She scoffs. "Dad doesn't care what I wear." She stands and adjusts her tinier skirt. "I transferred out of your myth class." I'm not sure she's talking to me— she's facing toward Piper's group of cheerleaders and football players. "I'm sure you're devastated."

"What are you taking instead?" I ask. But she's already three feet away, walking toward the dark mass of goths collecting and forming at the bottom back of the Greek like a shadow that grows with every soul it devours.

PIPER

Justin's been staring at Jolene since lunch started— and he's doing it again. I wouldn't mind; I'm not interested in him that way, but she's not even that good-looking. I don't get it. She has a mouse nose, and her eyes aren't even shaped like human eyes; they're like animated princess eyes—cute in cartoons, but kind of horrifying in real life. And her lips could definitely stand to be bigger. If I had an upper lip that thin, I think I'd kill myself. I'd get it filled at the very least. She should be embarrassed. And she's got these huge calves. Like, gross. And her breasts are abnormally large for someone so skeletal. I bet she got them enhanced. Probably that's why she went to France. Then no one would notice she missed school a few days and came back with a chest. This whole ballet school thing is obviously a cover. Why can't anyone else see that? They're all too distracted by the results.

"I don't get it," I tell Justin. But even when I talk to him, he still doesn't look my way. It's not like I always hold 100% of his attention, but usually he spreads it among lots of girls. It's really annoying when it's just one.

"You don't have to," he says. At least he acknowledges that I've said words.

"She's hot," Quinn's boyfriend's friend Weston says as if anyone asked him.

"Heard she dances ballet," some guy on the edge of our group says, making the guys around him laugh like ballet is somehow tantalizing.

Ugh. "I don't see it," I say.

I'd appeal to Courtney and Quinn to back me up, but they're sitting on the step above me and Justin, talking about some singer I can't stand.

It's annoying they don't talk about something that interests Quinn's boyfriend's friend Weston so that he'd stop butting in on mine and Justin's conversation, but then that might interest Justin, too, and then I'd seriously be bored.

"I wonder if she's dating that guy," Justin says, still staring at her.

I can only roll my eyes—wait, who does he must mean by "that guy."

"Logan?!" I ask. "No." I shake my head, trying to remember earlier today in our classes. Had there been any sign that they were together? Were they holding hands when I wasn't paying attention? They are around each other a lot...

"I wonder who would know," Justin says, almost to himself, and certainly not taking my "no" as a definitive answer. "Asking her sister is out."

"Why's that?" I ask, pretty certain he has no reason to have said what he said.

"Because they used to make out," Quinn's boyfriend's friend Weston says, finally coming in useful and drawing Justin's attention our way—for once.

"What? When?" I ask.

"Before I started dating Tay-Tay," Justin says.

Where is Tay-Tay? She usually eats with us during lunch. She must either be doing some cheer thing with Kaila, or some completely other thing with Jesse.

"So, before she went goth?" I ask.

"Obviously," he says.

How did I miss this? Mary was, past tense, one of my best friends. How did I not notice they were hooking up?

"How did I not know this?" I ask out loud this time.

"I didn't, like, broadcast it."

"And now you think her sister's hot?" I ask.

"I don't think." He shares a smile with me before giving it back to Jolene. Then he speaks the worst sentence I have ever heard him speak in the years I've known him. And he breathes it, as if to himself. But, lucky me, I catch all of it. "I'd better keep her away from Anthony."

Disgust and confusion, but mostly disgust, fill every facet of my brain and my being.

"Why?!" I ask, deliberately not hiding my abhorrence.

The idea that he would need to keep Jolene away from Anthony is ridiculous. I must have heard him wrong, and if I didn't, he must be talking out of his butt. He can't be implying what he is definitely implying— that if Anthony met her, he'd fall for her. No, that absolutely cannot be it.

"Oh," he says. "Sorry, Pipe. Forgot you liked him."

That's not the response I want.

It's probably true that everyone knows how I feel about Anthony, but I mean, come on. Imagine having a crush on one of your best friends for years, and everyone feels perfectly comfortable talking about it in front of everyone else.

"What? Psh. No, I..." I'm not a good actress, so I give up trying to save face, and just watch her, like Justin does, like we all do.

Would Anthony really be interested in her? Ugh. Could he already be interested in her? No, of course not. That's crazy. First, he's way more down-to-earth than that. He's not about to fawn all over her like Jesse in chemistry, drooling all over the beakers. Second, she's way beneath him. She's a nobody—no, she's worse than that; she's a freak's little sister. Sure, she's cute, demure, and mysterious, and probably speaks French and all that, but Anthony is quarterback, shredded and—well, Anthony. He doesn't talk a lot, and he's not exactly the life of the party like Justin is, but the few friends he has are popular. And he acts like it's not true, but there isn't a girl in school who wouldn't sacrifice one of the blond virgins squirming in health class to get a date with him. I mean, there's no way he'd go for her over every other single girl in the entire school, including me. Not possible. Justin's probably just on crack.

But if he's right at all—if there's the slightest chance Anthony might fall for her—then maybe someone should make sure she's already dating someone when that happens.

Worst-case scenario, Tay-Tay—the cheer captain who single-handedly kept me out of cheer this year—is out a boyfriend. Oh, no! She'll be devastated.

I laugh and cough at the same time—choking on my diet soda.

27 DEBRIEFING

JOLENE

Operation Miniskirt was obviously a disaster. It was supposed to skyrocket me into popularity, make the planets align, and bring peace to the jocks and geeks, but instead it probably did more damage than good. A bunch of boys stared, making my skin crawl to get away, and several girls sneered and whispered horrible insults, while technically also staring.

To be fair, there's a good chance I would have gotten a lot of attention just because maybe people have heard I've been in France for a year, and maybe they would be curious. I think the skirt was like my imported European junior high shoes—and came across as showy—except a hundred times worse.

So, when Mary and I get home, I cross through my bedroom, swing open my bookcase door, carefully step over the clothes I've left on my closet floor, reach my chest of drawers, trade my tiny skirt for sweatpants, push my other clothes in the drawer out of the way, and slip my miniskirt underneath.

I haven't given up. But this was a failed experiment. I need another.

28 THE DAY I MEET
ANTHONY WHITAKER

JOLENE

In the morning, I again get down to breakfast after Mary has left. My mom's also gone—she's in LA, working for the week, which leaves my dad and me.

Instead of a miniskirt, I wear dark, distressed jeans, brown ankle boots, and a purple peasant top that gathers and has long sleeves that slightly expose my shoulders. As always, I've pulled my hair to the side in a loose braid, and today I don't bother with a sweatshirt. Yesterday, it warmed up so fast that the only good my hoodie did was keep my lunch company in my locker—apart from aiding in Operation Hide Sleeveless Top.

I'm not sure what today's mission will be; I'm still obfuscated by yesterday's. If my plan was to get guys to like me, which would, in theory, force the girls to at least pretend to like me, it worked as well as the dead pointe shoes in my dance bag that I keep forgetting to replace.

I figure I'll have to do some under-playing—lying low and letting people forget about what I wore the day before. I'll shrink back and let the boys answer the teacher's questions, making sure I'm not too visible—or that I at least don't want to be visible. I'm just an easygoing, super pretty girl who's totally approachable and not at all promiscuous.

But it's not just the missions. I didn't like yesterday. Do I really have to do everything Caradine did just to make sure guys don't overlook me? Anyway, as I've said, it didn't work—well, it worked, like, it got Justin's attention, but it didn't work as in, it didn't make me popular, or dateless-proof.

Maybe I can work on that—on Justin. Maybe he's my key into their world. Is that using him? Does it matter if I know he'd use me in a heartbeat? We can use each other—except I'd be using him and he'd be doing nothing ever. Maybe it wouldn't hurt to be seen with him, though—I could keep my distance, but be around him, right?

I don't have much time to think about it. As I dig through the cupboard for a cup, I get a text from Logan that he's arrived. I'm running a little late. I grab a banana off the table and open the fridge to get my lunch, and this is the time my dad decides is perfect for having a long, drawn-out conversation.

"Hey honey, I didn't get a chance to ask you how your day went yesterday."

He got the chance. He was home all night. I was home all night. There was literally nothing stopping him from making the trek up to my room and having a chat with me.

"Did you make any new friends?" he asks.

"Was I supposed to?" I say as I put my lunch in my backpack.

"I just thought, since you were gone for so long, you'd want to come back and make some more friends—"

"I mean..." I pull my backpack over my shoulders. Of course, I would have loved to make new friends yesterday, and of course, I don't want to talk about it with my dad.

"I just thought that now you're a junior, you'd want maybe some other friends."

"I gotta go."

"Well, honey, it's just that Logan's a bit of a—well, he's a bit of a—and you'll probably want to start dating soon..."

It's worse than I thought. He doesn't want to talk friends—he wants to talk boyfriends!

"Are you worried I'm going to go out with Logan? What's wrong with Logan?" Uh-oh—he's not outside the door, is he?

I look out the window at him and Jess sitting in his van. Ugh. That van...

"Well, it's not so much, 'what's wrong with him.' He just—"

"Is this because he drove me to school?"

"No..."

But I think yes. I think he's worried that, because Logan drives me to school, that must mean we're desperately in love with each other. Why do parents do this? I wish they'd just slack off the ropes a little and realize that a lot of the big deals they make aren't big deals at all, because you've already considered what they don't think you've considered. I love Logan, but not the way my dad worries I do, and I feel kind of bad for Logan that my dad, apparently, doesn't think he'd be good enough for me, when we're not into each other anyway.

"Bye, Dad," I say as I walk out the door, hearing a quiet "Bye, honey" fade behind me.

My friendship with Logan is built upon our similar tastes in, well, everything. Except he likes more movies than I do. Even though all my favorites are favorites of his, he has more favorites. If that makes sense.

On the way to school he tells me about a movie he saw at the beginning of summer that I missed. He might have taken what I said to mean I missed seeing the film because I was in France, busy, but I didn't mean it that way. I missed it because I plain and simply wasn't interested at all in seeing it. I'm not always one to shy away from a butt-load of violence or any kind of action movie, especially a historic one, but this one—ugh. For one, the preview made it look like there were zero women in it, and according to Logan's drawn-out retelling of this "masterpiece," there weren't. And I can't stretch my brain enough to comprehend why a group of warriors from the thirteen hundreds would meet up with a giant robot, and I'm not curious enough to waste three hours of my life finding out.

He continues telling me about said movie as we enter mythology and sit in the same seats as the day before.

I don't think Mr. Laramie has ever turned on a heater in his life. I'll have to remember that if I take him again next year, to get him in a later period. Tomorrow, I'll definitely have to bring my sweatshirt, or a jacket, or something.

"Then, you know what he does?"

Shoot. Maybe I can respond with a vague answer that looks like I've been listening.

"Um..." Brilliant.

"He stabs him through the freaking neck!"

Oh good. He's so in love with retelling this story that it doesn't seem my devoted attention is 100% required.

But it doesn't matter anymore because someone sits down in front of me who puts a full and complete stop to Logan's retelling, especially because she sets her backpack down, turns to me, and begins to animatedly talk to us.

"I love your backpack! Where did you get it?" It's Piper Thompson.

"Paris." Wait—that's not entirely true. I got it on our weekend trip to Italy, but I might as well not go into details since I still don't know why the heck she's sitting in front of me, engaging in pleasant and complimentary conversation—

Shoot! Telling girls I got my stuff abroad is what got me in trouble in junior high! I was just talking about this in an earlier chapter, too!

But instead of rolling her eyes and glowering at another girl, she leans in and smiles. It throws me off a little, to be honest.

"Oh, that's right!" she says. "You spent a year in France. Right? Did you see the Eiffel Tower?"

I'm so caught off guard I forget who I'm talking to and a sarcastic "no" slips out. But I manage to stop myself from adding, "I spent a year in Paris and never saw the Eiffel Tower."

"Really?" she asks.

I laugh, trying to ease any embarrassment I might have caused her. Some people don't take easily to being the butt of a joke, even a harmless one. Like, Beau once stopped talking to me for a week because I laughed at him for asking Helene if it was raining outside when she came in dripping wet and putting away her umbrella.

"No, I'm kidding. I could actually see it from my bedroom." Maybe that was too much. I don't want to brag again. I'm fully aware the year I've spent is not something everyone can do. But again, and un-typically, if it phased her, she hid it.

My response, or maybe my acerbity, gets the attention of Quinn and Courtney, who are near enough to overhear and must be wondering why Piper's sitting with me and not them.

They suppress smiles and glance at each other, and I wonder if it's me, or maybe they don't always get along with Piper.

PIPER

174

I ignore Quinn and Courtney's little glares. They're probably mad at me for not noticing their new shoes that are just newer versions of their last ones, or haircuts that I can't possibly notice because they're wearing their hair in ponytails.

They're such little sheep. If they had any sense at all, they wouldn't follow everything I do. But being them, they start panting for Jolene to tell them all about France. As if I were only speaking to her to be friendly.

JOLENE

"Shut up!" Quinn shouts, causing a few people to look over. "Your aunt's a fashion designer, right?" I guess they must have heard as much from Mary because I've never spoken to them in my entire life except to tell them to knock it off when they kept kicking their kickball at me while I was sitting in the grass, playing with the flowers. "Did you go to Paris Fashion Week?"

"Yeah. All of them."

Quinn and Courtney gasp, and I worry I've gone too far again, but, like Piper, they lean in—breaking all the public-school norms I've had to meticulously navigate over the last several years. It's like I've suddenly come out of an asteroid field. I'm not even sure I need to suppress my more science-fictiony metaphors—that's the level of freedom I feel!

"Well, my aunt was exhibiting, so we kind of had to..." I drop off the end of my sentence after realizing almost the entire class is staring, eager-eyed, at me.

These stares beat the penetrating ones from yesterday, but they're still intimidating.

"I've been to Paris!" a girl whose name I'm uncertain of says a few seats behind me.

"Nobody cares," Piper says.

I almost turn to see who spoke, but Courtney stretches out a hand and places it on my arm, freezing me out of shock.

"Did you go to La Ménagerie Rouge?" she asks me.

"Sort of," I say. "We didn't see a show or anything, but my aunt's friend threw a party there."

"At La Ménagerie Rouge?" someone asks.

"Must have been a rich friend," Quinn says.

"It was Iphigeneia Mischka?" I keep hiking my voice up at the end of what I'm saying, hoping timidity eases any feelings of jealousy one of my listeners might indulge.

"The Iphigeneia Mischka?" Piper asks.

I guess she's heard of her, whereas I hadn't. She was in a huge movie, but it was, like, the one movie I didn't see that year, as luck had it. I watched it in France later, but I didn't think it was that good. She was good in it though.

"How many Iphigeneia Mischkas are there, Piper?" Courtney asks her.

Piper sinks back into her chair as Quinn leaves her desk, leaning on one closer to me with her knee on the seat.

"Do you have any pictures?" she asks.

"Yeah." I take my phone out of my back pocket, open my social app, and flip through my profile page until I find the group of photos of me at La Ménagerie Rouge.

I hand it to Quinn, who takes it and starts flipping through them.

"Oh," she says. "Courtney's asking to follow you. I'm just gonna allow it. Don't mind me. Is that Oscar Ivanov?"

"He's in this picture of you in this boat, too!" Courtney adds, looking at my account on her phone.

"Look at how he's looking at you..." Quinn says.

Piper stretches over to see—not smiling.

I take a minute to look back at Logan. He's reading a book, nonplussed. He lifts his head and smiles at me, reassuring me he doesn't mind that our conversation ended.

I'll have to let him tell me more about his movie later, or possibly even watch it with him when it comes to streaming next week.

"Jeez," Piper says. "A lot of these have Oscar in them."

"He was super nice and really good friends with my uncle, Caspian."

"That's your uncle?" Courtney says, pointing to a picture of Cass standing at the helm of *The Eleven*. "Oh. He's cute."

"He's married to my aunt," I say, as if it weren't obvious.

"I'm just looking," Courtney says in an innocent, singsong voice.

PIPER

177

It was not my intention to have Quinn and Courtney swarm in this much. On one hand, they're obviously influenced by me, which is great and all, but if I'm going to steer Jolene, I can't have these two dummies messing it up. They might compliment her too much without throwing in some cautionary digs to keep her ego in check, or after I keep it in check, she might seek them out for approval instead of me. They might even introduce her to Anthony. This is definitely getting out of hand.

JOLENE

"Cell phones away," Mr. Laramie says on his way to the front of the class. "Back to your seats."

"I want to interview you about Paris Fashion," Quinn says, turning off her phone.

"For the school paper?" Piper asks.

"For my socials, genius," Quinn says, scowling.

"Yeah. You're sitting with us at lunch," Courtney says as she and Quinn put their phones in their pockets and take seats right next to us.

"Yeah," Piper says. "Absolutely..."

Before she turns around to face the front, I glimpse that face I've come to always expect, that junior high face, that face that turns to her friend and whispers, "show off."

I'm not sure where it came from, or if it was always there, hiding under the surface, but something about how Piper looks gives me the impression that my welcomed company during lunch is anything but.

29 CHEMISTRY

JOLENE

When class ends, Courtney and Quinn ask me to hold up while they put their backpacks on and walk with me toward our next class. Piper joins us, too. On the way, they quiz me all about France: which landmarks I saw, which museums I visited, which plays I attended, which stores I shopped at, which restaurants I ate in, but mostly, they ask about Oscar Ivanov. Were they—he and Iphigeneia—the only celebrities I met? No, but they were the most frequent. How tall was he? Was he more gorgeous in person? Did he always speak with his accent? But every time they bring him up, Piper asks about something else, so as we walk into chemistry, I answer her question about whether I had escargot.

"It's really not bad at all," I say as she makes a face. "I mean, they smother it in garlic and butter so..."

This gets a good laugh out of Courtney as the bell rings.

"Take your seats," Ms. Magpali instructs us. "Attendance is going around. Mark yourself present by circling your name on yesterday's seating chart. Do not move spots. Sit in the same seats as yesterday. They are yours for now and forever. You are married to your desk."

"Aww, too bad," Piper says, looking anything but that she means what she says. "Guess you have to go sit over there now."

"We'll continue this later," Courtney assures me.

I don't get it. Piper was the one who sat down and started talking to me. Why is she now acting so annoyed that her friends are talking to me, too?

I find my seat in front of Logan, who isn't looking at me.

"Hey," I say to him. "What happened to you? After class, you just took off."

"Did I?" he asks, still not looking at me.

I must have upset him. But really? It wasn't like I was being mean—just making friends. I thought he was cool with it...

"No talking," Ms. Magpali warns. "Class has started."

Logan gets the attendance, circles his name, and passes it to me. I take it and circle my name as someone sits down next to me; must be Danny, returning to his seat from yesterday, so I turn to hand him the attendance, but a guy reaches to take it. He smells clean and expensive—his outstretched arm is the perfect amount of tan, like he's only outside when he's driving a convertible. This guy is not green-haired Danny.

"What are we doing?" Justin whispers.

180

"She wants us to circle our names on the roll chart," I whisper back, letting go of the attendance that he then sets in front of him. "She wants us to keep the same seats as last time..."

He makes a face, like, "We'll see about that," and erases his and Danny's names from their spots, and switches them so Danny's by Piper and he's by—well, me.

Did Danny take his seat? Is that why he's here, because Danny didn't want to sit by me anymore?

I turn and check but only catch Piper looking confused and upset. No one's in the seat he was sitting in yesterday.

I turn back front.

He can't be sitting next to me because he wants to sit next to me. He just can't. But nothing else makes sense—not that this makes sense. But—what's that Sherlock quote? "When you have eliminated the impossible, whatever remains, however improbable, must be the truth."

Despite myself, despite how I feel when he stares at me, despite all my instincts to run—my face flushes. I turn away to hide it, and to check Logan's expression. Did he see what just happened? He did. But he isn't smiling. He looks put out, which there's no excuse for.

It's not even that I like Justin, which, if I did, why should that bother Logan? It's just really flattering that he singled me out. That's all it is. It's a memory I can look back on and smile about. I'm not going home and writing "Jolene Evangeline Granite" a million times in my diary, although really that doesn't sound that bad, euphonically speaking.

181

Danny eventually comes in and approaches us.

"Hey, man," he says to Justin, glancing at me, then back to him. "I think you're in my spot."

And I'm sure that's it. Justin will apologize, retrieve the roll, make the corrections, and move to sit with Piper. Only that's not what happens.

"Nah," Justin says. "You were sitting back there, man." He points to his old seat by a still-glaring Piper.

"Oh." Danny shifts his backpack higher on his shoulder, and I think I catch a whiff of why he may not trust his memory. "Sorry, bruh."

"It happens." Justin cracks his thumb knuckle as Danny hauls his skateboard and science book back to the lab tables.

I turn toward the front and feel Justin's eyes all over me. I really wish I had brought my jacket.

30 ABBY SOMEONE

JOLENE

After class, Logan still doesn't talk to me. I go to French, and after trig, I return to my locker to switch out my math book for my lunch. He isn't anywhere. Piper is though. She comes over to me, smiling—a good sign, as I'm shutting my locker door.

"We sit at the top of the Greek in front of the art classes," she tells me as if everyone in the school doesn't know where the most popular kids sit.

She links her arm through mine, and we continue that way all the way to the Greek when we run into a pilgrim, who, when she turns her head, I recognize as my fellow ballerina, Lindsey Calisher.

Piper snorts at the sight of her in costume, laughs, and too loudly says, "Wow, Lindsey! You've finally found a cult that would accept you."

I'd laugh, but I'm too busy being mortified. In the weeks since I've been dancing in the same ballet class as Lindsey, we've developed a certain decorum. This isn't it. In our recent and ongoing battle of who can outshine and outclass whom—using words like "whom," by the way, helps—we've always been civil, apart from the occasional glaring.

To her credit, Lindsey doesn't slap Piper across the face.

"I'm playing Abigail Williams in *The Crucible*," she tells us. Upon getting no recognizable response from Piper, she continues. "We're performing scenes from last year's production to get freshmen interested in auditioning for this year's shows."

"Well, if that won't do the trick, what will?" Piper says, looking at me, expecting a laugh. I almost smile, but it's more apologetic and directed toward Lindsey.

But Lindsey just sighs. "Hi, Jolene."

"Hi, Lindsey," I say as she walks past us.

This is the first time I've ever felt bad for Lindsey Calisher. Until now, I honestly didn't think that was even possible. She's just so... Lindseyish.

As the first two to arrive at Piper and her friends' spot in the Greek, we sit and pull out our lunches. I've got a turkey sandwich on whole wheat bread, a tangerine, a bag of carrots, and a Diet Coke. I pull it all out of my brown bag, flatten it, and lay the items on top.

"How do you know Abigail back there?" Piper asks me.

"Abby? Ballet."

Piper turns her nose up as if I had just said I knew her from our time living in the mud together, in a swamp colony where we ate mosquitoes and wore hats made of used bandages.

"Ew. Sorry," she says.

184

"I love ballet," I say. "It's why I went to Paris."

She stops talking and looks around for, I assume, someone else to talk to. I welcome the break.

LOGAN

It's not that I mind her making friends—that's perfectly fine. I'm glad for her even, and maybe I'm making too big of a deal over it, but I thought she'd turn back to me after Quinn and Courtney had sat down, and then I waited at the door for her, but she hung back and walked with them. Then, she barely had a word for me in chemistry after Justin sat by her. And was I included in the invitation to join them for lunch? Doubtful, and even if I were, I couldn't, not with Piper Thompson there.

When Piper broke up with me after the two best weeks of my junior high life. She said she should see other people, and I should see nobody ever. It was awful. No, I couldn't join their group for lunch. The awkwardness would end me.

So, I stand at the top of Greek, holding the stuff I bought at the cafeteria—a cola, an apple, a sandwich, and a chocolate chip cookie—staring out over the vast theater.

Maybe I should go back inside and find a place to sit in a corner where someone passing by could mistake me for a member of a nearby group. But I hate the cafeteria smell.

Maybe I can sit with someone from the Star Warriors' club, someone from swimming, or someone from band—the trumpet guys aren't so bad, except

185

Isaiah. He makes jokes about my mom's limp and then acts all shocked when I so much as mention the scar on his face from when his dog bit him.

Have I been standing here too long? Better take a seat fast before someone says anything.

And that's when I see her bright-pink hair standing out among a group of hungry art goths.

I dash over to where they're sitting a few seats down from where I've been standing by the cafeteria exit.

"Can I sit here?" I ask while sitting and trying to make myself invisible.

"Sure, Logan," Mary say.

I peek up at her as she asks, "Where's Jolene?"

"She's sitting with her new friends." I jut my chin in Jolene's direction.

"Jolene doesn't make new friends." Mary laughs, but seeing is believing. "Oh. She's making friends out of my old ones."

She cracks something in her neck, and I turn to the guy next to me. I don't know him, but I've noticed him. His mohawk and red hair are hard to miss.

"Do you know any good clubs that meet during lunch?"

MARY

She looks almost exactly like me sitting up there at the top of the Greek between Piper and some other popular junior sheep. She wears her hair differently than I did, having a fancy French haircut, but it's similar in color to what mine was.

186

Well, if she wants that horde of vipers as friends, she can have them.

Piper didn't exactly offer a continuation of her friendship when I cut off all my hair and got a nose ring. To her, I was only worth the price of my popularity. She wasn't about to hang out with people lower than her in the social sphere, not unless she felt her popularity could take it. And apparently, Jolene's not too much of a risk. Well, that's great. Good for her.

I almost choke on my pear.

31 RED ROCK AND WHITE ROCK

PIPER

Courtney, Quinn, Quinn's boyfriend Todd, his friend Weston, Tyrus, and some other people who sit on the sides, never saying anything, and hope we allow them to stay, join Jolene and me at our lunch spot. But I gotta tell ya, being nice to Jolene isn't helping me like her any better. She didn't even laugh at my hilarious dismemberment of Lindsey. And Quinn and Courtney fawning over her is really annoying. What are they expecting to get out of it? Both of them are on the higher end of popularity. They don't need to suck up to her, and I doubt they're also trying to gain her trust, keep her away from Anthony, and set her up with Justin. But they can't actually like her. Ugh. I don't get it.

"I love your hair," Courtney tells her, not eating the apple in her hand, just holding it, letting it get brown. "Did it take you a long time to learn how to get the braid this way, or is it just what it naturally does?"

"No," Jolene responds. "It took for-freaking-ever."

This seems to comfort Courtney, and her face warms like a flower in the sun, and I gag a little on my sandwich. What would Courtney want to braid her hair like Jolene for anyway? Her hair's in a natural afro and curly and gorgeous, and Jolene's is beachy, wavy and dumb.

"Right?" I ask. "I was just about to tell her I'm going to shave her hair and steal it if she doesn't watch it."

I'm about to continue, and change the subject, but once Quinn and Courtney get going, they're like a steamroller.

"But you have the bone structure and features that you'd probably look good even bald," Quinn says, simpering. "You know those women who shave their heads but are still really pretty?"

"Right?" Courtney agrees. "A lot of guys can't even pull off a shaved head."

"I like buzzed hair on a guy," Quinn says, then covers her mouth and turns to her floppy-haired boyfriend, Todd. "Except on you. I like your hair."

"Coach said he'd shave his head in the Greek if we win tonight," Todd says. He hasn't shut up about the fact he made varsity football since he found out at the end of last year.

"Is that motivation?" I have to make sure we do not go back to talking about Jolene's hair. "I'd like to see the entire team shave their heads."

"Even Anthony?" Courtney asks with an annoying side-eye.

"Why stop there?" Todd continues. "Why not the whole school?"

189

"Why would everybody shave their heads if the football team won?" I ask.

"Why would the team?" Todd throws back.

Then Todd's friend, Weston, pipes up with, "Know who's weird looking without hair? Guys who can't grow beards."

"Like who?" Quinn asks, not taking her mouth off her straw.

"Like all of them," Weston says.

"How can you tell who can't and who just doesn't?" asks Quinn. It's a stupid conversation, and still about hair, but at least it's not praising Jolene's.

"They look boyish," Weston says.

"Everyone looks boyish," Jolene says.

I scoff. Behold! The all-knowing Jolene speaks! Let us hear what wisdom of men and boys she learned in far-off kingdoms and crap.

"Cause they're not French?" I ask, adding plenty of accusation to my tone. She needs to be put in place a little after all of Quinn and Courtney's fawning.

"Cause they're not adults...?" Jolene says.

I'm really starting to hate her. She's already let attention get to her head. Who does she think she is, talking back to me like that?

"Todd," Weston says out of nowhere. We all look at him.

"I can grow a beard!" Todd says.

"Then prove it," Weston teases. "Grow one."

"I can't grow one right now."

"I could if I wanted to."

"Then do it."

"I don't want to."

190

This back and forth is seconds away from driving me crazy when Courtney asks, as she leans toward me, secretively, "Piper, remember that guy you dated for, like, two weeks in junior high?"

"You'll have to be more specific." I turn to her, taking a sip of my diet soda.

Quinn laughs, and I smile—finally, someone with a sense of humor.

"He keeps staring at you." Courtney nods her head across the Greek at a group of art freaks, and sure enough, there's Logan Monnel staring in our direction. Pitiful.

I smirk and take another sip.

"That might actually be my fault," Jolene says. Do you see why I hate her?

"No," I assure her, flipping my hair. "We dated."

"I know..." she continues. "I mean, we're friends. I usually eat lunch with him. He's probably just wondering why I'm eating with you guys..."

The more words spew out of her mouth, the more I want to smash her face with my soda can, but I have to admit she's probably right. I mean, she could be anyway. But does she have to be right in front of everybody? I really need to put her in her place now, and subtly, so she doesn't hold it against me, but thoroughly, so she shuts up.

"You're friends with Logan?" Saying his name hurts the roof of my mouth and makes me gag, like when they x-ray you at the dentist.

"Logan's really cool..." she says.

I hate when people stand up for people. I'm ready to open a debate about the humongous faults of Logan

191

Monnel, but a bigger problem emerges from behind the art building in the form of Kaila Jones and Tay-Tay Breiman in their black and purple cheer uniforms. Did the skirts get shorter this year? Quinn and Courtney's don't seem that short.

"Hey Tay-Tay. Hey Kaila." I heard if you use people's names, they like you more. I smile up at them and turn to Chris—one of the desperate guys sitting on our group's edge. "Scoot over."

He looks at me, probably surprised I even know his name, but doesn't budge, so I scoot a bit so they can sit on my bench.

But they look at the cleared-out spots and stay standing.

"Do you guys know where Justin is?" Tay-Tay asks.

She's been doing this ever since they started dating last year—acting like she doesn't know where he is, just to draw attention to the fact they're dating. Next she'll bring up being cheer captain.

"He's down in the Greek," I say. "It's Friday. He's hosting the class comp with Jesse."

"They both are?" Her voice drops its squeaky cartoon cat quality. She darts her eyes around as if she didn't mean to say what she did out loud. I try not to smile too much at catching her disappointment in finding out her boyfriend and her make-out buddy are occupied. But I can't help smirking at Quinn and Courtney, who've caught it, too. Unfortunately, that leaves the only one making eye contact with Tay-Tay is Jolene.

"Is that your backpack?" Tay-Tay asks her.

"Yeah," Jolene says.

"I thought those were only available in Italy," Tay-Tay says.

Jolene swallows. "I was there last year." She talks like a dying lamb.

Tay-Tay stares at her, as if no one's allowed to leave the country without her permission. No, it's more impressed than that. Like she's surprised someone left the country without her permission.

"Let's just go to your house, Kay-Kay," Tay-Tay says to Kaila. I'm sorry — "Kay-Kay?" It's a nickname I've never heard before. How sad is it when you make your friend's name sound exactly like yours? So cutesy and gross.

We all say bye to each other, and Kay-Kay and Tay-Tay walk away, leaving me able to laugh at them to Quinn and Courtney.

"Widdle Tay-Tay and Kay-Kay couldn't stay-stay," I say in Tay's baby voice.

They laugh, but Jolene just looks confused, apparently not finding my hilarious remarks funny like everyone else.

There's a reason this weird girl is only now coming into the spotlight, and it's not because she's spent the last year in France.

"She's not going to watch her boyfriend host his first class comp?" Jolene asks.

Is this concern for Justin?

"They're probably fighting again," Courtney says.

"What 'again'? It never stops," I say.

"Kaila said Tay killed Justin's entire aquarium over the summer, all because he didn't want to go to White Rock," Quinn says.

"I heard it was just one fish, and it was an accident," Courtney says.

"That's not what Kaila said," Quinn challenges.

"And they went to White Rock. She posted that picture of them with that stick she thought was a snake—"

"That was Red Rock," Quinn says, taking a bite of lettuce. Not even lettuce from a salad. She literally packs a sandwich bag with a big leaf of lettuce in it every day. Courtney does the same thing. I don't remember who started doing it first, but it's a testament to whichever theorist first likened people to sheep—probably Aristotle. I mean, haven't they ever heard of carrots—something with flavor?

"It's the same thing," Courtney says.

"Then why is one called White and one Red?" Quinn asks.

"It was probably Red Rock, but she thought it was White Rock," Courtney says.

"Sounds like her," Quinn adds. "She's dumb enough to think that stick was a rattlesnake—she's dumb enough to think Red Rock is White Rock."

"Ugh." I moan. "Why does he put up with her?"

"I know, right?" Quinn asks. "She's not even pretty."

Quinn's boyfriend Todd's friend Weston snorts.

Quinn, Courtney, and I glare at him. He's not allowed an opinion on this, being a boy and all.

"She has some angles," he says.

I scoff.

"Her eyes are really pretty," Jolene says. "And she— I don't know—looks athletic..."

"I mean," Weston says, moving his arm as if to back up what Jolene says.

"I guess she has some angles," Courtney backpedals.

"Which ones?" Quinn asks, calling her out.

"Like Jole said," Courtney says, and I half miss the rest of her sentence, bewildered that she's given this creature a nickname, even one as uninventive as merely shortening it. "Her hair's cute, and she has pretty eyes—"

"So does my dog," Todd says.

Everyone laughs, even those on the outskirts of the group.

"You're so gross," Quinn tells her weird and embarrassing boyfriend.

"That's my point!" Todd says his voice quivering. "I'm not in love with my dog!"

"You so are," Weston says, not helping his friend.

I'm so sick of this conversation. Courtney and Quinn keep laughing like Todd and Weston are funny, as Todd keeps trying and failing to explain what he means. Maybe it's funnier if you're eating lettuce.

This would all be more bearable if Justin were here and not down in the Greek. He'd call them out on how lame they're being and steer the conversation to something interesting.

Of course, if he were here, then Tay-Tay wouldn't have left, and we'd have her and Kay-Kay. I'd have more opportunities to get on Tay's good side, maybe try-out for cheer again at the semester break, but it's nice to take a break from having to lick her shoes constantly.

195

I don't get why she doesn't dump Justin for Jesse. He's not as cute as Justin, but he's just as popular. He's ASB vice president to Justin's president, but he also plays football. Maybe she enjoys hogging both of them.

I can't wait to see her expression when my new friend steals her boyfriend out from under her. I'll act all like I had nothing to do with it, and be like, "You're so much prettier. I don't know what he sees in her."

But even if she goes out with Jesse, she'll have fallen a few social pegs for being dumped for Scary Mary's little sister.

And then when Justin and Jolene are together, it won't matter if Justin's able to keep her away from Anthony. She wouldn't toss Justin overboard for him, not when Justin's ASB president, while Anthony's claim to fame—apart from being quarterback—is not talking to anyone at parties. He spends them leaning against the wall by himself, making sure nobody drives home drunk, or shooting hoops in the backyard with Justin's autistic little brother.

So, if he's such a dud at parties, why do I like him, right? Trust me, if you saw him, you'd get it. He's got, like, twelve dimples when he smiles, and he's tall and lean, but muscular, too. He's swarthy like a pirate, but clean and with nice, square teeth. Usually, he just wears T-shirts and jeans, cause he's not rich—like Justin—but he makes everything look good, even if it's not super expensive. His haircut is pretty normal. It's not buzzed around the sides or anything—just floppy. Every time I see him, I want to run my hands through it.

I mean, there's no reason he wouldn't be into me. I run three and a half miles a day, I throw my shoulders back so my boobs look bigger; I spend a half hour every morning contouring my face, and I know I have the best hair out of all the girls in school. His lack of asking me out is inexcusable. And it's not like he's dating anyone else, either! He went with Amanda Potts to last year's prom—she asked him, but it didn't go anywhere after that, and she went off to college anyway. Before that, he had asked Renee Harlow to Winter Formal, but Justin told me it was because her mom had just died. They were childhood friends, and he wanted to be sure she went and had a nice time since it was her senior year, and she hadn't ever been asked to a dance before. She was considerate enough to get hit by a car while riding her bike and died three months later, but even before that, it wasn't like they were dating. They'd just say hi when passing each other in the halls, which was embarrassing enough. I mean, she never wore toenail polish when she wore flip-flops, which was all the time. Who does that? But for homecoming that year, I asked him, but he had already said yes to Angelina Rodrigeuz, even though later I heard he asked her after I had asked him, but I don't put a lot of weight into idle gossip. Plus, why would he ask Angelina? She has a huge scar like on her forearm from when she stopped her cat from scratching her little sister. It used to be really hideous. It's mostly healed now. Watch, she tries to get mauled again. Attention crazy much?

But whatever. A dance isn't the only time you can get up close to a boy. Class competitions are fantastic for this. They're when two representatives from each class does a challenge in the Greek during lunch on Fridays. Once, the competition was a chicken fight. Girls from each class got on the shoulders of guys from each class, and we battled it out. Being a sophomore, I had to be on another sophomore's back—not Anthony's—so I teamed up with Weston, Todd's friend. But we got all up close to Anthony and Tay-Tay before they took us down.

Except, I don't think they're going to do that comp again since when Tay-Tay eventually got pulled off Anthony's shoulders; she hit her head and had to be rushed to the ER.

There was nothing Anthony could have done, but he's felt bad about it ever since. Now he's always checking in with people and making sure they're doing okay. Even before that, he was always like there for people. It's so annoying. Why can't he just be there for me?

"We should go down and be in the class comp," I say.

No one moves a muscle apart from lackluster chewing. "What? I'll go. Where's Anthony?"

"Who's Anthony?" Jolene asks, chewing on an orange, not even curious enough to look up.

"Whitaker," I respond.

She doesn't show any sign of recognition. I don't know how she doesn't know him. Everyone in town knows him—like everyone. Our gardener saw him one Friday morning, when we had an in-service day, so a bunch of us hung out at my place, and said hi. I guess Anthony did a lot of work on this guy's Mustang or something. Anthony works at a garage in downtown Goleta. It's not surprising he leaves an impression, and everyone likes him. He's even friends with the school security guys, so they let him off campus during lunch. That's probably where he is now, which is sad but good.

Apparently, Jolene hasn't met him, and I can keep that going a bit longer. I mean, I seriously doubt she's his type but give me a couple of hours and it won't matter anymore. She'll be dating Justin and too taken to flirt with his best friend. And even if she and Justin break up down the road, Anthony wouldn't date his best friend's ex.

"How do you not know who Anthony Whitaker is?" I ask her loudly, hoping everyone sees her feel this shame. "He's the quarterback this year?"

She continues to stare at me blankly, and it occurs to me that the same loyalty Anthony owes Justin to not date his best friend's ex, might work on Jolene if she thinks we're friends and learns about my claim on Anthony.

So I add, "He's the single most gorgeous specimen this school has ever known."

"Aww," Todd's friend Weston says.

"Hurtful, Piper," Todd says.

I wave my arm, dismissing their complaints. They must have noticed that Anthony's worlds more attractive than them, in every way, from every angle— every feature beating out everyone else's features in the entire school. You may think you have a good nose? Maybe the best chin? You're wrong. And on you, his chin wouldn't look as good as it does on him.

"I was gone," Jolene says, subtly reminding us all—again—that she spent a year in Paris. Get a banner, why don't you? "It's not like he went up and down the locker halls shaking hands with everyone..."

"He should," I say, and I picture him walking down the locker halls, taking the time to say hi, and smiling at everyone, like a prince reaching out to his peasants. I see him handing a young, hungry boy a loaf of bread, putting his arm on the back of an old widow, contracting a horrible disease because he got too close to them—ew. Too far.

"He is a senior, though," I say. "So, I guess I can see how you wouldn't really—no. Irregardless—"

"It's just 'regardless'," Quinn says.

I shoot a death glance at her and continue. "Irregardless, you should know who he is. He's so gorgeous."

32 THE GAMES

JUSTIN

Jesse's a creep, and I'm pretty sure he's making out with Tay behind my back, but I don't have any proof, and she keeps saying I'm horrible for believing what everyone says and that they're all just lying because they're jealous of us.

She makes a good point though: everyone is jealous of us, probably because we're both attractive, popular, and rich. For a lot of guys, they gotta be good at sports too, but I don't have to bother with that.

I prefer being in charge, so I ran for ASB president, knowing I'd win. I was seventh grade president, eighth grade president, freshman class president, sophomore, junior, and now ASB. I considered going for vice-president—no sense having too many obligations. When I was seventh grade president, I'd run around, stressing out, getting blamed every time something went wrong—but then my dad told me if I make a mistake, blame the vice president. Dad said, that's the vice president's job—that's what he—or she—is there for. Nobody outside of leadership has any idea what I do anyway—or, more importantly, what I don't do. All they know is I make announcements in the Greek with my vice-president, Jesse, and host the class comps every Friday.

It's a good day, and not just because Tay-Tay's walking toward the upper parking lot. She won't be watching every move I make, trying to find something she can pick a fight over later, and right now I might just give her plenty of fight-fuel because I've got no intention of not letting my eyes wander where they want to wander—or over who they want to wander over.

The only downside of the day is that I'm not the only one who's noticed her. Not that I think any of them pose a threat, but their nerve bothers me. If only I could broadcast that they all need to shut up and sit down.

"Lupe got ugly over the summer," Jesse says as we stand on the stage at the bottom of the Greek, unwinding the microphone cords. My goal as president is to update our sound system into the twenty-first century and get Bluetooth tech.

"Lupe Ruiz?" I ask. "She looks exactly the same."

He has no comeback. "You know who's lookin' hot though? Sonja Peterson."

I exhale through my nose. Sonja Peterson plays volleyball, never wears makeup, and dresses like her parents have stock in a sporting goods store.

"You'd have to go to all her games," I tell him.

"Nuh-uh," he says. "You go to everything of Tay-Tay's?"

"Yes," I say. It's true, but it's not like I go for her. My friends all play football or basketball, and those are the only things the cheer team performs at. It's not like they compete or anything—except they go to away games, and I don't go to those. I'm not crazy.

"You know who's looking really hot? That French girl—what's her name? Mary's sister..."

My blood heats under my skin. I rub the back of my ear for something to busy my hands with, so I don't choke him.

"Thinking of asking her to Homecoming. Gotta ask someone hot—I'll probably be Homecoming King..."

"Mary's sister?" I ask. "Is that what you're going to call her when you ask her out?"

"No," he says, but his voice rises defensively. "Do you think she only speaks French?"

"She's not French, idiot. She's from here. She just went to France. She's Mary's sister."

"Oh," he says, like the moron he is. "Maybe I should ask out Sonja instead—just in case."

Best idea he's ever had.

"Wonder where she's sitting," he says.

"She's over there, by Piper." I plug the end of my cord into the amplifier.

He looks over at their group.

"No. I meant Sonja," he says.

I roll my eyes. Why would anyone care about Sonja? First of all, it'd be like dating a pole. Second, even girls who don't wear makeup wear makeup to dances. She might look like a freak with it on. We don't know! Third—wait. No time for thirds. We're starting.

203

Jesse faces the student body and greets them with arms wide—like Moses. "Good afternoon, Winchester Canyon High School, and welcome to your first class comp of the year!" Everyone cheers.

I glare at him for starting first. If he gets in the habit of acting like he's president, I'll have to do something. But it's not hard to take over. "I am Justin Granite, your ASB president. This is Jesse Morrison, vice. We have a few announcements before we get started." Shoot. I've forgotten all of them. I had them memorized in order, but Jesse going first threw me off. "Jesse's gonna tell you what those are. Go ahead, Jesse."

He clears his throat. "Alright, the first football game of the year starts tonight at seven—freshmen! We Avenging Angels are big on school spirit, so I expect to see you out there cheering tonight!"

He's buying time. He's on the football team, of course he remembers that one. I bet he's forgotten the rest. To be fair, nobody cares about anything else anyway. You see those fliers and posters all over campus. They're always left up too long, and nobody—oh! There are posters behind us.

I pivot and point at the fliers taped to the wall behind us of various teams, clubs, and sports advertising for whatever. I motion for Jesse to announce those. If he still misses something—well, what can you do? That's just Vice President Jesse.

He stares at the posters while addressing the group. "The Color Guard is holding auditions again. Yearbook is looking for more photographers, and you can pre-order your yearbook in the ASB store, by room H-thirty-one, and the chess club—which is a thing we have—I didn't know that—is looking for members, so join the chess club, if you're so inclined."

"That's it?" I ask.

Jesse balks at me. He must have no idea if that's it.

He starts to move on when a shout blares out from the stands. "Senior fundraiser!" someone yells. Thanks, someone.

"Right," I say, acting on top of it. "I'll take it from here, Jesse." I'm about to inform the populace about this senior fundraiser, which starts on a date I forget, and is for graduation—probably—but Jesse, annoyingly, beats me to it.

"Yes!" he says. "Seniors, we start fundraising for Grad Nite on Monday. All seniors need to drop by the ASB store to pick up their fundraising packets Monday morning during nutrition break, lunch, passing period, or after school."

"So, anytime Monday," I say, simplifying.

"Yes."

"Alright."

"Alright!" he says toward the audience, faking more excitement. "Freshmen, new upperclassmen, girls who were in another country for a year, class comps are lunch competitions where volunteer representatives from each class compete against the other classes. And Justin's going to tell us about our class comp."

I'm keeping score in my mind of all the times he acts like he's in charge. So, it takes a second to reply, but I do so in a way that hides how annoyed I am. I didn't get to be president by showing emotion.

"Thank you for that introduction, Jesse," I say. If you're the one thanking everyone, you're the one in charge. "What we have here is what's known as a water balloon toss. We need two boys and two girls from each class. Pairing up girls and girls, boys and boys, class against class. You're going to toss the water balloon back and forth. If you both catch it, you take a step back. This continues until there's one intact water balloon left, the team of which is the winner of—"

"Two gift certificates to Riptide!" Jesse waves them in the air.

"Right," I say. "So, two girls and two boys from each class, come on down here."

And it starts.

PIPER

I'm definitely competing in the water balloon toss.

"Where is Anthony?" I ask again for the 900th time. He's usually here by now, munching on a ham sandwich.

Oh, I forgot I decided he's probably off campus. I wish he'd let me know before he leaves. I'd go with him. Who did he go with? Who's not here? I don't have time to take inventory. If I'm not fast, other juniors will go down, and I won't be able to.

I grab Jolene's arm. "Come on. We're going down."

"No, no, no, no, no..." she says, pretending to be shy. I guess that's a thing.

I toss her arm back to her and skip down the steps into the Greek with Todd and Weston trailing behind. If she won't come down where Justin can watch her, fine. I'll take the popularity boost and exposure and worry about hooking her up with Justin later.

JUSTIN

Piper, Todd, and Weston stand at the bottom of the Greek in the grass. Two seniors on football join them, and a girl I don't know.

"You know that girl?" I ask Jesse. He shrugs and shakes his head, so I motion for her to come over. "What year are you in?"

"I'm a senior," she says, sounding offended.

"We need more freshmen," Jesse says. "Freshmen! What did I just finish telling you about school spirit! We need seniors—seniors! Hey, isn't your sister a freshman this year?"

"Guineth!" I yell at a little blond dot at the far corner of the Greek. "Get down here and bring Christie with you."

"We need more male freshmen," Jesse says.

"Boys."

"We need two little boys to join the balloon toss."

Another senior girl I know from grade school joins the girl I don't know, followed by two girls wearing junior varsity cheer uniforms, making them either juniors or sophomores, I'm guessing sophomores, and four guys I know to be sophomores and freshmen, one of them being my little brother, join the others, followed by Guineth and her best friend, Christie.

Guineth stares at me wide-eyed—probably nervous about entering her first class comp. I remember my first class comp. We—oh, no. She's pointing at our

207

brother, Noah, and shaking her head. She doesn't think he should play.

"He'll be fine," I mouth to her and wave an arm for her to stop worrying.

Guineth has waist-length blond hair, blue eyes, and before the year even started, everyone knew who she was: Guineth Granite, Justin's little sister. All my friends know her as the little girl who asked them to play house with her when they came over to shoot hoops when we were kids. They didn't want to join Guineth in her little plastic kitchen back then. But now? Now I get to be the protective big brother whenever I'm around them instead of cool friend guy. One of the reasons I prefer my smaller group of friends to an extended group. Anthony and Matt don't gawk at her or tell me how hot she is.

Noah, on the other hand, is completely different. When he was two, he was diagnosed with autism. To say he's frustrated watching his twin sister shine her way through life while he struggles every step of the way is a gross understatement. He looks like us. He has blond hair and all, but fewer people know he's my brother.

"I'm not going to be happy until we get Anthony down here," Jesse says. "I know for a fact our quarterback can throw a water balloon." He looks at me with a grin, like I should know what he's talking about. "Remember?" he asks when I say nothing.

I shake my head.

"My eighth birthday party..." He tries again.

But I seriously do not remember.

He moves on, rolling his eyes. "Alright." He counts everyone. "I think that's it. We have four freshmen, four seniors, four sophomores, and—we need another junior girl."

Perfect.

I look out over the enormous crowd and spot her sucking on a straw sticking out of a Diet Coke, looking right at me. Our eyes click. She frowns, looking curious. I look away, acting like I didn't just lock eyes with her.

"Where is Jolene Stansen?" I pretend to search among the students. I find her again and smile.

She freezes like she hopes I can't see her if she doesn't move.

"Come on, Jolene."

She stiffly shakes her head, then whips it around, taking in every single eye on her, curling into herself.

It makes me laugh a little. She reminds me of a lost kitten.

"Hold this." I pass my microphone to Jesse—scale the steps three at a time, and stand a few steps below her, leaning in on the leg in front of me. "Come on," I say.

She shakes her head again, looking as if I'm asking her to jump out of a helicopter.

I'm going to have to pull out some charm. "*Rejoignez-moi, s'il vous plaît?*"[20]

She tilts her head. Impressed?

"Oh," she replies. "*Je ne pense pas.*"[21]

---

[20] Join me, please?
[21] I don't think so.

And my limited French is spent—unless I want to ask her something she'd probably consider incredibly rude.

"You know," I say in English. "I'd look really stupid going back down there without you."

"Yeah," she says, "but I'd look really stupid down there..."

She's making it a challenge.

"How about you look stupid now if I promise to look stupid later?"

She considers my proposition for, like, a split second before responding. "Or—you can look stupid now, and I'll look stupid later."

I bite my lip and look down at her neck, slowly on down her body and even more slowly all the way back up to her eyes. "Promise?" I ask with a grin.

She looks bashful, excited, and disgusted at the same time. I can't guess which emotion is winning.

But she sighs. "Yeah. Alright. I'll look stupid now." And pockets the phone that was on the bench next to her, grasps my outstretched hand, lets me pull her up, and takes her place in the Greek while I return to the stage.

MARY

He leads her down into the Greek like Hades leading an ignorant, hesitant, and giddy Persephone down to the underworld.

My appetite goes with them.

I trudge back up the steps to the top of the Greek, toss what little's left of my lunch into a trash can by the cafeteria exit, consider adding the rest of my lunch to it, but put my earphones in, make sure the noise cancellation setting is on, and go for a walk.

PIPER

The way she leaps down the stairs makes me want to smack her. She's all graceful and gazelle-like, holding his hand as he leads her down into the amphitheater.

They part before they get to the bottom. He goes to the stage, and she lines up with her line directly across from me. If I didn't want to win so badly, I'd hurl the water balloon at her head the second the music starts. I know! I want her and Justin to be together, but come on. You have to admit that was disgusting—all that "Oh, no, I couldn't possibly go down in the Greek, it's just not French enough. Well, if you insist!" crap.

But instead of dousing her in water, after Jesse and Justin play the music for the game to begin, I gently toss the balloon to her and catch it when she lobs it back.

We step back and do it again a few more times until Guineth Granite's friend breaks their water balloon and screams, making the sophomore boy next to her jump and miss his water balloon as well.

We're far enough apart now that I really have to concentrate. The grass is a little muddier than I realized, too, and I'm wearing sandals, so I have to be careful not to slip or even get the sides of my feet muddy. If I fall in front of the entire school—well, at least Anthony isn't here to see it.

33 BALLOON TOSS AND KEEP AWAY

ANTHONY

It doesn't feel like a Friday. School starting on a Thursday has thrown my entire week off. Even in my jersey that we have to wear to school on Fridays— game days—it still feels like a Tuesday. If I had remembered it was a Friday, I wouldn't have agreed to join Tyrus, Isaiah, and the two Alices for a taco run. But as we walk closer to the Greek, I hear the music and the cheers—it's Friday. It's Justin's first class comp, and I'm missing it.

We turn the corner and walk along the top edge of the Greek, where down inside, my fellow students toss water balloons back and forth while Jesse and Justin stand on the stage blasting music and refereeing.

Tyrus reaches his hands over his head and touches every beam we walk under, eyeing the Alices out of the corner of his eye while he does it. But they don't seem to notice.

Alice Windsor talks about a band she and the other Alice saw last weekend while twirling her long dark ponytail, and Alice Sistine, who looks like Alice Windsor but blond, listens.

Isaiah glares at Tyrus, who hasn't stopped slapping the beams. Isaiah can't reach them without jumping, which he does.

"You didn't get that one," Tyrus says.

"Yeah, I did."

"Look how high I can reach," Tyrus outright tells Alice and Alice when they don't congratulate him.

They roll their eyes at him, then at each other.

"How high can you reach, Anthony?" he asks.

I shrug.

He goes back to slapping the roof, and I return to my Coke.

"Anyway, he asked me, like, fifteen times for my number," Alice Windsor says.

"The guitarist's brother?" Alice Sistine asks.

"No. The bassist."

"He was standing near the bassist because he was the guitarist's brother."

"No, he was the bassist."

"Then how come he called the guitarist his brother, wasn't on stage with them, and looked like he was in junior high?"

Alice Windsor sighs, crosses her arms, and watches the comp in the Creek.

Someone screams. It's Piper. She's soaking wet and swearing at the top of her lungs. Then she crosses the Creek, and smashes mud into the face of some poor brown-haired girl, who wipes the mud out of her eyes, takes her neighbor's water balloon, and hurls it at the back of Piper's head, officially soaking her.

213

Piper turns with a face that makes me worry for her partner. Then, she looks up at the entire school watching her, clears her throat, and tries to arrange her wet clothes.

She walks over to the brunette and says something that makes them both laugh, Piper more so. I don't recognize this girl she's talking to—but I can't look away.

I watch her brush the muddy stray hairs that have fallen out of her braid out of her face and respond to Justin, who calls her over and helps her rinse the dirt off.

She takes the elastic out of the bottom of her braid and lets the hose Justin holds for her run down her hair as she leans over the bushes, pulling her hands through her muddy tangles. Justin's sister gives her a towel she soaked in the balloon bucket, and the girl wipes away all the grime or at least most of it. Some stays around the corners of her forehead and near her ears.

She laughs with Guineth about something that makes Justin squirm and roll his eyes. I want to know what they're saying, but the crowd makes too much noise. I wish we had gotten here sooner. I wish I could have watched the entire thing, maybe caught where she had been sitting before joining the class comp.

She acts friendly enough with Piper, but they can't be that close. Piper would have mentioned having a new friend. She mentions everything.

"We should have stayed," I say.

"You wanted to do the water balloon toss?" one of the Alices asks.

214

Piper walks over to the girl, takes the towel, and dabs at the places she missed, scolding her, or at least it looks like she's scolding her. The girl just stands there, acting like Piper's giving her a spa treatment.

I laugh. "I have to go." I throw my drink in a nearby trash can and sit on the nearest bench. People are sitting here already, but I'm not sure who they are—I haven't moved my eyes off the girl at the bottom of the Greek. "Who is that girl with Piper?" I ask what I guess is a person to my left.

"Jolene?" tentatively answers a voice I recognize as Quinn Wayne's.

The bell marking the end of lunch rings loudly in our ears, but it's not enough to distract me. Everyone starts to leave. I make my way down into the Greek, but too many people are coming up. What would I even say if I caught up with her?

Jesse comes up the stairs and only sees me trying to come down when he's two steps below me.

"There you are," he shouts. "We were wondering where you've been!"

I step to one side, but he mirrors me.

"Get this—I saw Coach in the hall after fourth and guess what he said he'd do if we win tonight—shave his head!" He props his mouth open expectantly, but I dodge him.

"He does that every year."

"Yeah! And he's gonna do it our year, too!" Jesse says after me.

But a large group of girls filling the stairs makes me turn around and head back up the few steps I had gained. I'm on the top row again. I've lost her. No—

there she is. She's walking up the stairs with Piper by the stage.

I maneuver around a few students, trying not to lose sight of her. Up ahead, she parts with Piper, who starts coming my way.

"Hey, Anthony!" Piper yells as I pass her.

I turn to see what she wants while keeping my pace going backward.

JOLENE

When I head off to history, I'm soaking wet, wondering if I still have any mud left on me, or if that hose sufficiently cleansed me.

Shoot! My phone! No way it's dry after that.

I reach into my back pocket and take it out—or take out what I thought was my phone. It's very not. The cover is a pretty iridescent dark purple I recognize instantly as Piper's. I must have seen her phone on the seat, thought it was mine, and pocketed it before the competition. Easy to believe I was distracted—Justin was being... distracting.

"Wait, Piper." I turn around to go back to her. "This is—"

Having abruptly stopped walking while still looking at the phone, I smack into something tall and solid. While falling, my thigh scrapes a support beam, and my shoulder and head knock against the edge of the propped-open art room door. I land on my thigh, butt, and elbow, but the pain seems to come from everywhere. Worse still, I've fallen in front of the entire school—or everyone who's lingered anyway.

All this after managing to get absolutely covered in mud during lunch. I must be leaving an excellent impression on everybody. I'm sure they're all super impressed with the newly returned girl, who's filthy and can't walk straight.

A hand reaches down, and a voice I've never heard before says, "Oh, I'm so sorry. Are you all right?"

Somewhere nearby, Piper says, "Jeez, Anthony. Kill her, why don't you?"

Is this the Anthony Piper was talking about?

Another hand joins the other hand, and they lift me up to standing and don't let go.

"Piper, I have your phone." I hold it out to her. She takes it from me and inspects it. I cringe and hope I didn't land on it. I don't think I did.

"I must have had mine in my backpack and thought yours was mine." But trying to explain is hard—not because I hit my head—but because before me, still holding my arms and steadying me, stands the most gorgeous guy I've ever seen. I didn't know they could look like this. He's tall—crazy tall. So tall, you'd see him and say, "That guy is tall—hot and tall." He also has kind, gorgeous gray eyes, brown floppy hair, if you can see that high, and a smile that puts other smiles to shame. Shame on you, bad, lesser smiles. He's got a firm jaw and sculpturally perfect cheekbones and wears a black football jersey with the purple number twelve on the front under the letters "WCHS." He still supports me with his arms, and I feel his skin and Atlas-sized muscles under my fingertips.

"Let me take you to the nurse." He smells like the eucalyptus surrounding my house. And when he

217

speaks, his voice comes from right above my ear. It's so smooth, and the heat from his body's so warm I want to wrap it around me and fall asleep in it.

"No, I'm fine," I say. The last thing I want is to be a burden to this glorious archangel. But it's the first thing I want, too.

"You sure?" he asks.

"Look at her—she's fine," Piper says.

I hadn't noticed she didn't go to class yet.

He lets me go, eyeing me cautiously, and I stand up straighter. Not the best idea. The world rushes around my ears, and for a moment, I think I might black out.

I wobble a little and instinctively stretch out my arms. But as I do, he catches me up again, and this time, I'm even—temporarily—embraced, encircled, and snugged into his chest.

"Let me take you to the nurse," he suggests again, slightly more insistent.

"Oh, come on..." Piper moans.

"I was just a little woozy when standing," I say. Woozy? Woozy!?! This is my word choice?! I'm fluent in one and a half languages, and woozy is one of the first words I say to him?!

He supports me with one hand and raises the other.

"How many fingers am I holding up?" he asks.

His hand is a little fuzzy. Probably not a good sign.

"Yikes," I tell him. "You've got a lot of fingers, bruh. Maybe we should take you to the nurse."

"Okay, come on," he says.

"She's cracking jokes! She's fine!" Piper protests.

But he already has one arm around me, propelling me forward toward the office.

"Maybe I should carry you," he says.

"Oh," I say. "It's not come to that."

PIPER

I watch Anthony supporting Jolene away toward the nurse's office.

I don't notice Justin closing in behind me until he speaks. "What happened?"

I pivot so I can lean toward him to answer while watching them get smaller and smaller, hobbling as they go.

"He knocked into her, she hit her head, and he's taking her to the nurse, and I'm an idiot," I inform him—wait, I'm still mad at him. He gets an elbow in the ribs.

"Ow!"

"How come you didn't sit with us during chem?" I ask.

His answer is a smirk, a glance at Jolene, a knowing glance at me, and a walk away.

I grind my teeth as the words Justin said yesterday pop into my mind: "I'd better keep her away from Anthony." And there was me—I did everything in my power to parade her in front of the entire school.

34 THE HEALTH OFFICE

JOLENE

He holds the door and me as we slide into the nurse's office together. It's a small room with a long, high desk separating the entrance from the nurse's desk. A Dutch door keeps unwanted teenagers from gaining easy access to the beds or to Nurse Magparagalan's stuff.

As we approach the desk, she peers up at us from behind curly dark hair. She plays a cute animal game on her handheld device, which she quickly tucks away when she sees us.

Her eyes behind red-rimmed glasses brighten at the sight of Anthony. "Whitaker, didn't expect you until practice."

"Yeah. It's not me this time."

"I think it was just standing up dizziness," I say to him more than to the nurse, trying to convince him my injuries are not as bad as he thinks. "That's a thing, right?"

"You've got a big bump on your head," he says, pressing it down a little with a teasing grin.

"Ow," I say, slapping his hand away—playfully, of course.

"If you didn't have a bump, it wouldn't hurt," he says.

I can sense him smiling, even though his smile's so way up high.

"That's not true," I say. "My head is naturally tender right there."

He turns to Nurse Magparagalan.

"She fell and hit her head," he says at the same time I say, "He knocked me over."

Nurse Magparagalan looks bewildered at him. "What did you do—tackle her in the hallway? 'Go, Number Twelve?'" She rolls her teasing eyes. "Come on back."

Anthony still steadies me as the nurse holds open the partial door, and we walk into her office, then through a full door into the patient room.

The room has three beds, a bunch of cabinets, and a station on wheels with a laptop on top.

Anthony stretches out his arm to hold the backpack I'm taking off, and I let him. I sit on the edge of a bed as he leans against a cabinet facing it.

Nurse Magparagalan scooches over on a rolling stool and puts a blood pressure cuff around my arm.

"I was only dizzy when standing up," I tell her.

"That's good, but we'll check you out just in case." She's silent for a moment, then the cuff goes loose, and she slides the stethoscope off her ears. "Can you tell me what day it is?"

221

"Friday the second," I tell her.

"Good," she says.

I hope she doesn't ask me a hard math question. Wait. I'm okay at math. If she asked, I could probably answer it. Would that impress him? What is the matter with me?

"What grade are you in?"

"I'm a junior."

She looks at Anthony for verification. He shrugs.

"I think she is," he says. "She was doing the water balloon toss with another junior..."

He saw me doing the water balloon toss?

"You don't even know her, and you knocked her over?" the nurse asks, shaking her head and rolling her eyes.

Anthony opens his mouth to answer, but nothing comes out.

"Where does it hurt?"

Oh! She's talking to me.

"My head," I say. "But only a little. And I hit my shoulder, and my leg..."

She takes off the cuff, stands, and starts feeling my head.

"Does this hurt?" she asks.

"A little bit," I say.

She brings her eyes level with mine and shines a light in them. "Follow my finger with just your eyes." She zooms her digit all over the place. "And how about now? Any dizziness?"

"No," I say. "Just embarrassed."

"Don't be." She pulls her stethoscope onto her ears. "Number Twelve over here knocked you down. Deep breath."

"It was an accident," Anthony tells Nurse Magparagalan.

"Yeah," I say. "He was accidentally walking backward."

The nurse moves her stethoscope to my other side. "Deep breath again."

"It's how I expand my social circle," he says.

"Really?" I look over at him. Why haven't I been staring at him this entire time?

He's smiling and has my backpack shoulder strap wrapped over his folded arms.

"No, but I was looking for you." He rubs his neck, smiles with half his mouth, then looks away from me to the floor, turning ever so slightly red.

"You were?" I ask. There's a chance the dizziness might return.

"Wanted to ask you what your water balloon tossing secret was and if you'd consider joining the football team," he says.

"Ahh."

It's hard to tell if he's just flirty or funny, or both but also sincere.

"Can you show me where your shoulder hurts?" the nurse asks.

I slide my sleeve down and expose my aching shoulder blade.

She inspects it, and I'm suddenly distinctly aware of Anthony's presence. Is it usual for a boy to stay during the examination of the girl he walked to the nurse's office after knocking her over at lunch? Is it normal for boys to walk girls to the nurse's office at all? There's nothing stopping him from being sent to class, except that neither Nurse Magparagalan nor I have said anything. She seems friendly enough with him, and I'm not going to tell him to go. Stay forever, for all I care.

The nurse finishes bandaging my shoulder.

"What about your leg?" she asks.

"I think it's just bruised." I'm wearing jeans that go to my ankles. If I were bleeding, it'd be showing.

"Well," she says. "I don't think you have a concussion. Take painkillers for the bump, and if you start feeling nauseous, tired, or dizzy, come back, or go to urgent care. Here are your tardy slips."

She hands Anthony and me slips she pre-signed. We thank her. Anthony holds the door for me, and we leave the nurse's office.

I walk on my own two feet and everything—but I miss being supported by him. As far as walking methods go, I prefer being right up next to him, one arm around his neck, while one of his arms wraps around my waist.

He still holds my backpack. I start to wonder if he'll give it back when he tosses it over one shoulder, his own backpack on two, and continues carrying it for me.

"Where are you headed?" he asks.

I wish it were to a small bench under a nearby tree where we could just sit and chat for the rest of—well, ever, but I worry I've already taken up too much of his time.

"American history, with your coach," I say, remembering Coach Tinino must be a coach of something, and that something is football.

"My friend Justin's in that class."

Ah, so he's friends with Justin. I'm not sure how to play it. Do I admit to knowing exactly who he's talking about? Do I admit to acknowledging other men exist at all?

"Justin...?" I ask.

"Justin Granite?" Anthony asks back.

"Oh, okay." I act as though I may have heard of him. But I wouldn't object in the slightest if I never saw Justin again, and every pore in my skin wants to spend more time with Anthony. Seriously—why weren't his arms around me again? It seems so stupid to have space between us. What good is it? Who invented having space between people?

"How long have you and Piper been friends?" he asks me. Were we friends? I wasn't sure.

"About three hours."

"I'm Anthony Whitaker, by the way." The right side of his smile rises higher than his left. "If you haven't read my back."

I return his smile. "I'm Jolene Stansen."

"Oh!" he shouts, realization dawning on his face. "You're Mary's sister! You spent last year dancing in Paris!"

I feel my face flush.

"How was it?" he asks, seeming genuinely curious.

I take a deep breath. I'm not used to talking about myself, except to Logan and my mom, but not to Anthony Whitakers.

"Frustrating?" I ask cautiously as if searching for a better word but landing on one that'll have to do. "At first, I didn't understand what the teacher was saying—then I wished I didn't."

This gets a good laugh out of him, so I feel at ease to laugh, too, and I'm beginning to think we might never get to an awkward moment.

"Do you dance in town?" he asks.

We've reached my class, but neither of us admits it. We stand, talk, and dare the door to say anything about it.

"Yeah. I got back in time to start *The Nutcracker*."

Half my life is *The Nutcracker*—of course I got back in time for it. It's inevitable in the life of a ballet dancer—death, taxes, and *The Nutcracker*.

But this time, unlike last year, I'm actually cast in it. I consider telling him my teacher invited me to audition for the Sugar Plum Fairy, but I don't want to brag, and there's also a good chance he may have no idea that's the best role in the ballet. So, I leave it off. I also don't want to get into the politics of it all, and how even though I worked my butt off at an intense war-zone-inspired ballet school, I still have to try out.

"I don't want to intimidate you"—strangely enough, he doesn't. He should intimidate me. He's the type to do it, but I'm not threatened at all. I'm nervous, a little, but thrilled, and he makes me feel at ease, like if I slip up and say something wrong, he'll understand what I mean and won't take offense to it—"but my sister dances ballet."

"Really?" I ask.

I want him to tell me absolutely everything that has ever happened in his entire life.

"She's very good," he says, "even better than some seven-year-olds."

I smile and nod my head to show how impressive that is.

I wonder if he knows how his face lights up when he talks about his little sister. It's the most adorable thing in the world. I want to put it in a teddy bear and cuddle it everywhere I go.

"I guess I'll see you tonight," he says, completely throwing me.

Did he ask me out when I wasn't paying attention? Maybe I do have a concussion...

"Huh?" I tilt my head to the side.

"Oh!" he says, laughing slightly and shaking his head. "Sorry—I just assumed you'd be at the game. I usually hang out with—"

"Football players and cheerleaders?"

"Or just everyday citizens who go to the games..." He's quiet for a moment as if debating whether to say something, then eventually adds, "But it'd be cool if you did come. I'll be the one with this twelve on my back."

I smile again. A part of me loves the idea of going to the game tonight, sitting in the stands, watching Anthony play, knowing he'd be pleased I was there. But another part of me worries—he's so attractive, he's probably got at least six other girls ready to go to the game tonight—scattered in the stands, each thinking we've been specially selected by the QB to be in attendance. Each pathetic and pitiful, squealing every

227

time he makes a touchdown and biting our nails when he gets tackled.

I push this thought out of my head. Is it probable that he's got absolutely every girl in school dying of love for him? Yes. But did I have any proof he flirted with all of them? No. So, I'm determined to plow ahead cautiously optimistic.

"Right," I say.

JUSTIN

They're chatting, standing near the open door of the classroom where, inside, Coach Tinino bores us all to death with his football diagrams of the Revolutionary War.

They're taking forever. Is he not going to let her come to class?

JOLENE

"I'm really sorry about knocking you over," Anthony says.

"It's okay. It was an accident."

"Have a good weekend, if I don't see you," then adds, "Oh." He hands my backpack to me, smiles, and walks away.

I feel like I'm glowing when I enter the classroom, but I don't care. Anyone who saw us together is welcome to guess why I'm beaming, and they'll be right. Why hide it? It won't last long enough anyway— butterflies never do.

I hand my tardy slip to Coach Tinino, and avoid Justin's gaze, but I sense his curiosity stuck on me, like film on pudding that's been sitting out too long. He's probably wondering why I'm late and why I look so happy about it. I don't care. I don't care about anything that happens between now and the next time I see Anthony. All I care about is that there is another time—maybe even tonight, maybe in the hallway between classes. But that's not likely. I've never seen him in the halls before—I would have remembered. What would it be like if I do see him in the hall again? Would he go out of his way to find me? What would I say?

JUSTIN

Finally she steps in, all smiles—somehow head-to-foot. She looks back at him out the door while absent-mindedly fiddling with her side braid that's still a little wet from when I held the hose for her.

She hands a note to Tinino.

He glares at her. She's a smidge taller than he is, although that might just be because of her shoes, which are stylish, taupe, and have a slight heel.

Tay-Tay usually wears tennis-shoes—I guess she has to as part of her cheer uniform. She doesn't wear it every day, but often enough.

"Name?" Tinino asks her.

"Jolene," she says.

He glares at her.

"Oh, Stansen," she says, head ducking between her shoulder blades.

229

He scribbles something on the note as she takes her seat next to me, like I hoped she would.

Yesterday I sat by the far wall, but walls don't have long slender legs the color of milk that you know would quench your thirst if you could just get your hands on them.

Today I picked a seat by the one she sat in yesterday, and since humans are creatures of habit—or because she wanted to sit by me—she did not disappoint.

I raise my eyebrows at her—silently asking what's going on, to which her non-verbal response is an eye roll and a shake of the head as if to say whatever it was is too much to explain. Super helpful, Jolene.

"You're half an hour late, Stansen," Tinino says, tossing her late slip onto his meticulously disorganized desk.

"I had to go to the nurse," she says.

Tinino turns back to his diagram of Xs and Os, and I lean in toward her.

"What happened?" I ask, catching the smell of mocha and coconuts. Of all the girls I've known, I've never smelled this perfume on any of them. Maybe it was native to France. Maybe it was just her...

She bites the corner of her bottom lip. I want to bite it, too. She says something, but I'm not listening. I like the way her mouth moves when she talks. Whatever lip gloss or lipstick she had on this morning has all washed away from the mud and the hose. She'd look better if she reapplied it. She should have ditched Anthony and run into the bathroom and fixed her hair again while in there.

"Piper said Anthony knocked you over or something," I say, reminding her I'm still here, trying to talk to her.

Alice Sistine's iridescent polar bear hair swings—she turns her head so fast to stare at us.

"Yeah," Jolene says. "I had to go to the nurse. See?" She peels back her sleeve, exposing her creamy shoulder. There's an ugly giant bandage ruining it.

A mix between wanting to serve her up—clavicle all the way down to her toes—and devouring her for lunch, and hunting down and shooting Anthony, battle for priority in my mind.

"Anthony walked you to the office?" Alice asks, scowling at Jolene's shoulder.

"He was just being nice," Jolene says.

Alice eyes me as if to say she doesn't believe he was "just being nice" and turns back front.

My stomach sinks. Alice's irritation concerning Anthony and Jolene spending the last half hour together feeds my own.

I sneer at Jolene's bandaged skin. She seems to notice, gets slightly pinker, and pulls her sleeve back up.

35 SAVED BY THE BATHROOM

JOLENE

If I run into Anthony in the hall—just the thought of it reminds me of earlier, when I literally ran into him and was pressed up against the twelve on his chest—I don't want to be walking with Justin—I don't want Anthony to think I'm with Justin, especially when they're friends. I don't know if they have bro-code or something, but after history, Justin follows me out of the classroom.

"Here's your pencil back," he says, offering back the one I lent him during class.

"Oh no. Keep it." I once gave out my favorite pen to someone who asked, and he never gave it back, so I carry around a bunch of spares.

We turn a corner, and I get an idea.

"I..." I jut my thumb at the bathrooms.

"Oh," he says, panic filling his eyes. "Okay. I'll see ya."

I've learned from Logan that guys are terrified of getting between girls and the bathroom, and sure enough, Justin walks off and I turn into the pink-tiled room.

Girls fixing their hair and makeup crowd the mirrors. It's just as well. I always feel self-conscious doing my makeup in public, so despite all of it washing off at lunch, I leave my face the way it is, awkwardly wait along a wall for a few minutes, watch a few cat videos on my phone, then leave.

When I come out, I go to my locker and find Logan on the floor, transferring his books.

"I'm sorry about lunch," I say. "I kind of got roped into it. You could have joined us if you wanted..."

He looks ashamed. "It's okay."

"You want to tell me about the rest of that movie?" I should have made sure I remembered the name before I brought it up.

"Maybe later," he says. He zips his backpack and stands up, then shuts his locker with his foot.

"You wanna kill some zombies tonight?" I ask. Oh, wait—no. Well, maybe making plans with Logan tonight, instead of going to the game, is okay. Would I like to go? Sure, but not by myself, and I know it would be the last thing Logan would want to do.

"You know the update went live at nine," he says, eyes all bright and Logan-y.

"I didn't know there was going to be an update," I tell him.

"Yeah," he says. He continues telling me about it all the way to class.

36 ESCAPES AND ALICES

MARY

I thought if I escaped lunch, I would escape Jolene. But, like always, I was wrong. Not long into my creative writing class—I have to take two English classes this semester since I failed one last year—we're divided into groups to create a writing prompt to later give to another group. The idea is that we all do each other's prompts and come up with brilliant short stories. My group regretfully comprises the two Alices, who were once my friends, and two guys who play baseball and wear cowboy hats as if they live on a farm or have ever even seen a horse.

"Hey," says one of the baseball players, leaning toward me, reeking of cologne and chewing tobacco. "You're related to that girl, Jolene, right? You're her cousin or something?"

The Alices exchange glares. I bite my tongue literally—not to stop myself from saying something, but because my jaw tenses and snaps shut so fast, my tongue just gets kind of caught.

"No," I say. "My cousins are all dead." It's not true, but it's funny.

"Thought both your last names were Stansen," he drones on.

"It's the third most common surname in America." Also not true.

"Anyway," Alice Sistine says. She's not chewing gum, but if she were, she'd be smacking it a lot. "Our prompt should be something like—"

"Wait," the other Alice says, "I thought she was your sister. The girl who went to France..."

I was so close. We almost started actually working, moving on from the topic of my family tree. I wonder what it would be like if my mom never met Jolene's dad.

"She was my sister," I say. "But pod-people took over her body. It's an epidemic in Europe. Happens to everyone there. This is why I stay away from Montecito."

"So," says the other baseball player, "she's your sister...?"

"Pod sister," I say. "Technically pod half-sister once removed... by the aliens."

They look at me in the expected fashion. Right. Time to get back to work.

"I think our prompt should be," I say, "'write about someone you wish had never been born, and the impact their lack of life would have on a personal and global scale.'"

37 WHEN KEEP AWAY FAILS

JOLENE

Piper, I'm finding, can be unrelenting. After school, she meets me at my locker and asks so many questions so quickly that I can hardly answer the first before she asks another: "Then what happened?" "What did he say?" "What did you say?" "Did he laugh?" "Then what happened?" "Did he offer, or did you ask him to?" "Then what happened?"

"He walked me to my class," I say, placing my books in my locker.

"AND!?" She literally makes me jump. "What did you talk about?"

I take the apple I didn't eat at lunch and put it in my backpack.

"He asked me about Paris and ballet—oh! His little sister dances! And he was so cute about it. How sweet is that?"

Fire shoots out of her eyes. Maybe I shouldn't talk about his being cute in front of her.

"WHAT ELSE?" she asks.

236

I don't know what information she's looking for, or what she expects to hear that she hasn't yet. It's like I'm telling a mystery, and she can't wait to see who the killer is—but I don't know! Or maybe she's afraid we did something more than talk and walk. Maybe I should tell her we did. Maybe I should say we found a broom closet and made out until we realized school was over, but I don't think she'd take the joke well. Plus, it's not funny. The fact it didn't happen is depressing.

"He asked if I was going to the game tonight." I zip up my backpack. "Actually, he just kind of assumed it, and when I—"

PIPER

Jolene's telling me, basically, that Anthony asked her specifically to be at the game tonight. The details aren't clear yet, and Jolene's withholding. I'm not a patient girl. I lick my lips to prevent myself from screaming at her to hurry it up.

"He asked if I was going to the game tonight," she says.

Of course he did. His whole life is his dorky little sister and football.

She says something else, but I don't listen. If she went to the game tonight, she wouldn't really be anywhere near Anthony. She would, however, be very near Justin. Tay-Tay wouldn't be there either because she'd be on the field cheering...

"You should!" I yell, with no idea where in her blabber I'm interrupting her.

"What?" she asks, turning her head, one hand on her locker door.

"You should come to the game tonight!" I'm still yelling. "You can sit with me and Justin! His girlfriend's on cheer, so she won't be joining us, thank goodness."

"You really don't like Tay-Tay," she says.

"No—it's not that. It's just that Justin doesn't, and frankly he's right not to. She cheats on him with Jesse. We all know it, but he doesn't want to be girlfriend-less, so he acts like it's not happening. But if there was a girl he liked who was interested, and he thought she'd go out with him, he'd switch to her in a heartbeat."

"Guys actually do that?" she asks, disgust on her face. "Date a girl they don't like unless a sure thing is ready in the wings?"

"Girls do, too," I say. "Who wants to be single if they can help it?"

"I'd rather be single than with someone I didn't like, who was cheating on me," Jolene says stupidly.

"But I've noticed the way he looks at you," I say, pretending I didn't hear her.

"Anthony?" she asks, a little too wide-eyed.

"No!" I yell again. "Not Anthony! We weren't even talking about him!" She's worse than I thought. I'm going to have to do something. So, I play it up, take a big breath and sigh. "Although, I mean, he's kind of the greatest. I've had a crush on him since junior high—"

"Justin?"

238

"Anthony!" I frown, then turn back to gushing. "I think he's planning on asking me to Homecoming..."

She looks down at the bottom of her locker and shuts the door a little too hard. I resist gloating.

"How do you—what makes you—why do you think—"

"Oh, I don't know," I say, throwing in some giddy, bubbly bouncing. "Just the way he, like, says my name, and flirts with me, and hints at it..." I make my shoulders dance as I act.

If him talking to me is him flirting with me, and not hinting at it at all is hinting at it, then this isn't a lie.

"I mean, who else would he ask?" I ask.

She exhales through her nose and presses her lips together, jutting out her lower jaw.

I let my smile broaden and pretend not to notice her obvious disappointment.

"So, that's settled," I say. "You'll come to the game tonight and steal Justin away from Tay-Tay."

"Wait. No—"

"You don't think he's attractive?"

"No. Of course he is! It's just, sometimes he—I'm just not sure I want to jump into a relationship with him—"

I sigh, letting her see how annoyed I am. Letting her think she's being ridiculous and any number of girls would leap at the chance to jump into a relationship with him, which is true—they absolutely would.

She scrunches up her mouth and eyebrows and drops her voice, saying, "And I seriously doubt I'd be able to split them up—even if I tried."

I laugh loudly.

239

JOLENE

Piper's laugh is forced and unnerving. "That's what's bothering you?" she asks. "He as good as told me he'd dump her for you."

I look around. She's talking louder than I've ever spoken, let alone about people who could be nearby.

But no one's watching. They're all just walking past and hitting up their lockers, laughing, joking, not caring that Piper Thompson is inviting me to hang out with her and the most popular kids in school tonight.

"You guys would be so cute together—oh! And we could double to Homecoming!" Piper says, clapping her hands together.

I picture pulling up to Homecoming in a limo with Piper, Justin, and Anthony—everyone looking at us and talking about us. But if Piper ends up going with Anthony, it might actually be more painful to go in their group. I wouldn't be able to escape them. What if they kissed? Oh, gosh, what if they were cutesy?

"It would be so good for him," Piper says. "Tay's horrible. Did you miss the part where she's cheating on him? Everyone knows it. It's like a running joke."

"Piper..." I say, with nothing to add. I don't know what to say to get her to stop pushing us as a couple.

"Okay, you're too good for him. Fine," she says, not looking at me. It's not fair. I didn't mean I was too good for him. I don't think I'm too good for anyone. "But come tonight anyway. You'll be the only girl in our group I can stand."

I take a deep breath. If I go tonight, is there a chance she'll keep trying to get me together with Justin? I probably can't rule it out completely.

Worst-case scenario, she pushes in front of Justin, and he makes a big deal about it at lunch in the Greek, announcing to the entire school how stupid his friend is trying to hook him up with someone like me.

Best-case scenario, I go to the game tonight, solidify my friendship with Piper, and then maybe run into Anthony Monday at school and tell him I was there. He might even be able to see me tonight, sitting with his friends...

Maybe I should just stay home. If he's flirting with Piper and hinting at asking her to Prom—I mean—Homecoming, maybe he's just one of those charming guys who flirts with everyone, and pathetic girls like me keep falling for it. If that's the case, then what am I even doing?

But—but sometimes people are mistaken. I was so sure Beau was the best dancer in the class. He acted like he was. He had me convinced I wasn't as good as he was, but he was the one who couldn't keep up. What if this is like that? What if what Piper says isn't exactly what reality is? And what if I'm right? Ugh. That might not end well either. If I go after Anthony, I'm fairly certain Piper will never talk to me again. Would the entire popular sector shun me on her behalf?

It's just a game! I'm going to a football game. It doesn't mean I'm stealing Justin away from Tay-Tay, and it doesn't mean I'm going after Anthony. It just means I'm going with my new friend to a game. Period. End of story—but not really, I mean, keep reading.

"Okay," I say.

Elation lights up her face. She turns on her heels and starts walking away, yelling over her shoulder, "I'll pick you up early, we'll grab dinner, and go to Justin's party after the game."

"What?" I ask her strawberry blond shape walking away from me, as something stirs in my stomach. All I've agreed to multiplied in a matter of seconds. What if it multiplies again?

I take a moment to regain my bearings and remember what I should be doing at this time of day. I check my watch. Crap—it's twenty minutes after school. Mary's waiting for me.

I rush through the hallways, cutting through courtyards, climb the steps to the upper student parking lot, and sure enough, there's her black truck, the only car in the lot. A little pink dot shakes furiously inside.

I try the door. It's locked. I wait patiently while she pushes the button to unlock it.

I slide in and put my bag on the floor.

"Shut the door so I can back out," she says through clenched teeth.

I don't want to upset her more, so I shut the door quickly.

"You don't have to slam it," she says.

I buckle my seatbelt, but she doesn't pull the truck out. She locks her jaw instead, looking straight ahead.

"I've been waiting for twenty minutes," she says, snarling. "I could have walked home by now."

I don't think that's true. We live way the heck out there. We could almost attend a school in Lompoc. It's actually not fair to let Logan drive me to school, as he has to go at least six minutes through back-streets out of his way.

"Sorry," I say. "I lost track of time. I was talking."

"To Piper Thompson."

"Ohhhh. That's why you're mad." Granted, I can't blame her for being mad I'm late, but would she be on so much fire if I was talking to someone she didn't used to be friends with?

"It's a fun little bonus." She just about spits as she speaks.

She goes about thirty seconds without saying anything, and I wonder if she's died of rage when suddenly, as if choking, she gurgles out, "Six people asked me if I was related to you today."

If I had one single, solitary penny for every time someone asked me if I was related to Mary Stansen during just my freshman year of high school, I'd be rich enough to buy a time machine, go back to Paris, and avoid this conversation.

"So?" I ask, daring her to be mad about that when I dealt with it nearly every day my freshman year.

She peels out, and we drive home in silence.

38 MY FIRST CURFEW

JOLENE

It's the second day of school and a Friday, so my only homework is reading *The Iliad*, which I can do tomorrow or Sunday, which means I have about three and a half hours to do about twenty minutes' worth of getting ready. I may as well get started.

I toss a bath bomb into my giant, clawed, beautifully enormous tub, get the water piping hot, and soak for about twenty minutes. Then I wash and re-braid my hair, going for a romantic Dutch braid, pancaking the sections, and spending the time to get it just right.

I wash my face, exfoliate, moisturize, reapply my makeup, push my bookcase aside, step into my closet, pick out the perfect outfit, and lift off the hanger a cute, warm jacket—not so cute that if I take it off and someone steals it, I'd have a hard time replacing it because I got it in Europe, but cute, and I toss it on my bed.

I search my closet for something to wear underneath. Anthony will be at the after-party. Maybe

I should wear something that shows some skin even with my jacket on, but Justin will also be there, so maybe not. Maybe something that brings out my eyes, like purple, or something sexier, like red—or maybe not...

By the time I settle on my favorite pair of jeans, boots, a light-blue gathered and corseted top that's wistful, romantic, and timeless, and my brown leather jacket with a furry lining, it's time to go, and Piper's texting me she's waiting outside.

Mary's sitting at the kitchen table with a banana and her phone, while my dad fries bacon on the stove. Mom's not home yet.

"I'm going out," I announce.

In Paris, my life was my own. I never had to ask for permission to go anywhere. I enjoyed being treated like a mature adult, and I intend for it to continue.

So, I act as if I already have it, a strategy I picked up from one of Eloise's assistants, who let me in on a few of her tips and tricks on how she got promoted so quickly.

She seemed proud and like she wanted to share but couldn't very well give tips to those under her, and those above her were sure to use them against her.

I repaid her friendship by sharing some of her load when I could, or when it was fun.

"Who? What? Where? When? How?" my dad asks.

"You forgot why," Mary adds.

"Why?" my dad asks.

"Piper and me. The game. School. Now. Her Jeep. Because we want to." I list them off on my fingers.

Mary snorts.

"Who's Piper?" my dad asks. "Since when do you go to games?"

"Piper's my friend," I say. "You wanted me to have friends. This is what happens when you have friends; they want you to do stuff with them."

"Alright. Oh, curfew..." I was hoping he'd forget. "I don't know—eleven?"

I sigh inwardly. I don't know how long Piper will want to stay at the party, but I don't have time to negotiate—she's waiting.

"Kay, bye," I say, and walk out the door.

MARY

I rub behind my right ear, debating if I should speak or not. I should just let Dad fret all night over whether his widdle Jolie is doing drugs, having sex, hijacking cars, or sacrificing babies at the game.

But I'm in a charitable mood, and Jolene has been annoying lately.

"You know," I say, taking another bite of my banana so he has to work to understand me. "I shouldn't tell you this, but you can track her phone."

His eyes widen like he's just stumbled upon the fountain of youth.

"Tell me more, and I've got a twenty with your name on it."

"Make it a fifty, and you've got yourself a deal," I say.

"How much would it take for you to go to the game and keep an eye on her?"

I squint. I would rather take my banana and shove it up my nose than go to a football game and watch Jolene and Piper laugh all night, flirting with Justin...

"Aren't you worried I'll do whatever it is you're worried Jolene will do?" I ask.

He has the nerve to laugh. "Not even a little!"

I exhale and rise from the table, not bothering to dispose of my half-eaten banana. Let him clean up my trash.

"Keep your money, old man," I say, and stomp loudly upstairs.

39 IT'S ALWAYS HIGH TIDE
AT RIPTIDE

JOLENE

Piper drives a teal Jeep poorly. She runs stop signs, reds, and over curbs, taking the off-roading capabilities as a challenge.

She pulls into the Riptide parking lot, gets out, and I notice she hasn't changed her clothes like I have. She hasn't even put on a different jacket but wears the same purple hooded sweatshirt she wore to school. Her jeans even still have the small mark on them from when some mayonnaise fell out of her sandwich. I wonder if it occurred to her to change, but something prevented it—or if she doesn't obsess over these sorts of things like I do. Which of our actions is more normal? I'm betting hers.

We're led to a table, and I sit down, but Piper sneers.

The hostess looks at her with a confused face.

"The sun is really coming through that window," Piper says. "Can we sit somewhere else?"

The hostess leads us to a table away from the window, and I wait until Piper sits, then I take my seat.

The hostess hands us our menus. "Your waiter is Kylienna. She'll be right with you." She leaves.

"My mom says never take the first hotel room they offer, so I apply it to restaurants, too," Piper tells me.

I smile at her and browse the menu just in case they've added something new, or in case I spot something I've never seen before, or in case a craving jumps out at me, but nothing does. It's just as well, Piper keeps talking about what she's going to order and I can't concentrate.

"Should I get the side of fries or the steamed rice—ooh! The shrimp looks good."

"That does look good," I say, but I settle on the same sushi rolls I always get.

Riptide is open all night, so it's where everyone goes, for any reason, always. I've been back for just a few weeks, and I've already been here at least twice.

They have any food you might want—cheeseburgers, pizza, sushi, salmon, steaks, salads, Mexican food, Chinese, Thai, Korean, Indian, and barbecue, all in a beach-side shack that looks like you're dining under the sea. Mermaids, scuba divers, sharks, and even unsuspecting tourist legs are on the walls and ceiling. My favorite thing in the entire place is a big, giant, pink octopus holding different crustaceans in every tentacle. I've named him Kyle.

Kylienna appears. "What do you guys want to drink?" She looks at me.

"I'll have an iced tea," Piper says. "And we're actually ready to order."

Kylienna looks at me again.

"I'll have a Diet Coke."

She writes down our drinks, then looks back at Piper.

"I'll have the Thai peanut salad," Piper says. "But I want the sauce that comes on the salmon instead of the peanut sauce."

"You know that's the same sauce they put on the fresh salad," Kylienna says.

"I know, but I want the peanuts that come with the Thai salad, and I don't want the onions that come with the fresh salad."

"Okay," Kylienna says. "And for you?"

"Could I please get an eel roll and a Riptide roll?" I ask.

She writes it down.

"Oh!" Piper says. "And we have gift certificates." She pulls them out and places the gift certificates from the balloon toss on the table.

"Alright," Kylienna says. "Be right back with your drinks." She takes the gift certificates and leaves.

"Where did you get those?" I ask.

"I snatched them during the water balloon war."

"I thought the Swedish junior varsity twins won..."

Piper just shrugs and leans in. "So, Justin usually goes for girls who are interested but not too interested. Know what I mean? And he's really competitive, especially with Anthony, so if you act like you're only there for Anthony, it'll drive him mad."

I inwardly sigh. Did she forget that I didn't want her to set me up with Justin, or is she acting like she forgot?

"Um," I say, "I thought you just wanted to hang out..."

"I do." She sits back. "This is how I hang out."

"Sorry. It's kind of making me feel like I'm about to go on a date..."

"Have you dated anyone before?" Piper sips her iced tea.

How is the answer not obvious? I'm a trained dancer. My balance rocks. I can do fifteen *fouetté* turns in a row, but I nearly fall over whenever an attractive guy gets anywhere near me—I actually did fall over the last time. And even if I managed the whole boyfriend scene better, my parents didn't allow me to date before I left for France. I'm not even entirely sure they'd be on board if I got a boyfriend now, but I just shake my head.

"What were the guys in France like?"

My mind goes to Beau. For months, I obsessed over his opinion of me, only for him to drop off the face of the Earth. Jean was nicer and didn't treat me like a bag of meat. He was worlds different from Beau. If I ever saw Jean again, I'd say hello and maybe even ask if he wanted to grab a bite and catch up. If I ran into Beau, I'd slap his face.

Then, of course, there's Oscar. He never treated me as anything more than his friends' niece, but sometimes, late at night when I can't sleep, I wonder if things might have been different if we didn't always have Eloise or Caspian around—or if, that one time it was just the two of us at the café by Caspian's condo in Cannes, picking up breakfast for everyone else—what if he didn't hold my hand only because he didn't want it in the tabloids?

251

Of course, I'm crazy. He obviously was more interested in the croissants than he was in me. The idea of a movie star liking me when I couldn't even get a high school basketball player to ask me out is ridiculous.

If I'm honest, I wouldn't want to date any of them. Beau? Definitely not. Jean? No, and even Oscar—I felt like I always had to be impressive around him. There was no time to calm down, lean back, be myself. Maybe I'd get more comfortable after several years, but why put up with that when some guys make me comfortable instantly? Guys with floppy brown hair and twelve written on their chests. Of course, I didn't know Anthony when I was abroad. No. My head was filled with someone else, someone I haven't thought about since I got dressed for school this morning, someone I'll probably never see again.

"I don't know," I answer. "I spent the whole time thinking about a guy I knew back home."

"Anyone I know?"

"Matt Craddick." I watch in horror as her mouth falls apart.

Oh, so what if she does know him? Who cares? Even if she tells him I like him, it's not like I'll ever run into him.

"I know him!" she says. "He's like a good friend of mine!"

"Of course he is. It doesn't matter. He's probably off somewhere at some college—engaged to Caradine."

She smiles but doesn't respond.

"What?" I ask.

252

She shrugs and suddenly seems to find the coaster stack sitting on the edge of the table fascinating. She picks one up and studies it as if it says more than just "It's Always High Tide at Riptide."

40 THE GAME

PIPER

When we get to the school, we present our student discount cards, buy tickets, grab programs, and pay for the expensive option with colored photos and details of all the players—Anthony Whitaker, senior, quarterback, number twelve, weight: 210, height: 6'5, stats: blah, blah, blah.

Then we head up the five stairs onto the bleachers.

The football team still warms up and stretches on the field across from the other team: Oxnard.

We walk in front of the crowd, a wall separating us from the field. I stop halfway, and place my arms over the railing, trying to find Anthony among the helmeted team. Then I notice Jolene doing the same thing, so I turn, lean my back on the rail, and search the stands for Justin.

"There he is," I say, nodding in his direction.

He sits on the fifty-yard line next to Weston Prior, Quinn's boyfriend's friend. Jolene and I climb the steps toward them as the teams leave the field and the marching band makes its way to the back to start the pre-game show. They reach their formation and play *The National Anthem.* Everyone stands, and I'm forced to push past people to get next to Justin.

Weston stands on Justin's other side, and Jolene squeezes in next to me.

The stadium is filling up fast, so I don't bother trying to make out anyone else I know. It wouldn't matter if I saw anyone I'd rather sit with anyway, not tonight.

The Star-Spangled Banner ends, and everyone sits as the band strikes up the fight song. Then the football players run out, bursting through a giant "Avenging Angels" poster held by the spirit squads.

The kickoff is kicked, and this is when I try to pay attention. Some guy takes the ball and runs. A whistle blows, and everything stops. I shift my focus to the cheerleaders. I bet if I were down there with them, Anthony would have asked me out by now. It's all Tay-Tay's fault. She probably knew he'd ask me out and didn't want us competing against her and Justin for most popular couple. That's the real reason she didn't let me on the team.

I turn to Jolene, who bites the corner of her mouth and watches the field. I switch to Justin, who bites the corner of his mouth, watching Jolene.

JUSTIN

Before the first play even has a chance to begin, Piper says, "Come run to the snack bar with me." She rises and pulls on Jolene's arm, making her rise with

255

her. She turns to Weston and me. "You guys want anything?"

"A Coke," I say.

"I'll take some nachos," Weston says as I pull out my wallet and hand Piper a hundred.

"Here," I say. "Get whatever you guys want."

Piper turns over the bill. "I'm not bringing you change."

"Oh no." I laugh, looking back at the game as if I couldn't care less. Which I couldn't—except that was all I had, and now I'll have to remember to get cash back next time I go somewhere.

When they turn their backs to us, I turn my head back to them and watch as they bounce down the stairs, gawk at Anthony like all the girls do, pass the crowd, and go out of sight.

41 MY DECAPITATED
FAUX-BRONZE CHEERLEADER

MARY

I rage-clean when I'm mad, so my room is spotless. It sucks because there's nothing left to do when I'm angry again seconds later. Maybe I'll go for a run.

My running shorts stare up at me from out of my chest of drawers. I don't want to have to change, though. I take them and throw them onto the floor. Best to get the place a mess again, so I'll have something to do later.

I suck on my lips and stare at the wallpaper. When I was about nine, Mom redecorated my room in pink pastel stripes. Why is this still how my room looks?

I turn my murder music up and let the female vocals scream about burning and death while I peel the pink wallpaper off my walls. It's not easy work, and after a few minutes, my fingernails hurt. But it's satisfying to feel the paper lift and see the bare, scratched wall underneath.

257

The hard-to-peel spots are easier to remove once I get a damp sponge to rub on them. Sometimes they come up in big, long, satisfying sections that fall to the floor while I play over my earlier conversation in my head.

I wonder if Dad would worry about me if he didn't have a daughter of his own to worry about. Or would he not worry about anyone?

I think about Justin. If he hadn't scaled the Greek steps for my sister, it doesn't mean he would have done it for me—but out of all the girls on planet Earth, why did he have to pick her?

A stubborn piece of wallpaper won't come up, so I lean in and trip over my carefully tossed shoes. I pick one up and throw it at the other side of my bedroom. It knocks over a cheer trophy on its blazing journey. We never competed. They gave everyone a trophy at the end of the year. But now it lies dead, in pieces, on my floor; another something for future angry me to clean up.

I sit on the ground next to the faux-bronze cheerleader's severed head. She's lucky she's not real, or she'd be in a lot of pain right now.

I know the answer—he scaled the steps for her because something about him likes something about me, and she's me—if I were perfect. If I had been born to Mom and Dad, I'd be her: she, who never rage-cleans, who has perfect teeth, hair, thighs, butt, and then I'd be at the game right now—with him.

I chuck the head at my bookcase, putting a dent in my collection of Poe poems.

42 THE OFFICIAL PLAN
TO BREAK CURFEW

JOLENE

The snack bar is right outside the stadium, near where they sell tickets. Piper and I get in the moderately short line, behind some students and an older couple.

"Did he really give you a hundred bucks?" I ask.

"How many M&M's do you think we could buy?" Piper asks.

I point to the sign reading "M&M's $1.00." "I'm thinking a hundred," I say.

"I meant hypothetically," Piper says.

"Oh. Hypothetically, probably, like, thirty-five."

We get to the front of the line, order, and pay. Piper takes the change, we grab our snacks, and make our way back toward our seats.

"That was for you, by the way," Piper says while cramming the rest of Justin's money in her back pocket.

"Yeah?" I ask.

I don't like that. Is he so insecure that he thinks he needs to wow me with money? Does he think so little of me that he believes it'd work?

"Yeah," she says. "So, now just act like you're hardly interested—better yet, you're only here to watch Anthony play."

"So, just be myself?" I ask.

Again, she acts like I haven't repeatedly told her I'm not interested in Justin.

"That is not what I said," she says.

We get to the bottom of the steps going up to Justin and Weston, and Piper suddenly stops.

"Oh," she says. "You got up first."

I narrow my eyes. "Did we just go on a snack run so we could change seats?"

"And I got a hundred bucks," she says with a grin.

I lead the way up the stands until we get to our old spots. We slide in, and I sit next to Justin.

"Here, Weston," I say.

He reaches over Justin, something I have no intention of doing, so I pass Justin Weston's nachos.

"Thanks, gorgeous," Weston says with a wink at me.

Justin glares at him, then at me, then back at him. "Wow, bruh."

"Oh," Weston says. "Thank you, too, Justin..."

"Not that."

"You're also beautiful?" Weston asks, scrunching an eyebrow in confusion.

Justin rolls his eyes and turns to the game.

A little taken aback, I do the same and search the field. Anthony's standing on the sidelines watching his teammates. That must mean our defense is playing.

I wonder if he's completely consumed by what's happening with his team, or if even the smallest part of him is thinking about me...

Piper nudges me hard in the ribs.

"It wouldn't kill you to talk to him," she whispers out the corner of her mouth.

She might be right. It's probably not even that big of a might.

I take a deep breath and turn to Justin.

Something's been happening to me more and more. Since I've been back, it's happened so often that I've almost forgotten that it didn't used to happen at all. I'll be doing something and look up, and someone in my eyesight will look away real quick, like he, just seconds before, had been staring at me. Usually, they're too far away to tell exactly what part of me they've been staring at, but being this close to Justin—I know exactly where he's been looking.

I shift a little. The knot forming in my stomach squirms. Maybe if I say something, he'll realize my head is attached to the rest of my body.

"So," I say, "you owe me something embarrassing."

He smirks and leans against the back of the seat. It makes me uncomfortable having him behind me, but I don't want to lean back and join him either. Copying someone's movements speaks body language volumes—and the volumes are all romances.

Piper passes him his drink behind me. The movement makes me rigid and so uncomfortable that I lean back, despite really not wanting to.

"Is dating Tay-Tay not embarrassing enough?" He smiles wickedly.

Piper said he didn't like his girlfriend, and that she's cheating on him. Seems like Piper could be right, and maybe even on both accounts, but I get the feeling he might not exactly be loyal to Tay-Tay either.

His eyes move over me. We're too close. Did he lean back so I'd lean back? Because now we're practically lying down.

"It should be, right?" I say, sitting up. I'm aware I look like a dog circling its bed trying to find a cozy spot, but I don't care because I'm not a dog, I'm never going to be cozy, and this is certainly not my bed. "It's gotta be hard to be seen with a beautiful blond cheer captain."

"See? You get it," he says.

I can't tell if he knows I'm joking, especially because now I can't see him. Out of the corner of my eye, I can make out his burgundy leather jacket sleeve and royal-blue jeans, but that's about it.

"Do you talk about all your girlfriends like that?" I ask.

"Just the one," he says.

I hear him popping open his drink. "You like football?"

"Yep," I say.

It wasn't true yesterday, but it's been true ever since lunch. Has it really only been a few hours since I met Anthony?

Anthony and some others on offense switch places with the defense. We watch as they maneuver against the other team. A guy tosses the ball, and Anthony catches it. He takes a few steps back, ball raised, then seems to change his mind about throwing it, and runs

262

toward the goalpost. He gains a few yards before he's taken down brutally. We all suck our teeth, but a guy on the other team lends him his hand, helps him stand up, and the world goes on spinning.

A voice to my right says, "He's not that great, you know."

I gawk at Justin. Why is he ragging on his friend all of a sudden—especially after he almost got injured? Maybe it has something to do with my hands clasped in front of my hyperventilating chest. I rub my thumb into my palm to massage my hand, and act like I'm not completely pathetic.

"He's a bad friend," Justin says.

"Anthony?" Piper asks, disbelief apparent in her voice and sneer.

I hadn't realized she's been listening—

Justin bristles. "He canceled on me last week because his little sister needed stitches, and he had to take her to the ER."

I squint my eyes and tilt my head.

"What?" he asks.

"She's shocked at how cold your heart is," Weston tells Justin. "Huh, Jolene?"

Just as Justin turns to Weston, a voice shrieks from a few rows behind us.

"JOLENE STANSEN!"

We turn and there's Caradine Kreuger herself— Matt's girlfriend—sitting amongst some of the border friends scattered around us. Apart from a haircut, she hasn't changed much. She's even wearing her standard miniskirt, despite the dropping temperature. The most notable change is—at least to me—she's Mattless.

"Caradine?" Piper asks, seemingly just as surprised as me to see her. "What are you doing at a high school football game?"

It is weird she's here; she graduated last year, like Matt did.

Justin turns to me. "How do you know each other?"

"We don't—" I say.

Caradine calls me a name in a false whisper. I laugh at the absurdity of it all. Justin throws a glance behind his shoulder but adopts my attitude of unconcern.

"What's her problem?" he asks me as if I know.

Her ignoring me for an entire year used to bother me, but now this open hostility is just funny; funny and pointless.

"I don't know," I say as he turns to me. Suppressed resentment rises, and I raise my voice so she can hear me. "I was friends with her boyfriend, and I guess it still bothers her."

I don't look at her, but I imagine her seething.

"She doesn't have a boyfriend," Justin says, also loudly enough for Caradine to hear.

"She's not dating—" But applause and cheering interrupts my question.

Everyone rises out of their seats.

"Touchdown!" the announcer says. "Avenging Angels, number twelve, Anthony Whitaker."

We all stand and cheer.

"She's not dating Matt?" I yell over the crowd while clapping.

"They broke up months ago," he says as the cheerleaders pile into an old Volkswagen Bug with a WCHS Avenging Angels helmet instead of a hood.

264

It drives them to the goalpost where they form a pyramid.

"How many months ago?" I ask.

"Woo! Anthony!" Piper yells.

The kicker kicks the ball, making another goal, and so the cheerleaders dissolve their pyramid and squeeze back into the Bug, while those who can't fit run back to their spots in front of the field, and everyone in the stands calms down and retakes their seats.

All I did was stand up. I didn't move around at all, but when I sit down, I sit on top of something. I let out a yelp as the something wraps his arms around my waist, pulling me off balance as we fall backward. But Justin doesn't seem nearly as mortified as I am; he's laughing despite my profuse apologies.

"Sorry," I say again, tucking a stray hair behind my ear as he slides over and I regain my seat. I'm too embarrassed to look at him again, so I sit still and rigid, watching the game.

After a moment he asks, "Need a ride after this?"

I frown apologetically and shake my head. "I'm going with Piper—to your party," I say, still not looking at him, but not taking in the game either.

"I know the way, too," he says. "Piper doesn't mind."

"No," she says, taking a sip of her drink. "I don't mind."

"You can decide whether or not we drive with the top-up," Justin says, again trying to impress me with his money.

I take a big breath to buy some time. What I agreed to this afternoon is multiplying again. I'm just supposed to go to the game with Piper, stick by Piper's side the whole time, and not get too swept up into anything with Justin, but it's moving too fast.

The wind blows the strands of my hair that have freed themselves from my meticulous Dutch braid. It feels refreshing. I let it wash over my face.

The stadium erupts again as Jesse scores a touchdown.

Everyone stands and cheers, and it doesn't stop for about seven minutes when we all settle down and find our seats again. This time, I look first.

"What do you think?" He hasn't forgotten our previous conversation.

"About what?" I ask, pretending I have.

"About coming with me in my Porsche." He's showing off again.

"I don't know," I say. "I don't want to be rude and make Piper go all by herself—"

"She said she didn't mind," he insists. "How about if we win, you come with me to my party, and if we lose, you go with whoever, wherever...?"

43 MUSTARD AND MY LAST NERVE

JASON

Grocery stores on Friday nights are filled with college students buying alcohol—at least they are this close to Isla Vista. Everybody here has plans for something better tonight except for Matt and me. This is our plan.

I didn't even bother getting actual pants on, and shop in my jammie bottoms, Beavis t-shirt, and gray and yellow sweatshirt. I'd be embarrassed, but everyone in here is dressed just like me, except Matt, who goes everywhere in his basketball jersey, jeans, and black hoodie.

"Should I get some mustard?" Matt asks—maybe I'll open the pack of razors in our cart and kill myself.

"Do you eat mustard?" I ask him instead.

"Sometimes..."

I can't take it anymore. "Matt! It's Friday night! Let's go out!"

"There's a lot of sodium in this," he says, inspecting the mustard.

I grab it from him and drop it into the cart.

"Come on," I say. "Do you think that girl you like is wandering around a grocery store right now?"

He sighs. "Probably—probably this one, too..."

"Aww. It's too bad then that you didn't get together since you're both such losers."

He looks at me. Finally, I have his attention. "Let's go to Justin's party," I say.

"I have plans." He pushes the cart onward.

"Reading is not plans."

"I'm not stopping you from going."

"You kind of are; my car's still at Nick's."

He rolls his eyes, which is fair. My poor baby's always at Nick's. Anthony does a pretty good job patching her back up, but she's determined to fall apart again—saucy little thing.

We walk into an aisle that has a bunch of local college merch.

"I have to finish moving in." Matt tosses a UCSB beanie in the cart. "And I have to finalize my schedule. I know I want to major in business, but they want me to pick a minor, too. My grandpa says I should pick something sensible, like economics, but I suck at math, and my school counselor said a lot of students choose to minor in something fun. So, then I'm thinking, what about creative writing or screenwriting? But I've also always had an interest in music, like maybe composition—"

I scream. "Just come to the party, and I'll let you bore me to death with your college plans."

It's not that I love high school parties, but it's something, and it's better than this.

"Will you read my screenplay?" he asks.

268

Ugh, of course he asks that. His screenplay is this block of paper that rambles and circles. He told me the plot while he was writing it, trying to get me to help him through his more problematic places. It's about a young high school guy who has a big crush on a delightful girl in his math class, but he's torn because his girlfriend, mean as she is, is super popular. It's despicable that he tries to justify hanging on to Caradine for so long in such an obvious and boring screenplay.

I even tried to read it once. I got to the fifteenth page when I had to stop for my own sanity. Like, literally, reading this thing will drive you insane. He talks about entering it in festivals. I don't have the heart to tell him I wouldn't use it to wipe my butt. Promising to read it is promising to find a way around telling him it's a piece of crap.

"Fine," I say. That's how much I want to go to the party.

44 JUSTIN'S PORSCHE

JOLENE

I thought Piper was a bad driver. She ran reds because she wasn't paying attention. He runs them because he feels like it. He speeds, he tailgates, he races an Audi in congested traffic and cheers loudly when he wins. I should text my parents and tell them I love them.

"You hungry? We could grab a bite," he yells over the air, whipping past us.

I've given up trying to maintain my braid and let it fly all over the place.

"I ate before the game, and then during the game," I say.

"Let's stop for drinks," he says, taking an exit off the 101.

The car slows for the light, and I pull down the passenger-side visor and check the mirror. My hair's more than just a little wind-blown but doesn't look bad. It looks like I've been driving fast, in a fast car—not the worst look.

45 JUSTIN'S PARTY

PIPER

Everything is falling into place. Justin's driving Jolene to the party, and they left before me and aren't even here yet. If I'm right—and I am—I should have them together by the end of the night, and Anthony will realize Jolene's off the market. I wonder when he'll ask me to Homecoming—where is he anyway? I know he can't be as early as me since he had to go back to school on the bus, unload equipment, and shower, but other guys from the team are already here, and the cheerleaders just came in their uniforms.

One of them approaches me. I smile tightly. She doesn't know her reign as most popular girl is about to come screeching to a halt.

"Piper," Tay-Tay whines, "you haven't seen Justin, have you?"

"No," I tell her. I don't want her to shoot the messenger, so I don't tell her he's driving Jolene here. She'll figure it out. "Maybe he stopped to pick up something for the party."

"Where's that friend of yours, the one who was sitting by Justin at the game?"

"Who?" I ask. "Oh, Jolene? I wouldn't call her a friend." I scoff to sell it. "She's just this new girl with, like, zero friends. Justin and I were joking that she looks like one of those ugly dogs that you kind of feel bad for."

Tay breathes out a laugh. "You know I wanted you on the team, right?" she says. But come on, she's captain. If she wanted me on the team, I'd be on the team. "We took a team vote, and I was outnumbered." Oh. "You should try out again at the semester break."

"Okay," I say. Yeah. After Justin breaks up with her, and I start dating Anthony, she'll be begging me to join cheer. What a condescending slut!

Hopefully, arranging her and Justin's breakup tonight won't take too much of my attention so I can spend the bulk of the party with Anthony. Speaking of which—

Whenever we're at a party, Anthony usually leans up against some wall somewhere by himself. Sure enough, there he is—on the far side of the room, past the crowd of dancing teenagers actually having fun— single-handedly supporting the wall from falling down on us.

I don't know how he manages to be by himself so much. You'd think people would constantly harass him. Maybe everyone's caught on that he's pretty boring at parties. You can't keep his attention for longer than ten seconds before he excuses himself to help the host with something or some other boring

272

thing I would never do at a party—like helping clean up.

I push the throngs of idiots out of my way and nuzzle in beside him, back against the wall like him.

He checks his watch, probably anxious about leaving his little sister home alone with their mom.

I take a big breath as if to say, "Oh man, what a party." He smirks in response, lowering his watch arm.

I tilt my head up toward him while we stare off at who-knows-what. One of the football players screams something unintelligible at a larger football player. Anthony shifts. The dude calls the other a name and walks away, and I sense Anthony relax a little next to me. He probably was getting ready to interfere if things got too heated—typical.

I roll my eyes, then notice Justin's fourteen-year-old sister sitting on the side of a couch where a few football players sit, eyeing her in ways that I doubt she gets the full meaning of—and does she know each has a reputation for being a player off the field more than on? I almost worry if Justin's gonna get home soon and maybe keep an eye on that—it isn't my job.

"You know when Justin's getting here?" Anthony asks.

I'm about to answer with more truth than necessary, when I catch sight of something that alarms me, but I can't place why—Matt Craddick and Jason Canvis walk into the living room. There's something about Matt that someone said something about—maybe the uneasy feeling is just that I haven't seen him in a while. If that makes sense.

273

"When's the last time you saw Matt at a party?" I ask Anthony with a chuckle.

"How long have I known him?"

Then it hits me. "Oh no," I say.

"What?" he asks.

"Something Jolene said," I tell him. "That girl is driving me crazy!"

I don't really care who Jolene dates, as long as someone distracts her from Anthony. But if she still has feelings for Matt, I won't have the bonus of Justin dumping Tay-Tay. It was going to be so satisfying watching that smug smirk slide off her face. It'd make up for all the times she talked down to me, belittled me, acted like I wasn't there, didn't invite me to her birthday parties, didn't fight for me to join cheer. She'd regret how she's treated me—if she ever traced her breakup back to me.

Anthony looks confused, but I'm not about to elaborate.

JASON

Maybe I should go back to high school. There aren't nearly as many hot girls inside Matt's apartment as there are at Justin's party. Sometimes, there are a few when our neighbors come over, but I've already written them off as uninterested. Dillon was over once when I got out of the shower and didn't have a shirt on and laughed. Charlene just flat-out refuses to talk to me, even when I offer her half of my cupcake.

Britta and Cilla, Swedish twins wearing their JV cheer uniforms even though there's no JV football

274

games on Fridays, laugh with Justin's freshman brother, Noah. Shoot, if he can get them to dance with him—

"Hey, Britta," I say. "Bet'cha've been wondering where I've been at."

The trick to distinguishing between the two twins is Britta always wears her big, curly blond hair down, and Cilla likes to wear it up. I wonder if they prefer it that way, or if they're just tired of everyone confusing them all the time. Maybe they don't always keep the same hairstyle, and people confuse them, but they never bother correcting them.

"We heard you dropped out of school," Britta says in her Swedish accent. "You should have stayed."

So, I've been missed. I had no idea Britta cared.

"You would have learned not to end a sentence with a preposition." She turns and walks away.

"That's a little prescriptive," I say to Noah.

He shrugs.

PIPER

I'm not sure what I'm going to say to Matt to make sure he doesn't absolutely ruin everything, but I head toward him anyway. I have to act fast. But Caradine, who I didn't know was here, beats me to him. Apparently, it's not enough to sit in the bleachers during the football game and view high school boys from afar.

She emerges from nowhere, grabs Matt's shoulder, and says, "I saw your girlfriend tonight."

I grind my teeth. That's all I need—for him to realize Jolene is coming tonight. He'll reconnect with her, and that'll be the end of everything: my entire afternoon of planning!

I push her arm out of my way. "Excuse me, Caradine. Isn't there a Little League game you should be at?" I drag Matt a few feet away, so Caradine would get the hint, and leave us alone. "What are you doing here?"

"Aww," he says insufferably. "It's good to see you, too, Pipe."

"Well," I say, thinking fast, as I'm prone to do. "Turns out Justin's dad's kicking everyone out. So—"

"Very funny," he says. "Where's Justin?"

Fine. That wasn't my best lie. Justin's dad never cares about anything. Justin could have a party on the roof during a fire, and his dad would be chill.

"He's driving somebody here," I say, "so he's taking his time—hopefully."

At least, I think that's why they aren't here yet, although, knowing how he drives, it's possible they're in a ditch somewhere.

"Tay-Tay's already here—" Matt says.

"No. Not Tay-Tay."

"Good," he says with a roll of his eyes.

"That's what I've been saying!" I slap his arm excitedly. No one seems to care whether Justin dates a cheating slut except me, and now Matt.

"I've been waiting for Justin to get rid of her," he says. "So, who's his new girl? Do I know her?"

Crap sandwich.

"Um," I say. "How do I know if you know her? I don't know everyone you might know. I mean, I've never seen you two talking or anything. So—"

"You're being weird. Who is she?"

"Jo-Jo Standwichsen." I hardly open my mouth when I speak.

"JOLENE STANSEN?"

How did he get that out of what I said?

I throw my head back and exhale loudly. "No. Justine Montgomerswitch."

"That's not a real name."

"Prove it."

"How does Justin know Jolene?" he asks.

I scoff. "Everyone knows Jolene—"

"How?"

"They go to the same school."

"So?" he asks. "That doesn't mean he knows her."

He does like her. If he didn't, he wouldn't want details. Great. I'd better cut him off before he gets too carried away and holds what I'm about to do against me.

"I'm setting her up with Justin, so he'll dump Tay-Tay. Don't ruin this for me, you stupid"—I slap his arm—"handsome"—slap again—"giant." Three slaps total, plus the one from earlier.

The corners of his eyes fall, and his chin juts up. "Does she like him?"

"Tay-Tay?" I ask. "I mean, I think she does—"

"Not Tay-Tay."

"Yeah!" I say. "He's all she ever talks about!" Not a lie. We've been talking about him a lot, at least today...

"Really?" he asks.

"Uh-huh. You bet."

Then, my life gets even worse. Anthony joins us.

"Have you guys seen Justin?" He towers over me, slightly taller than even Matt.

"Justin?" I ask. "No. He's not coming."

"He's driving Jolene, so he's 'taking his time,'" Matt says.

"He's driving Jolene?" I don't like the way Anthony says her name, like it's—well, I guess he didn't really say it in a certain way, I just don't like that he said it. "He's gonna do it wrong. I should be driving her."

I exhale loudly, again. "Well, she likes Justin. So—" But they aren't listening to me.

"How do you even know her?" Matt asks.

But Anthony isn't listening to Matt either. His head's turned, and he's looking at a commotion behind us. Noah and the Swedish JV cheer twins who won the class comp earlier today laugh—well, the twins laugh.

Anthony raises his eyebrows.

"Who is that weird kid?" someone asks.

"That's Justin's little brother," someone else says, also laughing.

Anthony turns back to Matt. "Oh. I tackled her in the hallway. 'Go Number Twelve.' Excuse me." In three long strides he's standing over Noah. "Hey, Noah."

"Hey, Anthony!" Noah's eyes, like everyone's, light up when he sees him.

"How're your ants doing?" he asks.

"Oh! Real good!" Noah says. "You wanna see them?"

"Let's do it," Anthony and Noah leave the room.

Of course. Thank you, Noah, for making Anthony leave. I remind myself my dentist told me I've got to stop grinding my teeth.

"You guys know where Justin is?" Jason asks, suddenly with us.

I'm about to ignore him when Matt beats me to it.

"Piper, you have to find a different way to break up Justin and Tay-Tay," Matt says.

I turn on him, my frustration beyond a little sizzle. Not only do I have to deal with Jolene and her refusal to play her part efficiently and Matt and his obstruction, but now Anthony's whisked away by Justin's needy brother. It all flares up to the surface.

"She's into him, okay? Drop it," I yell at him.

"You're using her," Matt says, annoyingly calm.

"I am not. They're going to be great together. Best couple ever."

It's getting warm in here. Or maybe that's just all the blood rushing to my head.

"He doesn't have anything in common with her. He thinks Harry Potter is Zelda, and Zelda is cereal."

"What?" I ask. "No. He doesn't. Why? Is Jolene some sort of Slytherpuff? She failed to mention she was bookish."

"You don't even know her," he accuses.

I scoff, feigning offense. "I love the girl. I don't care if she's read for pleasure."

The front doors burst open. Justin enters the house, heaving a consternated-looking Jolene along with him. He plants her next to him, stretches out his arms to the group, and shouts, "TWENTY-ONE - ZERO!" to

279

which the student body in attendance explodes in cheers.

I roll my eyes, but when I turn around, Matt's gone. I frantically search for him, but it's too late. He's making his way toward her.

JOLENE

I'm beginning to feel not so much like a person but more like a child's blanket that's taken everywhere, appreciated, loved even, but also completely worn out after being dragged all over town.

When he yells the score of the game to the crowd, he lets go of my arm, and I can breathe long enough to take in his house. It's huge—mansion-like, larger than Mamie's, with a view over Goleta instead of the Eiffel Tower. It's also more modern, with angles and stark colors—lots of blacks, whites, yellows, branchy plants, and strange, painful-looking triangular art.

There's an enormous staircase leading to the upper stories—I can imagine getting lost and being unable to find my way out. It's a daunting thought since everything is drowning me: the blaring house music, the partiers, the vaulted ceilings, the low lights, the smell of sweat and freshly mopped floors, not to mention the emotional pressure from Piper and now from Justin. He's taken a car ride to mean that we're some sort of item. It's all made so much worse by the fact everyone knows he's dating someone else, but nobody seems surprised or to care, except me. And that's not even my biggest complaint about it. There was no training in France for navigating situations like this. *Pirouettes?* Yes. *Fouette* turns. *Oui.* High school parties? No.

"Can I take your jacket?" Justin asks me as he pulls his arms out of his.

I rethink the revealing light-blue gathered and corseted top I'm wearing. "No, thanks. I'm fine."

I search for Anthony.

"I'll be right back," Justin says. "Want a drink?"

"Just water."

He leaves, and I feel my muscles relax. But I'm only given a short bereavement when I feel a weird sense, like someone's looking at me.

I turn, and there he is: Matt Craddick, standing feet away. I was right the year before when I thought Matt-gaze would be something you could feel. My body tenses up again in surprise, confusion, and panic. I take a moment to stop gaping and shut my mouth. I was counting on never seeing him again—no, not counting—yes, counting. With all the plans I've made for the school year, I never once calculated on him actually being in my life again.

And he looks good. He wears a black basketball jersey and dark jeans. His hair is the same: buzzed short and black, but his smile has changed. There's an urgency now, and a radiating excitement. Or am I just projecting my own?

"Jolene," he says. "I can't believe it's you!"

My heart sinks a little. "Yeah. I guess I've changed a lot." Was I really that ugly before that I'm hardly even recognizable now?

"No," he says. "It's not that. It's just that I'm so glad to see you—I can hardly believe you're actually here."

281

I gape again.

"How was France?"

I never know how to answer that question. It's a country. I was there a year. It's a million different things. If we had the time, I could tell him chapters' worth of how France was, but I don't know how long he has, so he gets an abridged version.

"Very French." Very abridged.

He smiles—warm and inviting, like I didn't just give him a weak joke of an answer but something witty and fun.

"But how are you?" I ask. "Are you living in town?"

"Yeah," he says.

I've forgotten the sound of his voice and how it stills the air around me.

"My grandpa hooked me up with a place and a job. I'm going to UCSB."

"Mrs. Diefenbacher's alma mater," I say.

"How do you remember that?"

Suddenly, it feels like nothing's changed. We're still two kids in math class.

"It was on the final, along with how many pets she had."

But of course he didn't take the final. He was gone before that, and I was gone shortly after.

"It was?" he asks. "Let's see. She had three cats, two dogs, a frog—six?"

I make the error sound of a game show. "You forgot the rat in her garage. I forgot that one, too."

"See, I don't think that should count." He tilts his head to the side.

"I don't either. But she said it counted because she named it."

"Ratasaurus!" Matt says, remembering, a glow spreading across his face.

We're laughing like idiots when a cloud appears over us—Justin returns with drinks. The one he hands me is not water.

Before I can protest, he puts an arm around my waist and addresses Matt. "Stop talking to my woman."

The expression on Matt's face requires immediate damage control.

"I'm not—" But what do I say? Had I given Justin any reason to believe I was his girlfriend, or "woman," as he put it? How do I tell Matt I'm not interested whatsoever in this man whose arm is around me without embarrassing Justin? Or should I not care? Obviously, he doesn't care about what I think. I don't know! It all happens too suddenly, too fast! I can only grasp and stutter and hope he miraculously interprets my efforts. "He's not—"

"I'm kidding," Justin says. "Glad you came. Grab some food. Take some home if you want."

I scrunch an eyebrow and look at him.

He turns his gaze to me. "Come on."

Before I know it, he's pulling me away through the jungle of teenagers.

"I was talking to him—" I say.

"I didn't realize you knew Matt." He keeps one arm around me, the other dividing the house guests. The farther into the crowd we get, the further I'm in over my head. It's not so much his arm—since without it we'd quickly get separated by the crowd, and I'd be lost forever, like falling overboard on a cruise ship.

A girl I don't know waves at me as Justin shoves past her.

"Hi Jolene," she says.

I've never seen her a day in my life, and she knows my name. Is this what being popular's like? People just know you and want to know you? Is this because she thinks I'm with Justin?

He brings me down a hallway into a smaller room with fewer people. Some guys play a game I recognize—a first-person shooter that Logan says is "for party gamers," and a few girls sit around looking bored. I feel for them, but can't they take a turn, or leave?

Then something pulls my attention away, and the pull is strong. Nearby, looking at a wall full of Granite family portraits, are Anthony and Justin's freshman brother.

Now Justin's arm around me feels like it means something, and I wish I had thrown it off before we came in. But it's too late. Justin cinches it tighter, like a boa constrictor.

"Justin hates this one," Noah says. "He says he looks like a monkey."

Noah and Anthony laugh, and Justin narrows his eyes.

"What are you guys doing?" he asks them. Anthony and Noah turn and take us in.

"Noah's showing me his favorite Granite family photos," Anthony says. His eyes meet mine and smile. "Hi, Jolene."

If Justin's arm around me bothers Anthony, he doesn't show it. Maybe he's just skilled at hiding it—I hope. I wouldn't mind at all if he raged with jealousy, and started throwing things. He could grab Justin's arm, twist it, and Justin could yell and tackle him to the ground. They grapple until finally Anthony rises, triumphant. He throws me over his shoulder and carries me off into the sunset...

"Hi, Anthony," I say. "Good game. You played..." Is saying "well" too proper? Is saying "good" too mundane? Has too much time lapsed to say anything?

"Thank you, Jolene," he says, his grin meeting his eyes and having a little dance party. "I did play."

"Alright," Justin says, perhaps feeling the energy between Anthony and myself—or is that pitiful wishful thinking? Imagine if our energy were so strong other people could feel it. "We'll let you get back to your monkey."

"I actually wanted to see that," I say.

"Let's not." Justin turns me away from it—away from Anthony.

"How's your head?" Anthony asks, moving around Justin.

I've almost forgotten my earlier injury.

"What head?" I ask.

He laughs and points to me. "That one."

"It's fine," I say, smiling, blushing, doing all the things.

"Good. It'd be sad if it ruined you and made you all psychotic or something."

"How do you know I wasn't totally different before?"

"You're right," he says. "I only know you post-incident. What were you like before?"

"I wish I could remember!"

He laughs.

"Did you know Jason and Matt are here?" Justin asks Anthony. "You should go talk to them. Gotta maintain your friendships, now that we hardly see them—"

"But when I tried to talk to them—" I protest again, but I'm cut off.

"Okay. Bye," Justin says to Anthony, dragging me back the way we came, his arm around me again.

ANTHONY

I watch as Justin manhandles Jolene down the hall.

"Where are we going?" she asks him.

"Somewhere my friends aren't," Justin says.

"Weird you threw a party then." Her words are playful—but there's frustration in her tone.

I'm starting to understand why I got a weird call from Justin before the game—not a text—a call. He was on about loyalty, the Greek, and girls. I thought someone must have said something about Tay-Tay or something—nothing made any sense. But seeing him dragging Jolene down the hall clears it all up.

I'm almost torn. It'd be great if Justin moved on, left his cheating girlfriend, but not with Jolene. She's too sweet for him, too gleaming. He'd drag her down. She needs someone who'll match her warmth, her glow.

I turn to Noah. "You all right?"

"Yeah," he says. "I'm gonna find Todd and his friend Weston and see if they want to shoot some hoops out back."

"Good man," I say.

He gives me five down low, and I catch up with Jolene and Justin. I put my arms around their shoulders and stick my head between theirs.

"Alright," I say. "Let's go talk to Matt and Jason."

Justin looks at my hand on his shoulder and tries to shake it off without letting go of Jolene. "No, man. You go on your own."

He breaks away from her to shove me off, and I let him.

"Do you want to go with me to talk to Matt and Jason?" I ask Jolene.

"Sure," she says, her expression a mixture of bewilderment and exasperation.

"Okay. Fine." Justin throws his hands up in the air, like a kid at his birthday party who wants to play Marco Polo but is outnumbered by all his friends who'd rather just swim and splash around.

46 WHAT'S LIFE WITHOUT
A LITTLE MANIPULATION?

PIPER

I don't know which is worse—the boring party or the impossible friends who are actively trying to ruin my life. It's eleven o'clock, and Justin still hasn't dumped Tay-Tay. All he's managed is to drag Jolene all over the house for who-knows-what-reason and further annoy me.

But then, why have I noticed Justin's obvious pursual of Jolene—but Tay-Tay hasn't? Where is she?

There's a beam of red hair; I make my way toward it and tap Kaila on the shoulder. "Kay-Kay, where's Tay-Tay?"

"Don't call me that," she says.

"Oh. I thought I heard Tay call you—"

"Yeah," she says. "Don't call me that."

"Okay. Do you know where she is?"

She clicks her tongue and looks away. She's always clicking her tongue. Makes me want to rip it out.

"What do you want?" she asks.

288

"Where's Tay?" I ask her again, seething with polite bubbliness.

"Well," she says, sucking her teeth like they're sour. "She and Jesse just went into the kitchen, so where do you think?" She waggles her head back and forth like a dog's tail, and I want to smack her pointy little smirking face. But I don't have the time—or the nerve. She's almost a complete nobody, but she probably has some sway during cheer auditions.

I turn and rise on tiptoes to see better. Justin, Jolene, and Anthony come my way, so I shove people who don't move fast enough and head toward my friends.

"There you are," I say to Justin, placing my hands on his chest to prevent him from going farther or not paying attention. "I need to talk to you."

I grab his arm and pull him a few steps to the side. Knowing Jolene and Anthony, they won't be too concerned with what we're saying.

"Jolene told me she hopes you'll ask her to Homecoming," I tell him.

"Yeah?" He turns and looks at Jolene, a grin growing across his mouth.

It makes me almost feel guilty about lying through every single tooth I have—

"Too bad you're still dating Tay-Tay," I tell him.

The corners of his eyes and lips fall—the exact reaction I'm looking for.

"She's in the kitchen."

He walks off. This might actually all work out.

I turn back, ready to pull apart Jolene and Anthony.

JOLENE

289

Anthony and I get into the living room, and Piper comes up to us, then takes Justin aside. I search for Matt and Jason but can't find them anywhere.

"I don't see them," I tell Anthony who's got the height advantage.

If he's looking at all, he'll be able to spot them. He searches but shakes his head.

We stand awkwardly for a minute. I fold my arms in front of me and look at people's shoes. I don't want to be in his way if he wants to go talk to someone else. Of course, I don't want him to...

"What's going on with Piper and Justin?"

Is he asking because he's into Piper? How much information am I allowed to tell him?

"She's trying to break him up with Tay-Tay."

His eyes widen, I suppose at Piper's ambition. It makes me laugh a little, and his expression softens.

"Do you want them to break up, too?" I ask—oh. Does that sound like I want them to separate so I can date Justin? I just meant "too" as in "Piper does, too," not "I do, too."

ANTHONY

Does she want them to break up so she can date him? That would go along with what Justin and Piper said, but every time they're together, she looks like she wants to get away from him. Maybe I should be clearer about where I stand. I should let her know I only want them to split for Justin's sake, not because I'm into Tay, or something.

290

"He deserves better," I say, "someone nice."

JOLENE

Is he implying that I would be this "better," "nice" girlfriend, or is he saying I wouldn't be good for Justin either? After everything I've gone through, am I still not enough for these people?

He tilts his head back with a huge smile, then beams down at me. "But whoever that poor girl is would be too good for him."

Every tense muscle in my body releases, and I let it show.

"He's not always..." It feels like he's about to list reasons Justin wouldn't deserve a nice girl, but he trails off—maybe realizing he doesn't want to bash his friend too hard, but I can see his point. He wants his friend to be happy, but not at the cost of some innocent girl.

"Maybe we should find him someone who can't see very well," I suggest. "Then she won't know when he's ogling her."

Anthony looks at me for a moment, then lightly chuckles, as if he appreciates and sympathizes that I speak from experience.

"Weren't you wearing glasses earlier?" he asks, eyeing me sideways. "How's your vision?"

"Oh, but I'm not nice," I say.

"Really?"

"No. I'm very mean. I kicked a puppy once."

"No, you didn't."

291

"No, I wouldn't ever," I say. "I'd let it bite me—but I'm like, crazy mean."

He nods in agreement as if there's no way he believes me.

My phone vibrates in my pocket. I know who it is before I check it—oh. I thought it was going to be my dad, but it's Logan.

"Shoot!" I say. "I forgot."

"What?"

"I had plans with my friend Logan tonight," I tell him. "We were supposed to fight some zombies."

"Logan Monnel?" he asks.

I'm surprised he knows him. I let him know with my smile. "Yeah."

"He's your boyfriend?" he asks, raising the end the way grade school kids do.

"No. He likes—someone else, and I like—not him."

"'Not him'?"

I press my lips together and nod. He scratches his cheekbone with the back of his index finger.

"Fair enough."

He looks around, then at me, motioning his head toward the staircase. We walk over and sit on the bottom few steps, close to the railing in case anyone wants to get by.

We're silent for a moment, but it's not awkward— it's the way it feels when you've known someone for years and you trust they're not thinking horrible thoughts about you in the silence, mixed with the excitement of new feelings and the accompanying gastrointestinal butterflies.

The music's loud, but it's nice to sit with him without having to think up something to say. The singer says, "Get up and dance," over and over, and will probably keep his demand even after all the world burns.

Anthony leans over, tilting his head toward me while watching the party. "I know we just sat down, but I think we should get up and dance."

I laugh. He smiles, stands—oh, he's serious. He stretches his hand down, helps me up, and doesn't let go of me until we reach the dance floor.

PIPER

Anthony and Jolene are not where I left them. That's not good. Hopefully, they didn't go find a room somewhere. Maybe he's holding up the wall again, but they're all clear. I scan the dance floor and spot them. He's not hard to find, really, even though the last place I'd look is dancing. I've seen him dance before, at dances and stuff, but never in my life at a party. Ugh. All the walls are gonna come crashing down. Worse still, he's dancing with Jolene—not even in a group— just him and Jolene. I tried to make it clear to her, he's off limits, but she doesn't seem to get that showing him any attention at all is showing him far too much. I'm gonna have to step in.

I push through the crowd and grab Jolene's hand, concern all over my face. "Can I talk to you for a second?"

She nods, looks apologetically at Anthony, and allows me to lead her away from him and the dancers. Once we're out of earshot, I turn on her.

"I just had to say something before it got too far, because it was looking like you were getting really close with him, and I just can't do this to you," I say.

Her face is perfect—it looks like it's about to shatter, probably would if I flicked it.

I snatch up her hands and make a tear come out—I should be an actress, for reals, you guys. "I don't want guys to come between us, and," I act like this is excruciatingly painful for me, "earlier, before you got here, we were flirting, and he was hinting he was going to ask me to the dance, and I was, like, 'What about Jolene? It seemed like you were kind of into her', and he was like, 'Don't hold that against me. I was just trying to make you jealous', and I don't know why he's playing us like this, or why he'd go off and dance with you after being with me all night, but I knew you wouldn't let him manipulate and gaslight us."

JOLENE

I gape at Piper, aware my mouth must be so wide open a bird could fly in.

None of it could be true at all. I can't picture it. I can't picture her version of Anthony who'd go from girl to girl—not when he's been easy and sweet and didn't want to say mean things about his kind-of-mean friend.

She turns away from me and runs her fingers through her hair. If she looked at me, she'd see

294

confusion all over my face. I can't believe what she said about Anthony being insincere, but the fact she felt strongly enough about him to say it means this whole thing is a mess.

Nobody else hears Justin's little sister, Guineth. At first, I don't hear her either. I mean, there's no real reason she should have drawn my attention—she's a super pretty, blond, tan, freshman female Justin.

I've never even spoken to her. But as I turn away from Piper—no longer interested in staring at the back of her hair—I catch Anthony's gaze. He watches me with sad eyes, then turns and strides toward Guineth—excusing his way through the crowd. It's only then I notice Justin's sister trying to grab a picture frame out of the hands of a broad, blond gorilla holding it out of her reach.

"Stop!" she says. "Put it back!"

47 PARTY BATMAN

JUSTIN

I open the doors, walk down the hallway and into the kitchen, expecting to find Tay-Tay and some cheerleaders chatting away, but instead, she's sitting on my counter, locked in an aggressive lip war with Jesse.

I've heard they were cheating on me—I've heard it a lot, and I always thought I'd be furious if I ever found any proof of it. I'd throw things, I'd yell, I'd beat him to a bloody pulp—but I can't see the point now. I don't want to do any of that. I'm—hmm. I think I'm relieved.

"We're done, Tay," I inform her, turning and leaving the room—not even sure she heard me.

"Wait," she says. Behind me, there's a scuffle and feet scampering to gain traction on the marble floor. "Wait! Justin!"

I keep walking.

PIPER

I'm about to ask Jolene where Anthony's going when the doors to the hallway that lead to the kitchen fling open, and Justin appears, entering the living room.

I suspect Tay-Tay and Jesse were making out in the kitchen, and I thought Justin would be angrier than when we were all watching a movie and Noah's ants escaped and got all over his room. But he's calm— almost as if he walked in on his sister's cat sleeping rather than his girlfriend making out with Jesse.

Right behind him, Tay-Tay flies in, grabbing his shirt. "Excuse me! You don't just get to walk away and not talk about this!"

He faces her and tilts his head to the side.

JOLENE

"I'm just looking at it," the blond gorilla says to Guineth. He has no clue Anthony's making his way toward him.

Someone touches my arm—worried it's Justin, I turn and see Piper. She smirks pointedly, so I shift to see what she's looking at: near the door that leads to the kitchen, Justin and Tay-Tay fight.

"Give it to me!" Guineth says, stealing back my attention, still trying desperately to retrieve the frame from this guy.

From this distance and in this light, it's hard to tell what's in the frame, but it looks like a portrait of a beautiful blond woman—maybe Mrs. Granite.

297

PIPER

"I can't believe you're doing this right before Homecoming!" Tay-Tay yells.

I have to give her props for pulling out all the manipulative stops. Guilting him into staying with her when he's just caught her cheating on him with Jesse, his own friend—well, his sort-of friend—low carb friend—it's masterful. If it were a sport, I'd cheer.

JOLENE

Anthony reaches Guineth and the guffawing creep. He peels back the guy's fingers, releasing the picture frame.

"Ow! Ow!" the guy yells. "Come on, man!"

Anthony ignores his complaints, holding him by the back of his collar as if this guy were a rag he had just used to clean the floor by the toilet.

"You okay, Guineth?'" Anthony asks, handing her the frame, his tone big-brotherly.

"As long as he leaves my house," Guineth says, crossing her arms, anger and relief on her face.

"I was just joking!"

"Time to go, Mike." Anthony deftly marches him out of the living room.

PIPER

"What are you complaining about? Now you can go to Homecoming with Jesse, like we both know you want to," Justin says.

Tay-Tay flips her ponytail, shifts her weight onto one leg, and scoffs. "I don't know what you're talking about."

I take my props back; trying to gaslight him now is pointless. A smarter narcissist would do a better job manipulating this conversation. I would.

"Oh, I get it," Tay-Tay says. "This is because of Jolene Stansen." She waits, perhaps to gauge his reaction, before adding, "You think I can't see you flirting with her from the field?"

Hmm—maybe I have to give back those props again. He probably should feel at least somewhat guilty there. But it doesn't seem to land. Guess she didn't fully buy it when I told her we were just sitting with Jolene to be nice.

"This isn't about Jolene," he says, to which Tay laughs loudly and abruptly, making the few people in the room who weren't watching turn their heads.

But Justin shrugs. "Okay, fine. It is."

He ascends the first few stairs leading up to his room.

She grabs his arm again. "Wait, Justin!"

But so far, the only place Tay-Tay's efforts have gotten her is nowhere. All I need to do now to cement their breakup is ensure Justin doesn't take Tay-Tay back in these next few precious minutes. The last thing I need is for one of them to apologize and ruin everything. No—that would not distract Jolene from Anthony at all!

But Jolene's not paying attention again. She's watching Anthony. Ugh!

299

I grab her shoulders and start pushing her in Justin's direction. "Go after him!"

"What—why?" she asks.

Anthony suddenly stands in front of us. "Where'd Justin go? I gotta tell him he's paying for Mike's Lug."

"He's upstairs breaking up with Tay-Tay," I tell him, crossing my arms.

Anthony sighs, a hint of a smile breaking through.

"At least one good thing happened tonight." he heads toward the stairs.

"You also won the game," Jolene calls after him.

"Oh, yeah." He shrugs and scales the steps.

I'd watch him, but I'm too busy glaring at Jolene, looking at him like he were a little puppy, hands clasped in front of her chest and everything.

"He doesn't even care about the game—like winning is just something he does," Jolene muses, probably to herself. "And then he heard Guineth when no one else was paying attention and effortlessly disposed of Mike. It's like he's the party's Batman. He broods against the wall and only comes out for justice."

I miss my old life—pre-Jolene. I grind my teeth. If she won't willingly enter a relationship with Justin, I have to ease her into it—trick her into it. If she gets in too deep, she's the type who'll be too nice to break his heart. And he's the type to make it difficult. Although, now that I think about it, it might be enough if Anthony thinks Jolene's in a relationship with Justin. If he's upstairs when Jolene checks on Justin—that might be the best-case scenario yet. He'll think Justin means a lot to her, whether or not they start anything.

Now to get Jolene up there before either Anthony or Justin come back down.

I put my hands together like a saintly, patient nanny trying to communicate with a spoiled brat.

"Jolene?" I keep my voice even and sweet. "Our dear friend Justin is so—so close to being free of his terrible girlfriend. You're the only one who can stop him from taking her back—" I sense her objecting before she starts. "I'm not saying you have to go out with him. You just need to be there. Let him know Tay-Tay isn't his only option."

"But—"

"Please," I beg.

That does the trick. She looks up the stairs, and I know I've got her. I try not to smirk too much as she takes the first few steps. Instead, I simply let out a sigh. I am good at this—I should break people apart more often.

48 A LONG TIME COMING

JUSTIN

It's true what people say—Tay-Tay isn't bright. Anyone with any sense would know I don't want to be anywhere near her, but she follows me into my room anyway, opening the door I just slammed.

"How dare you break up with me!" I bet they can hear her voice downstairs. "You'd be nothing without me!"

I scoff. Over the last year, she has dropped little bombs like this. "You're so lucky to have me," she'd say, or "I'm such a trophy girlfriend," or "You're such a loser." It bothered me, but I laughed it all off when we were in public and said the same sort of things back to her in private. But now, I can't believe I ever put up with her. Well, no more.

She walks up to me, close, and puts her hands on her chest, right under her collarbone. "I am the cheer captain, and all you have is a slutty sister and Noah."

"Get out." I try to sound menacing, scaring her into it.

She clicks her tongue, turns, and drags her arm across my desk, sending my computer monitor, keyboard, homework, mouse, and magazines flying. "Oops." She goes out the door.

Anthony comes through it, squeezing past her. He bends down and helps me restore my monitor with me. Its screen got cracked, but I'm sick of this monitor anyway.

"Tell me she's mad because you finally dumped her," Anthony says as he puts the battery back inside my mouse.

I glare at him but let part of my face smile. The truth is, I wanted it to work out with Tay, but not because I enjoyed her company. I felt like because our relationship was so much work; I had to stay with it, because otherwise, the struggle would have been for nothing. And it felt like I had to have a substantial reason to break up with her. If I were going to hurt her that way, I couldn't do it and remain a decent person unless I had a solid reason. It was all stupid—you're allowed to break up with someone for any reason—but catching her red-handed cheating on me with Jesse, well that's a decent reason.

"Too long a time coming," I say.

"I'm surprised you didn't throw her out the window."

I laugh and twist my broken monitor so it faces the way I like it.

"Yeah, I just didn't want Guineth and Noah to have to explain to people why their big brother went to jail. I mean, I went out with her for a year. What was I thinking?"

We both laugh at my expense. A heavy load I didn't realize was there finally lifting from off my chest.

49 STEPS

JOLENE

Considerate of the Granites to have such a large house with such a huge grand staircase. I need the time climbing it to think—time away from Piper. But even now, thinking isn't coming easily. The air is thick with noise and beer, even removed from the mob way up here.

It's ironic; during the day, when there aren't as many people, it's probably peaceful here. It's just Justin, his twin siblings, and his dad alone in this house, way up on this hill, separated—like I am, down in my creek, from any neighbors.

The walls are all windows. You can tell where the ocean is: it's where the lights stop—the stars picking it up again in the sky.

Logan said the Granites were beyond rich. Justin's dad owns Granite Forge—one of the biggest arms manufacturers in the country. It explains their house, and why Justin's so—Justin. But I almost feel bad for him. It must be hard to find your girlfriend cheating on you at your own party—in your own house.

A noise on the landing startles me into looking up. I should have anticipated Tay-Tay—angry—running out of Justin's room, but I didn't.

Both my hands grab the banister in case she shoves me, but she doesn't. She brushes past, and I ease my grip, but then she calls out to me.

"You know—"

Why do I turn to face her? I don't remember making the choice, and when I do, I regret it. Her wet face isn't one I want to see, and this is not a conversation I want to have.

"He doesn't like you. He's just playing with you because you're the pretty new thing, but he'll get tired of you. It wouldn't be the first time he went through a girl in a week." She sniffs, tosses her ponytail, and proceeds down the stairs like royalty, instead of a recently rejected teenager—her posture all perfect, head up, graceful—apart from the repeated sniffs.

I shouldn't feel sorry for her. She cheated on him with Jesse. She was also beautiful, popular, not only could she get any guy she wanted, she had— simultaneously. But her eyes were red, her nose was running. It had all taken its toll. My sister's former best friend. Would Tay end up like Mary? Are we all destined to become Mary?

I reach the top of the stairs, finding my way too quickly. There's a hallway and three doors, each clearly marked: "Guineth's Room," "Noah's Room," and finally, "Justin's Room." I take a second to marvel at how they chose to spell "Guineth," then turn to Justin's door.

What am I doing? Piper says, "Go," and I go? Why!? Why am I listening to her at all?! Because she's popular?! Ugh, that's it—I don't want her to hate me. I've come too far. I've worked too hard to be pretty and popular, and I have it now. If I have popular friends, I must be popular. If I have Justin's attention, I must be pretty. Right?

Involuntarily, my lip crinkles up, raising my cheek, releasing a sneer on my face. Suddenly, getting what I want includes having what I hate. I mean, not "hate" really, but I don't want to date Justin. If I go through that door, I'll be sending a different signal. It'll be harder later to turn him down. I'll also be sending Piper a signal that I'll lie over and play dead whenever she wants me to, all so she'll like me. I'm not even sure I like her! She shows a lot of disregard for how I feel for someone professing to be my friend. And is Tay-Tay right? Will it be me running down those stairs in a few weeks, warning his next victim she'll be me soon?

But then—if I don't knock on his door, if I just turn around and go down the way I came, Piper will be furious. She'll yell at me something about Justin taking Tay-Tay back, and I guess he will. Piper will probably never talk to me again, same with Justin. I'll be right where I started: a single-friend entity, boyfriendless, ignored, snubbed for girls who knock on doors and have popular friends.

Maybe these aren't my only choices—Justin or bust. Maybe, but that's taking a big jump. Piper made it pretty clear Anthony couldn't possibly be interested in me as he's most likely gonna ask her to Homecoming. I struggle to believe it, but people don't lie like that, and if she did—it almost makes things more complicated. And even if I didn't want to be her friend, did I owe her some girl-loyalty to not go after the guy she's liked for years? Would I hold it against her if she did the same to me and went after Matt?

Matt—is he still here? I never expected to see him again, so I planned this whole thing to ensure someone like him would never overlook me again, but he—the real him—is literally downstairs right now, not overlooking me, and I'm about to knock on the bedroom door of Justin Granite's.

It's like a faulty circle: be pretty and popular to get someone like Matt; meanwhile, Matt's right here, but in order to get him, you have to be pretty and popular and date Justin—it doesn't make any sense!

I'm about to turn, to flee, to run down the stairs but someone's laughing behind the door. Tay must not have shut it all the way when she left. My curiosity takes over, and I creep forward.

"She's not cute," Justin's voice says.

I try harder to hide from them than to see them, but their voices are as clear as if they were in the room.

"Meh." That's Anthony's "meh."

I laugh a little quiet laugh. It's so like him.

"Her legs are hot in a skirt, I guess, but that's all I'll give her," Justin says.

I think about the first time I met Justin—the day I wore a miniskirt. Would he have even noticed me

308

without it? I've always thought he probably wouldn't have.

"Her voice is annoying," Justin says. "She's about the dumbest thing on the planet."

Is my voice annoying? Am I dumb? Maybe he took something I said sarcastically as serious, and it came off dumb? But what?

"Honestly, I don't even want to be friends with her, let alone date her, or be seen with her," Justin says.

"You do have terrible taste in women."

But I can hardly hear what Anthony's saying. I'm running down the stairs, tears racing each other down my face. I don't even make the choice to go in or run away, and my life falls apart.

JUSTIN

Anthony finishes plugging my phone charger back into my charging bank. Now that everything's back to normal, it's almost like I never dated Tay-Tay. There's a panda bear she bought me on my bed, but I can tear it apart and burn the pieces later.

"You do have really bad taste in women," Anthony says, "except Jolene, of course."

JOLENE

Each step down the stairs feels like my life collapses more and more. The farther I get from Justin and Anthony, the closer I get to Piper and the rest of the party. Should I find her and tell her I'm leaving? A smart sobbing girl would have looked for her while she was on the stairs. It would take forever to find her. Too many people would notice me crying and I'd never be able to show my face again. It'll be difficult to do that even if no one sees me. I'll have to move to France permanently and change my name to Leslie or something. Maybe I'll send her a text that I've left.

I do a quick scan of the room, just in case she's nearby, and there he is: Matt Craddick. He's looking at me too, with the same expression of shock and horror that's gotta be on my face. It's not my fault I ran into the room just in time to catch him locked in a full-body kiss with Caradine.

If I thought my life was over before, I was an idiot— stupid kid, foolish, and young. Now I'm older and wiser.

Disoriented as I've felt since arriving, I find the front door easily and heave the giant thing open. I didn't realize how heavy it was when Justin opened it earlier.

I break into the chilly night, slamming the mansion door behind me, breathing like my morning alarm has gone off, waking me from my nightmare. But of course, there is no alarm, and my nightmare rides on.

I make it about ten steps before realizing I don't have anywhere to go.

The air is still. The distance mutes and dulls the music and mob swirling around inside.

I put my hands behind my neck, shut my eyes, lift my head, sniff, open my eyes and take in the billions of stars that only shine this far out from the city.

The tears on my face feel like little icicles prickling my cheeks and sending a tingle down my spine. I wipe them away, but the tingle remains. Maybe it's not the frozen tears or the weather that are to blame. No—it feels more like I'm being watched. Oh yeah. Mike, the guy Anthony kicked out of the party, is bound to be somewhere nearby, waiting for his ride.

I turn to see where he's waiting and find two guys. Mike leans against the wall by the door. I must have run past him without even noticing. The other guy emerges from the house. He shuts the door behind him and calls out, "Jolene!"

I turn away. "Leave me alone." I wipe my cheeks again in case any leftover tears think about exposing themselves to the enemy, pull my jacket tighter, and cross my arms over my chest. The sticky sweat under my clothes has cooled, abetting the effect of the sudden temperature drop from the body heat in the house to the cold-blooded porch.

He stops a few feet behind me. I feel him there, like energy you can touch. Without looking, I can almost see him biting his cheek, squinching his eyebrows, and wondering how he could possibly say anything that would give me the slightest inclination to ever talk to him again.

There's something else there too, stirring in the soft but shivering distance, a yearning not only coming from him.

I shut my eyes and take a deep breath, nearly groaning. If he's out here to apologize, he's a prom too late.

"What's wrong?" he asks.

311

I scoff. How can I summarize the multitude of problems this night has gifted me?

But in my frustration and agony, a reckless disregard for every trepidation I've ever had sprouts inside of me. He wants to know what's wrong? Fine.

"I shouldn't have come here," I say, looking out at the gate surrounding the large driveway. "I was stupid to think things would be—never mind. It doesn't matter."

I'm too exasperated to go into details. I mean, what does he want me to say—that I thought I changed, and that now they'd all like me?! Sure! I did! And it seemed like they liked me for a while—but what a headache!

And he was worst of all! What is he even doing out here when he obviously is still choosing Caradine? I did everything I could to be the kind of girl he would go for, but he's still choosing Caradine! So, why is he out here?! He doesn't owe me anything, and I certainly don't owe him.

"Go back to your girlfriend," I tell him scathingly, looking over at him so he can see the resentment on my face.

"Go back to your boyfriend," he sends back. Hilarious.

"Boyfriend," I sneer. "I don't have a boyfriend."

"You're with Justin." He sounds surprised and shakes his head, gesturing to the house.

"Perfect." I sigh.

"Why are you so angry?!"

I turn and open my mouth to yell at him, but his expression is more concerned than I thought it'd be. I lose momentum. The tears try to come back.

312

"I'm tired, Matt." Pretending it's not what I'm doing, I wipe my eye with my ring finger. "I'm tired of everything exploding in my face and feeling like a loser."

"Why would you ever feel like a loser?" he asks. There's kindness in his eyes, but I don't let them fool me—not again. Not this time.

"BECAUSE THAT'S WHAT ALL OF YOU THINK!" I point at the manor, blasting music behind us.

"What are you talking about?" he asks.

"I overheard Justin and Anthony, and..." I sigh.

A bat flaps overhead, drawing my attention for a second before it distances itself past the trees.

"Jole," Matt says, still behind me.

I close my eyes and breathe deeply. He's only ever called me Jole once before. It was a rainy day, and lunch in the Greek was out of the question. Logan was home, sick. Eating with Mary was never an option. Large groups sat in rows and circles under the awnings around the top of the Greek theater. I searched for someone I knew. Logan was never sick, so I had never had to find someone else to sit with. I figured I could ask Lindsey and her group if I could join them; it would just be for one lunch period.

I started walking over to where they were sitting, leaning against the art building, when I saw Matt coming toward me with a sack lunch and a wide smile on his face.

We spent the next fifteen minutes standing, chatting near where a gutter let out at the awning, and a waterfall of collected rain poured into a puddle nearby.

Before I knew it, the bell rang. I had to eat my lunch during English class, but Laramie never minded. As we went our ways, Matt called me Jole and tapped my elbow with his hand. I felt that tap throughout all of class. I can feel it now as Matt steps to my side, his big, dark eyes frowning down at me.

"Justin's an idiot," he says. "Don't go out with him. I mean, he's my friend, but he's an idiot."

What's it to him? What could it possibly be to him? This question feels familiar in my head. Nothing has changed. He's still leading me around by the nose—giving me just a bit of hope without confirming actual feelings.

A chill reminds me—nothing ever came of that lunch. The next day, it was like it never happened.

I sniff. "Well, I'm not so..."

Little pieces of what's happening click: his posture, how he rubs his neck, stares at the ground, kicks the gravel underneath, his use of my nickname...

"So, who should I..." I start to ask.

All this time, he's been telling me how he feels without telling me. He's been asking me to confess it first without asking me. But now he's lived the consequences and spent a year without me. I've changed. Has he changed, too?

My lungs convulse, and my chest leaps. It's coming. He's going to ask me out. I'm seconds away from it.

"Unbelievable!" Caradine's voice calls from the doorway.

I look at her, then at Matt, whose eyes are closed and whose head's tilted back, a frown covering his entire face.

"Awesome." He speaks to himself.

"Right," I say. "I'll see ya."

"Jolene—"

I whip out my phone, ignore the missed calls from my dad, and call my sister. She answers. She must be bored.

"Hey. Can you pick me up?"

"No," she says. I guess she's not that bored.

"Please?"

"No."

I've lived with her stubbornness long enough to know how to deal with it and which bribe has the best success rate.

"I'll buy you tacos," I say.

I wait a few seconds before...

"Fine," she says. "Where are you?"

"Justin's..."

She groans and hangs up the phone.

I feel Matt still standing slightly behind me. I turn to him with what must be a terrifying look because he retreats a little. Then, he takes a step forward, regaining his lost ground.

"I'm not with Caradine," he says.

I have to laugh. It's the law.

"Cool." I have no more energy to worry about whether he'll ever admit to liking me. If I see him again and it's awkward, then good. Let it be awkward. It's better than being this frail little child, nervous and waiting—no more waiting.

"Jolene..." He apparently is not as done as I am.

"I don't care, Matt! Know what? I liked you before I left. I liked you a lot. But you were with Caradine, and I—"

"Jolene..." He reaches for me, but I recoil away.

"Could you just—go away?" I ask. "Please? I'm really not in the mood for any more fun little games."

He has the audacity to look offended but, more so, concerned.

"I'm not—" he says.

He's not what? I don't care.

"Caradine's waiting," I tell him, pointing at her with a flick of my eyes and a lean of my head.

He takes a few steps in her direction, then turns back to me, my back already facing him.

"Can I drive you home?" he asks.

"Bye. See you later." I'm almost in tears as I say it.

A part of me wants to run to him, grab his face, and kiss him until the sun comes up. But most of me, instead, just wants the world to stop spinning.

"Okay. Good night, Jolene."

I feel the distance between us grow as he walks back toward her.

"It's not gonna happen," he tells her so softly it's almost impossible to hear.

I pivot—he's holding the door for her. Then, after she steps in, he shuts it, turns, and sits down.

"What are you doing?" I ask.

"Nothing," he says. "Free porch."

I sigh, turn, and sit on the gravel. Not he, Mike, nor myself say anything until Mike's Lug arrives.

He exchanges words with the driver, tells Matt, "Rough luck," gets an eye roll in reply, winks at me, gets in the car, and rides off.

Matt stands up and leans against the building. I glare at him, but he doesn't appear to even see me do so, so I turn back toward the driveway.

I swear it's gotten colder.

Finally, Mary pulls up. She makes it past the security gate and drives in. I stand and wait for her as she drives up to me, stops, and I open the passenger door of her black truck.

I turn—is Matt still there? His back slides through the mansion's door.

I get into the truck, and we drive away.

50 THE RISE AND FALL OF
JOLENE STANSEN

JOLENE

For a while, we say nothing. She drives to Fairview, takes a right, and pulls into Tino's Tacos, known for having a late-night window.

I buy her some tacos, both of us drinks, and we get back into the truck, heading west toward home.

She tries to eat while she drives. I wish I had my license. It didn't make sense to get it in Paris, for reasons I've forgotten, but now I wish I had found a way to do it.

"You wanna tell me what happened?" she asks, mouth full.

"No."

"Okay." She shrugs.

"I overheard Justin telling Anthony I was annoying, ugly, and dumb."

"What?"

"Right? So, I ran for it, and on my way out, I saw Matt making out with Caradine."

I feel the tears threatening to return and embarrass me in front of my sister, but the rage intensifying inside me silences them, and I grind my teeth instead.

"But none of that sounds like you, though," Mary says after a moment of silence. "You're not ugly, dumb—I mean, sometimes you're annoying..."

"Haha," I say, not amused.

"'Oh,'" she puts on a voice, "'in Paris, we had cheese and crumpets at every meal, and no one ever farted or pooped, and it rained croissants and couture fashion.' We get it! You went to France!"

I snort.

"They probably weren't even talking about you," she continues. "They could have been talking about me, for all you know."

The tears find a way and stream down my face like that dumb waterfall of collected rainwater.

"I just feel so stupid!" I shout. "Why did I think that just because I've been gone a year, anything would have changed? Matt will probably never talk to me again, and—oh, my gosh, Logan! My life is such a colossal failure!" I sob into the furry cuff of my fitted brown leather jacket.

"Ugh," she says. "I can't believe this."

"What?" I ask between wails.

"I can't believe I'm in a position where I have to talk you up."

"What?" I ask again.

When we were younger, Mary and I got along about as well as an uncontrolled flame in a library. We fought over toys, friends, and attention on birthdays, and as we got older, it got worse—we stopped fighting completely. We stopped anything. I hardly know her.

"You have everything, Jolene," she says. "Everything. Do you know what happened to me when I went to Paris? Let's see, I shopped by myself. I went to the Eiffel Tower alone, met a crabby woman in the catacombs who fell on me, and I had to go to a French ER. I think I went to work once with Aunt Eloise and out to dinner twice with her and Mamie. And who is Uncle Cass? I've never heard of him. They didn't take me to fancy Ménagerie Rouge cat parties. They didn't buy me a new wardrobe, and they only offered to get me a fancy haircut after I got gum in my hair. The only person in our entire family who likes me is maybe Mom, maybe. She doesn't love me best— I know that. Even the goths prefer you to me. You should hear them talk about you." She takes a second to pretend to gag. "Even before you came back from France with your posh clothes and two thousand dollar euro hairstyle, you were still the most beautiful, fun, kind, annoyingly perfect person, and the most obnoxious thing about it is that you don't see it. It would be so much better if you were even a teensy bit of a snob because then I wouldn't feel so bad about hating your stupid face."

"You don't hate me."

"I know! That's what I just said!" She tilts her head. "If Justin, Anthony, Matt, whoever can't see you for who you are—I don't get why you're trying so hard to fit in with them when they should all be trying to fit in with you."

I always thought she hated me. I thought out of every living creature on earth, including Beau, Caradine, and Coach Tinino—who may never forgive me for coming in late—I thought she hated me the most.

"You're just saying that because you're my sister," I say after a few minutes.

"The only thing I do because I'm your sister is dye my hair so we don't look too much alike."

I snort, releasing the fierce misery of the evening. I look at her, driving with a smirk through the trees.

"That sweatshirt is ginormous on you," I inform her. "Where did you get it?"

She squares her jaw, and I'm not sure she'll answer.

"Justin," she says.

I feel like I've eaten a rock. While I've been telling anyone who'll listen about absolutely every facet of my year in France, Mary's been silent about her time here. That should have been enough for me to know it hasn't been great for her—that and her drastic shift in appearance. She hasn't reached out to me, but how much have I reached out to her? I should have asked her if she was still friends with Piper, what she thought of Justin, if she knew Anthony, or if she ever ran into Matt. Instead, I went out there blind—blind and stupid.

She parks at the curb, and we get out.

"Dad's asleep on the couch waiting for you," Mary says as we walk across the yard to the front door.

I roll my eyes.

She undoes the lock, and we step inside. She flies up the stairs, and I shut and lock the door, then turn to my dad. I was really hoping he'd be in bed and I could be like, "I didn't wake you up when I got home? I'm sorry—I forgot. It was super early though." But now I'll have to wake him.

"Dad." I nudge his shoulder.

He stirs and looks at me. "What time is it?"

"I don't know," I say, trying my hand at lying to my parents. Something I haven't done since I was twelve when I told them it was Mary who forgot to turn off the backyard hose.

Somehow, they knew instantly. Parents always knew. But maybe I'm smarter now, and more capable.

"Almost eleven?" It's not a lie if it's a question.

"The time I came in here. Amazing! Time has stood still."

I sniff. So much for being a more capable liar.

"It's twelve-thirty," I say, sitting on the coffee table.

"Yay, honesty." He sits up and yawns. "Keep it up. Where were you?"

"We went to a friend's house after the game." No rule insists I call it a party.

"So, a party. Were there drugs, beer, boys?"

"I don't think so, yes, and yes. But I didn't drink, and the boys were chill."

"'The boys were chill'?"

I glare at him rather than elaborate. After a second he sighs, and I can feel the end near—when I can go up to bed and recount every dreadful thing that happened tonight.

"Alright," he says. "A party that ends so early sounds lame anyway. We'll discuss punishment tomorrow."

He stands and motions for me to go first up the stairs, which I do.

It's cold up in my room. I turn on the heat and change into gray sweatpants, a white camisole, and my fluffy white robe. Then I brush my teeth, and crawl into bed, turning my electric blanket on.

My phone's blowing up with texts and missed calls from Piper. I hold my button down, slide the prompt to turn off my phone, and set it on its charger. What does she want from me? Justin's not dating Tay-Tay anymore. If she wants to know where I've gone, she can ask around, and Matt will tell her.

I turn on my side and spot the yearbook I had left on my desk, open to the picture of Matt I had circled with a red heart. Ugh.

I throw my covers back, cross to the book, and hurl it into the trash by my bed, sit down, reach into the trash, take the book back out, stand up, and put it on my shelf.

Once back in bed, I shut my eyes, and let sleep take me.

The next thing I know, I'm sitting on a gilded throne in a solid gold palace—wait, it's not all gold—jewels are carefully interlaced in the architecture and furnishings, ooh, even on me. I wear a blinding white gown that makes me wonder if they've found a way to weave diamonds.

I'm inspecting my garment when the immense doors at the far end of my hall open. A man to my left leans over to me.

"The thieves, your majesty," he says.

I nod, and my men lead those I thought were my friends into the room in chains and rags. Piper's hair is a mess. When they get to me, my guards motion for them not to come any closer.

Anthony, Justin, Piper, and Matt bow, prostrate on the floor. They're barefoot, and Anthony's shirt's missing. He rubs his rippling arms. I want him to look at me, but he doesn't. Too much shame, perhaps, to stand making eye contact with the one he's betrayed.

I let my eyes move on—a kindness to Anthony— and fix them on Justin, who has no problem looking directly at me. He wears a slight grin and a knowing glance. I tilt my head, wrinkle my eyebrows, and shut my gaping mouth.

"We're sorry!" Piper yells.

"We didn't mean it!" Matt says, sobbing. He breaks away from the group, grabs the hem of my glowing gown, and weeps. "Forgive me, please!"

I scooch away, the way a fly might evade a spider, and a guard hits Matt on the forehead with the butt of his staff and drags him back to the others.

The man on my left leans in again. "What do you want us to do with them?"

Intriguing question.

"Like what?" I ask him.

"Well," he says. He reminds me of Pierre, Mamie's butler in Paris. "You could throw them in the dungeons, or make them dance for you, or strip them of their titles and banish them from the kingdom—a classic—or execute them, of course, or..."

But I don't get to do any of these things. Instead, I get to get out of bed, walk Dogberry down the stairs, and let him out in the cool morning air so he can do his business.

In reality, I won't do anything to any of them. Best I can even hope for is they'll ignore me, and my life will go back to how it was—before Paris.

51 THE AUDITION

JOLENE

I want to go back to sleep, but I can't. Saturday morning ballet rehearsals start today to prepare for *The Nutcracker*. This morning, we get to audition for the Sugar Plum Fairy.

I love the ballet studio in the morning. I stretch my legs while wearing my black leotard, pink tights, pink dance sweater, black thigh-high leg warmers, and pink slippers.

Fog presses up against the high, cracked-open windows, letting the cool air mix with the stale smell of feet and sweat I've grown to love.

Besides our teacher, Lindsey Calisher is the only person there before me. She danced Sugar Plum during the year I spent in Paris, and from the look of her scowl, she'd like to do so again. I kind of don't want to take it away from her. Don't get me wrong, I'd love to have the part—I worked my butt off in Paris, and I'd like to think I've accomplished something, but I'd also feel bad if I was Lindsey and got demoted to Snow

Queen or something. Snow Queen would be a step up for me here; in Paris I wasn't even in *The Nutcracker*.

More girls, some I know, some I don't, join us, and eventually, our teacher leads us through a barre warm-up. She then calls us all into the center. I have a body language-only full-on brawl with Lindsey over the spot in the front, just off center.

Then Mrs. Reed teaches us the routine. It's simple enough: start in *quasi, tendu* four counts, *plié*, triple *pirouette, pas de bourrée*, step, step, *grand jeté*, step, *chassé, tour jeté*, and we pick our own ending.

Some of the girls forget a step. Some of their *grand jetés* look like regular *jetés*.

Lindsey completes all the steps technically but robotically. I recognize there's a chance I'm more critical of her than I am of the others.

They all seem nervous. But after dancing with Beau and Madame Patenaude, it takes a lot to intimidate me, at least on this ballet floor.

After dancing the audition, everyone claps, as we've all done for everyone. But Lindsey glares at me as I stand at the back of the class, making room for the next dancer.

I take it to mean I did a good job. I had ended with a double *saut de basque*, a move reserved for men that's not usually taught to women.

One day in Paris, I was early for my lesson—having misunderstood, yet again, French instructions—and sat in on the guys' class as they were learning this move. I stood in the back and tried it with them. Their teacher even gave me a few pointers, saying that even if I'm never asked to do a double *saut de basque*, the

327

technique might still be useful for me. It took a week of practice until I got it.

The rest of the dancers dance, and our teacher tells us to pack up and she'll email us the cast list.

I sit down and unwrap my toe shoes—peel them off, stand up, and unzip my dance bag.

Unzipping her bag nearby, Lindsey glances at me a few times before finally speaking. "Where did you learn that?"

"The double *saut de basque?*"

"Is that what it is?" she asks.

I nod. "I sat in on a men's class last year." I find if I say "last year" and not "in Paris," people sneer less.

Her eyes fall, disappointment smearing over her face despite my careful word choices.

"Oh," she trails off.

"It's nothing you couldn't do. I could teach it to you—"

"No." She looks the other way. "That's all right. It would probably take too much time—"

"I picked it up in about a week. You'd probably get it even faster—"

"No, thanks." She pulls on her jeans, slides into her street shoes, and leaves while wrapping a sweatshirt around her shoulders.

My dad picks me up, and as we're pulling into the driveway, before I have to surrender my phone again—they let me have it for ballet—I check my email, and there's the cast list for *The Nutcracker.*

"That was fast," I tell my dad as I click on the link to the list. There at the top, across from the words "Sugar

Plum Fairy," is Lindsey's name and mine. We're sharing Sugar Plum and Snow Queen. I'm glad. Lindsey won't hate me, and I'll get to dance the part. It's perfect, really.

"Good news?" my dad asks.

"I'm Sugar Plum and Snow Queen!"

"Honey, that's wonderful!" He hugs me awkwardly over the center partition and gear selector.

"Let's celebrate!" He opens his door. "I'll order pizza. Get inside and tell your mom, and hand over your phone."

I run into the house and find my mom hugging my sister in the kitchen.

"I won an art contest!" Mary points to what our mom's holding—a painting of a young woman with short pink hair crying into her reflection in a puddle. But the girl in the puddle has long brown hair and a cheerleader uniform on. I try not to read too much into it.

"That's great!" I say.

My good news can come later. I don't want to compete for congratulations.

"Jolene got the part!" My dad enters just after me, tossing his keys on the table behind Mary. "She shares it, but she got the lead!"

"Oh!" My mom hands the painting back to Mary. "Jolene! I knew you could do it!"

"Thanks—" I'm cut off by my parents squishing me in a hug sandwich.

Mary watches us with her lip curled up, clutching her painting over her chest.

She runs off, and I think about following her. I was hoping after our car ride home we might repair our relationship, but that might be harder than I thought.

I don't know what I'd say. Maybe it would be better to give her some time and ask her about her art contest when she's in a better mood.

Once upstairs, I unpack my toe shoes, hanging them over the back of my chair so they can breathe and calm down.

Even if nothing else has changed—if I hadn't gone to Paris, I would not have the lead role in the ballet right now. I should text Jean and let him know my good news and check on how he's doing. But my dad took my phone this morning as my punishment—wouldn't even budge when I told him I might get attacked at ballet and need to call the police—Lindsey was looking pretty close to biting for a minute, but no. It's fine. I was avoiding my phone anyway—dodging Piper. She can cope.

I change out of my ballet clothes and into sweats.

Where is my phone? Over and over I search for it then remember I don't have it—forget, remember, forget, remember. I need to distract my mind, so I go to my bookcase and pick a book I've read eleven times already. What is it about teenage vampires that so completely takes your mind off things?

52 A NORMAL WEEKEND

LOGAN

Late Saturday evening, Jolene arrives, apologizing for not texting first, and for ditching me the night before, and hungry to destroy some zombies.

We get our team out of a swarm and cross an almost deserted amusement park. A few zombies pose a threat, but they're easy enough to pick off as we run past.

"We had auditions this morning for Sugar Plum Fairy," Jolene says.

How is she just now telling me this?

"And!?" I ask.

"And I got it," she says, holding back chalance.

"That's great!" I shout as she smiles.

Shoot—I've accidentally shot a zombie that screams and charges me and alerts all other zombies to my presence.

Jolene tries to fight them off. She throws an explosive away from us, which causes a few of the

331

undead to leave me and go get blown up. Then she starts shooting the hoard off of me.

"I'm sharing the role with Lindsey. We take turns between Sugar Plum and Snow Queen every other night."

"That's awesome," I say, and die in game. "Now you get to dance both parts. That's fun. Right?"

She nods, still glowing, and not dying in game.

"How was the party I wasn't invited to?"

She checks my face, maybe to make sure I'm joking, which I am, and smiles a sad smile. "Terrible. The worst it could have possibly gone. Matt was there."

She tells me everything that has ever happened in her entire life, and by the end we're laughing, joking, and respawning. We give the zombies what for all weekend, and by the time we split on Sunday night, we've strategized a new plan to wipe them off the face of the video game.

53 THE BOY I'M COMPLETELY CRAZY ABOUT

JOLENE

I don't look at it—my phone. I know its alarm is going to go off any second, but if I don't look at it, I can get a few more seconds of sleep—nope. It goes off. I turn it off and throw my covers back.

Mondays have a way of always coming too fast. Hanging out with Logan helps the weekend slow down, though, and it's nice to know that even though everything's going back to normal, normal's really not that bad. Although it might end up being worse than normal. In fact, it probably will be. Monday has come, which means I have to face them. They'll probably all vehemently hate me now. Piper will never forgive me for leaving the party without telling her, for not jumping into a relationship with Justin, and for not texting her all weekend—my dad gave me back my phone last night, but I still haven't read her messages. Justin will be back with Tay, obviously. Matt—let's just forget about him, please and thank you. Anthony...

I take out my braid and re-braid it. I can't think about him right now.

The clothes from Paris glare at me as I bypass them, rummaging through the depths of my closet for something to wear. Screw looking cute and trying to make popular friends, and fit in, and get a boyfriend.

I dig down into my drawers stuffed with cute, new jeans and find my red and pink plaid pants. They used to be my mom's in the nineties. They're weird, and I love them. I pair them with a pink camisole and my light-blue hoodie. Fashion forward? Chic? No, and who cares? It's cute, and I feel cute in it.

Logan picks me up, and moments later we walk into myth and set our backpacks on our usual chairs. The thoughts and fears I've been trying to push aside all weekend overtake me. I'm not ready to face them— the students, not the chairs. I try to block it all from my mind by engaging Logan in conversation, which is easy if that conversation is about video games.

"I can't believe that mob last night." That's all I have to say.

"Did you notice I changed the setting after the fifth time?" he asks.

"You did? From what?"

"I put it on moderate."

"We probably would have been fine if you didn't use a sniper rifle. Just saying."

"Stop trying to change me." He grimaces. "I like using a sniper rifle."

"That's fine when you're far away somewhere, picking them off, but there are better weapons to use when you're stuck in a mob!" I laugh at his stubbornness.

"I like playing this way!"

"But you die every time, and I'm the one who has to leave the safe room to come get you."

"Just stay in there, and we'll go on to the next round."

"Oh." I hadn't considered that. I shrug. "Next time, I'll do that."

"Thank you."

"There you are!" Piper says, entering the classroom.

Here we go. It's a good thing the room doesn't have many people in it yet—fewer witnesses of the upcoming spectacle.

Her eyes are fiery and clash with her strawberry-blond hair. "Where have you been? You just disappeared Friday night, and you aren't texting me back. I expected to get here and find out you had died."

"I thought Matt would have told you I left," I say meekly as she sits next to me.

"He did!" She's still angry. "But I only found him after the guys and I searched the entire house looking for you."

"The guys?" I ask.

"Yes," she says, flinging her hair over her shoulder. "Justin, Jason, Anthony—the guys! I thought you were going to talk to Justin after they broke up, but Justin said you never did. What happened?"

"I overheard him saying I was ugly, annoying, and dumb, so that sucked, and I left."

Piper scrunches her eyes together, looking confused. She clicks her tongue and shakes her head.

"But that doesn't make any sense," she says. "Justin hasn't shut up about you all weekend. He was planning on asking you to Homecoming, but you ran off like freaking Cinderella."

"I heard what I heard," I say.

"Hm," Piper smirks, and quickly covers her mouth, but her eyes smile.

"Huh?" I ask.

"No. It's just—I mean, that's kind of on par for Justin. He's not really known for his sincerity." She smirks again. "He probably was just going to use you, then ghost you. He's done that to some pretty but less popular girls—no offense. At least you got him to break up with Tay-Tay, or maybe he would have done that anyway."

She keeps talking, but I don't process any more than this. I'm too distracted by how much I don't care. That party was not my last chance at high school happiness. Justin won't ask me to Homecoming, but he did dump Tay-Tay—who cares? I didn't like him anyway. And as far as Piper goes, if she wants to be my friend, then great. If not, that's cool, too. Who has the energy to worry about what people, who couldn't care less if you lived or died, thought? I spent the weekend freaking out over it. What a waste of time. There will be other friends and other guys. Guys who I'll fit with. Guys who'll get me, and I'll get in return. I may not get all the guys I'll ever want, but that's fine. It's probably for the best.

What would have happened if I had gotten Matt my freshman year? I would have spent a year apart from

336

him. We probably would have broken up during that time, and then if we saw each other at Justin's party, it would have been even worse than it was—or, we would have stayed together, and I never would have met—

Admittedly, that's the one thing that still bothers me. His is the one opinion that's not as easy for me to shrug off. What had he said? "You do have really bad taste in women"? Was Anthony just trying to pacify Justin, or did he really think I was in bad taste? It matched what Piper's said about him, but not at all what I got from him in real life, except in that moment...

My pencil breaks. I didn't even realize I had been pushing it against a metal bend in my desk chair.

Piper notices. She reaches a hand out to me and places it on my arm. "Hey," she says. "Justin's not worth it." She takes her arm back and busies herself with her thin, yellow water bottle.

A hand places a tiny pencil sharpener on my desk. I glance at Logan. I almost forgot about him. He gives me an encouraging half-smile.

Maybe all I got out of all this was a glimpse through the window. I was popular—or thought I was—for a day. And what did it do for me? Nothing. Popular friends aren't better than my unpopular ones. I'm still not dating Matt and probably never will. I easily could have offended Logan by going to the game, the party, and eating lunch without him. That would have been an unbearable consequence. I don't deserve his unwavering friendship, but the fact he thinks I do says something, right?

"Clear off your desks," our teacher says. "All you should have is a pencil. Your tests are coming around."

Popularity certainly has not resulted in better grades. I didn't even know there was a test today.

I sharpen my pencil, hand the sharpener back to Logan, take a test packet, pass the others behind me, and get to failing.

Piper complains about the test all the way to my locker. Logan walks a few steps behind us, then bolts off around a building, skipping a trip to his locker, probably eager to escape Piper's tirade—if only I could.

"This isn't the fourteenth century, not that they had pencils in the fourteen hundreds, but can't we have Scantrons that take more than just a number two?" she asks, leaning against the lockers as I twist the knob on my padlock.

"You hear about this thing?" a low voice says above my ear. I forgot how his voice sounds like a cool spring. I want to take my shoes off and stand in it. That's weird imagery. Forget I said it.

My body faces Piper, so I see her shocked expression before I turn to Anthony who's smiling down at me, holding up his cell phone.

"It's called a phone," he says. "Or, *Cellular phoniphicus*, if you want the Latin."

"Very scientific," I tell him.

Why is he here, talking to me? He hasn't even glanced at Piper, who has straightened up, flipped her hair, and can't seem to decide on which of us to focus.

338

He wears a navy-blue shirt with a white sporty logo on the front, dark jeans, and a navy-blue hoodie. Maybe his favorite color is navy, or maybe he knows just how good it looks on him. But he could wear absolutely anything and still be the most attractive guy in any room. Such is his power.

"Relatively new technology, actually," he continues, "dating back to a man named Alexander, who came up with it when he was working with people who were hearing impaired, in the Year of Our Lord 1876. I looked it up in class to impress you."

I can't help but smile, but this behavior contradicts everything Piper said, and what I overheard him tell Justin—

Wait.

Wait, wait, wait, wait, wait, wait, wait, wait—

Mary said they probably weren't talking about me—what if—wait—

But I don't have time to sort out what's swirling around in my head. Anthony's looking at me, expecting a coherent response. I can't just keep smiling at him like an idiot.

"Interesting," I manage. Well, I tried.

But he smiles easily. A man this gorgeous should not be this effortless to be around. I should be nervous, but he always puts me in a kind of state of cautious nirvana. It's different from being around Logan. Logan is easy, but there's no electricity. And it's different from being around Matt. I struggle for words around him—when I'm not screaming at him. With Anthony—I don't know—it's like I've known him my entire life, and everything I say hits exactly how I hope or better. He never misunderstands or misinterprets, and I don't need to read his brain to know it. I just know it. And I know it's the same for him. It has to be.

Except—Friday night. I misunderstood him then—or at least, it's starting to seem, more and more, like that must have been exactly what I did—misunderstand...

Suddenly it dawns on me that he brought up phones because he wants something. My number? Please let it be my number. Will I look too desperate if I just give it to him?

"Piper said you didn't call her back all weekend." He widens his eyes at me, playfully, like I have something to answer for.

"Oh," I say.

Apparently, he's spoken to Piper this morning, or maybe during the weekend—either way, he still hasn't so much as glanced her way since approaching us.

I exchange my notebooks with my locker and look up at him.

"Yeah," I continue, not wanting to give him all the phone-taken-away details. "I had a really busy weekend." It wasn't a lie, not totally. Killing zombies can be time-consuming.

"Psh." Half his lips smirk. "I don't care if you don't call Piper back—I'm glad you don't call Piper back. No offense, Pipe."

She shifts her attention from me to him, probably surprised at finally being addressed, but the moment lasts about five split seconds before his gray eyes are on me again.

"Leaves more time for calling me." He sounds frivolous and teasing, but he looks at me the way no one else ever does. His eyes sync with my mind. His smile warms me, like sitting on the beach in the summer. "If you want. Word is—now this is wild—what happens is, you put a number in, and you can call an actual person, or text."

"Amazing."

"Yeah. Do you want to try it out with me?"

"Oh. Like, I give you a number and we see if it works?"

"Exactly what I'm thinking. Hang on. First, before the number, let me put in your name."

"You want my number?" I draw my hand through my hair, unsure exactly how to maneuver. How do you give the guy who could crush your heart the ability to do so without peeing your pants at the same time?

"Well then, we can see if it works," he says, tilting his head.

"Right."

He types, swipes, then starts to read what he's typing.

"J-O-L-E-N-E?" he asks. I nod. "Stansen. S-Q-U-P-L-O-M?"

"The 'O' should be a 'Y'," I say.

"Oops," he says. "Change the 'Q' to a 'K.' Got it."

After the second it takes me to realize he's waiting for me, I tell him my number. He repeats it—correctly—as he types it in.

"We've gotta get your picture for it," he says, "for science." He takes a step away and holds up his phone.

341

I squish my lips together slightly while posing, the way Eloise's models often did—looking at the camera lens as if to say, "You asked for this."

He laughs lightly while capturing my image. I smile, embarrassed but having fun.

"Now one with both of us." He jumps in the shot and smiles at his phone with me. "Now a serious one." We pout at the screen. "Okay, more serious." He rages at the sky while I pretend to cry.

He lowers his phone and looks at it. I don't know why that makes me more nervous than his looking at me in person. But then he glances over and I change my mind; in person is way more intense.

He swipes a few times, grins, and shows me. "Aww," he says. "It's cute." He puts his cell in his back pocket. "Alright. Get to class, Skuplym." He turns and walks away.

I look back at Piper and wonder how long she's been glaring at me.

"I thought you said they were talking crap about you?" Her tone is accusatory, as if I lied in order to overthrow the government.

"I did too," I say, letting my shock and relief fill my voice.

She looks less haughty than she did in class and more hurt. There's a chance Anthony overlooking her bothers her more than she lets on, and she lets on quite a bit.

I try to sound unsure to boost her confidence. "And, I mean, it's not like we've never heard Justin talk like that about girls. He talked about Tay-Tay like that all the time—" I say. And the thought that had tried to wiggle itself out while I was talking to Anthony finally breaks through my crowded mind. "Oh, my gosh! He was talking about Tay-Tay!" As I say it, I know it's true.

I thought he must have been talking about me because I wore a short skirt once, but Tay-Tay's a cheerleader—she wears them all the time! And she had just left the room—of course they were talking about her! I was stupid to think anything different!

Piper's head tilts from one side to the other. Her teeth all but grind to stubs. "Mystery solved."

With Piper's rather reluctant agreement, a wave of relief washes over me, almost knocking me down. If her confirmation isn't enough to prove I'm right, surely Anthony asking for my number is. Right?

Piper slams my locker shut and walks off, obviously angry and easy to guess about what. It makes me bite my cheek. I don't like seeing her sad—even worse when I'm causing it. And maybe I shouldn't feel too thrilled about Anthony asking for my number. Just because Justin and Anthony were talking about Tay and not me, that doesn't mean I can disregard everything Piper said about him—or—well, it means we're back to me not seeing any of the red flags. Do I just take Piper's word that they're really there when she's such a locker slammer? Truth is, I have more reasons to trust Anthony than I do to trust Piper. She's done nothing but push me around since I met her.

I bring my backpack around my shoulders, tossing my side-braid in front so it's not trapped by the straps.

The drama and chaos is almost enough to make me yearn for the normal years—the years before Paris, the years I thought I'd see again after the—what I thought was—disastrous party. The simpler years— before I became close friends with a popular girl, before I screamed at Matt that I had once liked him, before I was tackled in the hallway by the hottest guy on the football team—wait. I take that one back. I take that one very much back.

I smirk, probably looking like an idiot to anyone watching. But it seems to me—when my phone buzzes in my pocket and it's an "It works! Amazing!" text from Anthony—it might have been a good thing after all that I went to Paris.

THE END

CHARACTER REFERENCE
In Order of Appearance

Jolene Stansen
  Teenaged ballerina
Matt Craddick
  Jolene's crush/Caradine's boyfriend
Mrs. Diefenbacher
  Jolene & Matt's math teacher
Danny Vegas
  Jolene & Matt's math tablemate
Tim
  Jolene, Danny, & Matt's smart tablemate
Caradine Krueger
  Matt's girlfriend
Logan Monnel
  Jolene's friend
Mary Stansen
  Jolene's half-sister
Piper Thompson
  Mary's popular friend
Dogberry & Horatio
  Jolene's Border Collie & ever-sleeping kitty
Lori Stansen
  Jolene's mom/works at a movie studio in LA
Steve Stansen
  Lori's husband/Mary's stepdad/Jolene's dad/
  architect
Eloise Duchene Grant
  Jolene's aunt/Steve's half-sister/Iris's daughter/
  Caspian's wife/lives in France
Iris "Mamie" Duchene

Jolene's grandma living in France
Caspian "Cass" Grant
Eloise's husband/living in France
Iphigeneia "Geneia" Mischka
Eloise's famous friend living in France
Oscar Ivanov
Eloise and Caspian's famous friend living in France
Madame Patenaude
Ballet teacher in France
Beau
Jolene's first dance partner in France
Helene
Jolene's dance friend in France
Jean
Jolene's second dance partner in France
Mrs. Reed
Jolene's ballet teacher in Goleta
Lindsey Calisher
Dances ballet with Jolene in Goleta
Veronika
Mary's friend
Jess Monnel
Logan's younger sister
Mr. Laramie
WCHS mythology teacher
Quinn Wayne
Cheerleader/Courtney's best friend/Piper's friend/dating Todd
Courtney Usher
Cheerleader/Quinn's best friend/Piper's friend
Kaila Jones

Cheerleader

Tyrus Krueger
Football player/Caradine's younger brother

Todd Elsinore
Quinn's boyfriend/Weston's friend/
football player

Weston Prior
Todd's friend

Ms. Magpali
Chemistry teacher

Justin Granite
ASB president/in Jolene's chemistry class/
Anthony's best friend

Jesse Morrison
ASB vice president/football player/in Jolene's
chemistry class

Jason Canvis
Matt's friend/roommate/high school dropout

Isaac Craddick
Matt's grandpa/owns his apartment building

Charlene Benedict
Matt and Jason's neighbor/Dillon's roommate

Dillon Mahony
Matt and Jason's neighbor/Charlene's roommate

Tay-Tay "Tay" Breiman
Justin's girlfriend

Guineth Granite (pronounced "GWEN-eth")
Justin's younger sister/frosh cheerleader

Christie Samuels
Guineth's best friend/frosh cheerleader

Noah Granite
Guineth's twin/Justin's younger brother

Anthony Whitaker
   Football quarterback/Piper's crush/Justin's best
   friend
Isaiah
   Football player
Alice Windsor
   Cheerleader/Alice's best friend/likes Anthony
Alice Sistine
   Cheerleader/Alice's best friend/likes Anthony
Nurse Kate Magparagalan
   WCHS nurse
Coach Tinino
   WCHS history teacher/football coach
Mike
   Football player at Justin's party